Revealed

NEW HEIGHTS PUBLISHING

www.suzannefalter.com

Book cover design by Caroline Manchoulas
www.ladylit.com

Book design by Danielle H. Acee

ISBN: 978-0-9969981-6-1

Revealed

An Oaktown Girls Novel

by

SUZANNE **FALTER**

Chapter One

Rosalind Choi stood on the deck of the meditation pool in her navy blue bathing suit, and glanced around at the other occupants, blissfully soaking. A wave of intense shyness slipped over her.

To begin with, it was a full moon, which, in Rosalind's mind, meant larger forces were at work. What she didn't expect was that this would involve getting naked in public. At the moment, she was one of the few visitors actually even wearing a bathing suit. But then this was Harbin, a place where anything could happen.

Harbin Hot Springs was a clothing optional resort a few hours north of the Bay Area, up in the rolling brown hills of Lake County. It was also home to a sterling group of natural cold and hot springs lovingly tended by grizzled older hippies, most of them wearing little more than a sweaty bandana headband and a pair of aging flip flops. Or maybe, on more formal occasions, a tie-dyed sarong.

Over the years it had become a haven for stressed out techies and others who wanted to escape the Bay Area fog, traffic, and non-stop hordes of people. By Friday night the meditation pool, under the gracious canopy of a massive fig tree, loaded with ripe fruit, had come alive with whispered chatter. This was in spite of the sign, expressly forbidding conversation and sexual activity of any kind.

It was here that Rosalind found herself an hour after she'd arrived. But then, she just didn't know the pools were going to be so…busy. She'd only been here twice before, and then on weekdays. But now, on a weekend, the place was entirely different. Even the protracted crawl of traffic up 101 had been daunting.

Glancing around nervously, Rosalind tugged the back of her bikini bottom more firmly into place as she slipped into the clear warm water. Quickly, she submerged up to her neck, eager to avoid the curious gaze of several men around her. She swam across the pool to a shady corner underneath a massive flower arrangement.

The September sun was gone, and the chill of the evening was setting in. Darkness gathered as the moon became brighter overhead. Rosalind leaned her head against the white plastered wall of the pool. She took a deep breath and allowed herself to relax slightly, shaking off the drive and her tension as her body unwound in the water. She watched the small wall sconces around the pool flicker on, one by one.

Rosalind took another deep breath and exhaled, consciously dropping her shoulders and loosening her jaw. Gone was the need to perform or impress. Gone, for the moment at least, was the pressure of her new job at the foundation she had started. Gone was the need to be anything other than simply who she was, right here and right now.

In fact, Rosalind was a closeted lesbian, now gamely doing her best to slowly, carefully emerge and create a life she actually wanted. Months earlier, everything that had once been hers crashed and burned after she exposed the corruption at her tech firm to a reporter at *The San Francisco Chronicle*. Her job had ended immediately, and with it her connection to her strict, evangelical parents—hard-working Chinese immigrants who'd sacrificed heavily for her education.

Gone was also any good cred she'd built in her six years slogging away in the tech business. All of that had been replaced by a new role, one Rosalind never could have imagined. Now she led women to speak out against the entitled 'bro' culture in the tech world.

Everything Rosalind had once taken for granted was now gone, and so she was set free. And yet, all that freedom came with a price.

Closing her eyes, she took a long deep breath and attempted once more to relax.

As soon as everything fell apart, Rosalind had found her way to Harbin on a friend's suggestion. She'd never thought of herself as a person who could actually go to a clothing-optional spa, but on a whim she showed up one afternoon. At that exact moment in her life, there didn't seem to be anything left to lose.

Quickly the hot springs became her sanctuary. But then, Harbin had also lost everything a few years earlier, in a wildfire that gutted the place. Now it was largely rebuilt, and doing its best to retrieve the funky spiritual essence that had once made it so unique. In Rosalind's mind, it was definitely working.

Opening her eyes in the twilight, she focused on a cluster of seven naked women on the pool deck. They entered the water together, holding hands. A few of them wore dandelion chains around their necks or on their heads. Three of the women were holding small glass jars with votive candles in them. One of them cleared her throat as if to address the group.

"Are y'all here for the Spiral Dance?" she asked in a lilting voice. The woman glanced around. A few people nodded, while others made their way purposefully to the stairs and climbed out of the pool.

Rosalind had no idea what a Spiral Dance was or what the woman was talking about. But instead of leaving, she decided to stay and see what happened. This was something the new Rosalind would do, she reasoned. Live a little recklessly. Be part of a Spiral Dance.

Why not?

More people filed into the pool now, all of them naked. They took their places along the walls of the meditation pool with an almost businesslike air about them. It appeared they were waiting for the event to begin.

"What's happening?" Rosalind asked the tall, blonde athletic-looking woman who had just slipped in beside her.

"You haven't been to the Spiral Dance before?" she asked, and Rosalind shook her head. "Then maybe you'd best wait and see," she replied. Then she smiled.

Rosalind swallowed. Not only did the woman's answer give her pause, but Rosalind was immediately struck by her. Maybe it was her voice, or her very level gaze—the sort a goddess might give the peons who surrounded her. Somehow Rosalind felt this woman's presence right down to her groin. She smiled at her new friend, all the while fighting back a flush of attraction.

"Oh…okay," Rosalind said, but the woman just put her finger to her lips and silenced her. Then she looked at Rosalind one more time, taking her in with a deep understanding gaze. Rosalind found she was unable to look away. Once more, she swallowed hard.

The awareness that she was drawn to this naked Amazon beside her totally unnerved Rosalind. She needed to get a grip immediately. Something was already happening. In the back of her mind, she wondered if she was ready for it.

At any rate, Rosalind was definitely not getting out of the pool. Not now.

The three women leading the Spiral Dance took a center position in the pool, holding up candles. "We are here to honor the endless cycle of birth, death and rebirth, just as we honor all of the cycles of the moon," one of them intoned. "There is no end to life, and that is why we gather in a circle."

The three began to chant in a low monotone as others in the group joined them.

There is no end to life…there is no end. There is no end to life… there is no end.

The three women entwined fingers, and slowly began to

move in a small, tight circle as they sang. One of the women held out her hand as others quickly stepped in to join hands and follow in the spiral. Those who were pressed against the walls of the pool began to slide into place, all of them moving in a perfectly fluid, slow-moving dance.

One by one, everyone slipped in seamlessly as the line moved steadily closer to Rosalind. Looking down at her bikini-clad body, it struck her that she should shed her bathing suit and join the rest of the naked revelers. She studied their bodies, drawing closer and closer together, like books on a shelf as the circle naturally expanded.

What self-respecting Chinese-American woman in tech would whip off her bathing suit and dance wildly in a pool with a bunch of complete strangers? And naked strangers, no less?

Certainly not her, that was for sure. But, just then, the tall blonde who was still standing beside her held out her hand wordlessly.

Numbly, Rosalind reached out and felt the woman's fingers close around her own. Then she followed, her senses overcome by the rush of the moment. Feeling their hands entwined was downright empowering. The blonde looked over her shoulder at Rosalind and she smiled as they joined the circle. Bliss was painted across her face.

Suddenly, Rosalind stopped and pulled back her hand. Ripping off her bikini top, she wadded it up and tossed it onto the pool deck. Then she did the same with her bathing suit bottom as the blonde woman disappeared up ahead of her in the spiral.

Quickly Rosalind plunged back into the circle. All around her bodies were weaving along at a faster and faster pace. A heavy butch dyke pushed up behind her and put her hands on her waist. "Come on, sweetheart," she muttered. "Grab on to the person in front of you."

Gulping, Rosalind glanced over her shoulder at the woman and did as she was told, wrapping her arms around the slender

Black man in front of her. Her thoughts blurred into the vortex of the spiral movement.

I'm doing this...I am actually doing this, Rosalind thought giddily. Faster and faster she moved as she joined the tightly whirling chanters.

There is no end to life...there is no end...

Rosalind found herself moving along in the anonymous blur of humanity, her words coming louder and clearer. It didn't matter who was in front of her and who was behind her, or even what she was singing. Nor did it matter that they were all enthusiastically, blissfully naked. Rosalind was connected to these people, these strangers, like she'd never been connected to anyone. They were all caught in a life pulse she could just barely grok.

Tighter and tighter, faster and faster the Spiral Dance whirled together as the water churned around them. Overhead the moon was framed between the trees. Rosalind looked up, and in that moment she felt completely alive.

She exulted, throwing her head back and chanting even more loudly. The circle continued for several more moments.

Finally the dancers began to slow down. And after another moment, they stopped altogether. Then, just as quietly and spontaneously as it began, the Spiral Dance ended. Dancers began slipping away into the night as Rosalind watched in mild amazement. Once again, she found her way back to her corner of the pool.

For a moment, she wondered where her bathing suit had ended up, but then that thought simply evaporated. Standing in front of her now was the tall blonde woman who'd led her into the circle at the beginning of the dance. She smiled and took Rosalind's hand.

Then raising it to her mouth, she kissed it, wordlessly.

Rosalind's mouth went dry as a shot of electricity traveled straight from her groin to her brain. She nodded, and blushed. The woman smiled and held Rosalind's gaze for another long, delicious moment. Then silently, she turned and walked toward the stairs out of the warm pool.

All Rosalind could do was to follow.

*

Rosalind drove through Harbin's dragon gate and sped past the gatehouse at the end of the drive. The last twenty-four hours had been like something out of a dream. She was giddy with excitement. And she was exhausted, as well.

Tasha, the tall athletic blonde who'd beckoned to her after the Spiral Dance, had just spent the last six hours making enthusiastic, and highly instructive, love to Rosalind. A top if there ever was one, Tasha took control of the situation and took her new pupil in hand as she taught her the fine points of lesbian lovemaking.

Tasha didn't have much to say, Rosalind had noticed. But then, Tasha didn't have to. Her statuesque beauty made her a striking companion as she walked along with Rosalind, her arm protectively around her waist.

With her spiky white-blonde hair, and her eyes as blue as a lake, Tasha demanded attention. Add to that her washboard abs, and the distinctive undulating rattle snake that was tattooed down her left leg, and really…she was simply breathtaking.

Tasha lived in Oakland, which Rosalind figured was some kind of happy accident. She was a yoga teacher, she said. "Sort of."

Rosalind was unclear on what that actually meant. She suspected Tasha actually did something else for a living, but what exactly? Rosalind wondered when she would find out.

Undoubtedly, she'd learn more about her mysterious and exciting new lover in the coming weeks as they got to know each other better. After climbing out of the meditation pool together, they'd basically spent every waking moment together for the next twenty-four hours. They'd shared a bed the following night, making love off and on, then continuing well into the next day with a few breaks for lounging in the pools.

And now, here was Rosalind, limping away in some kind of amazed primal shock. She'd done it. She'd found a lover, and more or less come out. At least to Tasha.

In spite of her shyness, Rosalind had actually, finally gotten this very creaky engine started, and the results were unbelievably hot. The new Rosalind was definitely in the driver's seat now.

When compared to the few anemic men she'd dated, Tasha was in an entirely different realm. In bed, she was just plain magic. It was as if her fingers, her tongue, and her taught muscular body had already encoded themselves into Rosalind's psyche. Rosalind surfed orgasm after orgasm, not quite believing any of this was happening.

But it was. Most incredibly…it was.

Tasha was even an activist. She started the group that monitored the Oakland Police Department's use of force against people of color. And of course, she'd heard of Rosalind. Everybody had, pretty much, since *The Chronicle* story on how she turned her former employer, a bro-happy start up that spread disinformation, over to the FBI.

Tasha was even up on her new foundation, asking Rosalind all kinds of questions about it.

As her car worked its way up and down the cascade of switchbacks, past the naked scorched Lake County forest, and the remnants of old tourist sites, her mind was gone entirely. Rosalind was busy thinking about dinners out with Tasha, and their Friday nights on Grand Avenue or Uptown. There was so much to be done. Riding bikes across the Bay Bridge, and long hikes in Redwood Park. Maybe they could get up to the Sierras, or out to the beach in Marin.

And then there were the protests, walking the streets of Berkeley with a signboard in one hand and Tasha's in the other.

They would be righteous and strong together, women who made a difference. They would make speeches together, and go to each other's press conferences. Right along with the chemistry, there was synchronicity for sure.

Rosalind shook her head and laughed. This was all coming true—everything she'd wanted was seemingly happening right here and right now. With this woman, this Tasha, who seemed to appear out of nowhere. And, miraculously, she lived in Oakland. It was all so easy. Effortless.

Just like true love should be.

Rosalind pulled in to Calistoga, and stopped at the convenience store for a coffee. Given that she was running on at most two hours of sleep, caffeinating seemed like a good idea before the two-hour drive ahead.

A moment later, as she settled the cup of steaming black coffee into the console in her car, Rosalind pulled out her phone. Why not send a welcoming text, she thought, for when Tasha gets home a little later?

Why not let her know she was thinking about her?

Rosalind's fingers flew across the phone screen, typing her thoughts in quick bursts.

Really happy we met…hoping we can see each other again soon. There are so many things I'd like to do with you. Tasha, you are miraculous. I'm so glad I met you!

Pausing, Rosalind took in what she wrote. Then with a little rush of delight, she pushed the send button.

It never occurred to her that Tasha might only have been a fling.

Chapter Two

Delilah shuffled the well-worn deck of Goddess cards as a flutter of fear spun up through her chest. It was strange to be afraid at such a moment, given that she and her friend Sally had been here many times before. Carefully, she handed the cards back to Sally.

A soft beam of sunlight slipped through the heavy velvet curtains, softening the darkness of the back room at Desire's Magical Garden. Formerly Delilah's college roommate, Sally was now the regular psychic on duty at this small occult shop in Oakland.

The store was packed with all manner of things related to goddesses, witchcraft, magic, and spiritual intent. The store was crammed with everything from crystals and wands to large dusty jars of herbs, and the scent of sage and patchouli were ever present in the air. It was the sort of place that had a large taxidermied owl perched high above the book shelves, wings spread wide.

Sally had been coveting this job for years, though it was only in recent months she'd finally found the courage to apply for it. And now, here she was, Desire's Psychic-in-Residence.

"What do you want me to focus on?" Sally asked her friend.

"Well…" Delilah began, but then hesitated. She swallowed, trying to steady herself. There was much at stake in her life at the moment. "A baby," she finally blurted out. "I want to find out if we're going to have a baby."

There. She'd said it. Delilah's most fervent wish had finally left the contours of her mind and been spoken aloud. It was something she hadn't even been able to bring up with her wife, Tenika.

A broad smile moved across Sally's face, and her eyes lit with happiness. "Delilah, that's great! And I can't say I'm surprised," she said. "Pick three."

Delilah did as she was told, placing the cards face down on the small round table between them. Thoughtfully, Sally turned the three cards over. Then she shook her head in mild amazement. "It's all right here. I see a baby!" she said. "And...wow." She looked up at her friend with a toothy grin. "Actually, I see more than one."

Delilah's eyes grew wide for a moment. "What?"

Sally studied the cards again. "I see twins."

"Twins?" Delilah paused. "Are you sure?"

"Well, as sure as I can be. It's a reading, so we see intentions and alignments, not necessarily birth weights and due dates, right? But I'd say it really does look like twins."

Delilah shook her head in amazement, trying to process what she'd just heard. "Come on...seriously?"

"Mmm hmm," Sally said, turning over two more cards. "Yet, there will be...resistance."

"Tenika?"

"Perhaps. Or maybe it's your own fear—or your family's? Would they support this?"

"Yes, no, I don't know. Whatever..." Delilah's voice dropped. There was no predicting what her uber-Catholic mother would do. She had a hard time wrapping her head around her daughter's interracial lesbian marriage in the supposedly heathen East Bay of California. It was hard to gin up a lot enthusiasm for it at the church Delilah had grown up in.

"Well, Tenika's family will certainly be fine with it," she said.

"Ah."

Delilah paused reflectively. "Twins..." she said in a soft voice.

Then she shook her head. "Wow."

"Take two more cards," Sally said. Delilah chose two, and Sally placed them face up on the velvet tablecloth.

"See, this is Lakshmi, and she's reversed." Sally motioned to the golden goddess on the card between them. The words 'Bright Future' appeared below her name. "I think your fear is going to be the real cause of the trouble here, Delilah. You have to trust that this baby—these babies—are coming to your life and Tenika's for a reason." Sally raised her eyes and looked at her friend tenderly. "You are meant to raise these children together. There is a lot of abundance of all kinds here, but especially abundance in love."

"But both cards are reversed, Sally. Nematoma, too."

"That's right, because this is the lesson inherent in this experience. Lakshmi wants you to stop worrying and go with the flow. And Nematoma reverses when she wants you to get back in touch with Spirit. She's saying clean out your space, go on a retreat, smudge your home. Spend more time meditating. Just... up the vibe all around you to get ready for these babies. It's as important as the multi-vitamins."

"Okay," said Delilah. Then she hesitated. "But Sally...what if Tenika freaks out? I have no idea how she'll react."

"You haven't talked about it?"

Delilah shook her head.

Sally looked at her friend curiously. "How come?"

"Because...well, it was hard enough for her to get behind getting married. I didn't want to push it, you know?"

Sally smiled. "And yet, there's no stopping the Universe, Delilah. These babies are on their way, no matter how much anyone resists." She drew three more cards from the deck and lay them down. "Yup. Look at this," she said. "This entire reading is about preparing for a massive change."

Sally regarded her friend with a smile of support. "It's time to get ready and welcome them in," she said gently.

Delilah tossed her long, dark hair behind her shoulder and closed her eyes. "But...but I don't even know how we're supposed to do this. I mean...where do we even start?"

"There are lots of ways. There are books and doctors, and fertility centers and adoption agencies." Gently, Sally patted her friend's arm. "But the first person you need to talk to is your wife."

Delilah's stomach gave a lurch of apprehension. "Okay," she said uncertainly. She so didn't want to upset the delicate balance of their marriage. Things had been going so well since they'd gotten married the previous year.

Sally smiled once more. "Trust it, Delilah. Everything's going to be just fine."

Maybe, thought Delilah. But first she was seriously going to have to work on Tenika.

That is where all of this would begin. Or end.

*

Tenika Cummins leaned on the push button that brought down the aging Toyota Tundra on the overhead lift. The hydraulics at the Driven Garage tended to moan at such moments. And they did, indeed, as the Toyota returned to the floor.

"Okay, sis, you owe me one," she told her business partner, Lizzy as she peeled the greasy latex gloves from her hands. "Your brake linings are all set."

Lizzy glanced up from the lube job she was still in the midst of in the next bay, and she smiled. With practiced efficiency, she poured the last of the synthetic oil into the gaping maw of the tiny Honda before her and gave the bottle a shake. "You are a true friend, T. Thank you."

Tenika shrugged. "Even so, you doing all the lube jobs today is a pretty even exchange. So I guess a beer would do it."

Lizzy glanced around and her eyes fastened on the battered old clock, formerly white but now yellowed with age. It had been hanging there for decades, since Tenika's uncle owned the garage.

"Hey! Look at that. Quitting time, already. Okay, beer's on me." Lizzy smiled again at her cohort. "You make it easy, T."

Tenika strode over to the big overhead doors out to the San Pablo Avenue, and pulled each of them down into place. Then she gave a yawn. "I've been dragging all day," she said. "I don't know what my problem is." She shoved her glasses up her nose and pulled the bandana off that had been holding her long black dreads in place. Tenika began unzipping the grease-stained blue canvas coveralls that hid her street clothing. "Let's get the hell out of here."

Driven, the only woman owned automotive garage in Oakland—let alone the Bay Area—was as busy as ever. The garage was empty now, save for the two of them. A steady stream of customers, mostly women, had come in all day long for repairs, or to hang in the now popular conversation corner.

A moment later, Lizzy pulled out the keys and locked the door to the garage as Tenika climbed into her truck parked out front. "Meet you there?" she called through her window.

"Yep," Lizzy said, glancing over her shoulder. She watched Tenika drive off with a pang of gratitude. It was Tenika's uncle who originally brought the two of them together. And Tenika's uncle who'd left the garage to his niece in his will. Given that it was the first Black-owned garage in Oakland, it was fitting that it had now become the first woman-owned garage as well—even if Lizzy was White.

Tenika insisted the ancestors were smiling on them these days, because somehow they were still keeping the flame alive.

Moments later, Lizzy pulled up to The White Horse and parked behind Tenika's truck. For some it might seem a little early to be hitting a gay bar, but they could always count on a fairly empty scene this time of day. Not to mention some good Guinness on tap, and a quiet enough vibe to relax in.

Tenika was studying her phone as Lizzy arrived. "You beat me," Lizzy chuckled. "As usual. What'll it be?"

A moment later, Lizzy ordered an Obsidian for Tenika and a Guinness for herself from Lloyd, the affable transman behind the bar. Then she settled in beside her business partner. Ru Paul's *Drag Race* held forth silently on a large television screen overhead.

"So?" Lizzy asked. Tenika looked up as she put the phone away, and Lizzy noticed she had a particular look on her face. There was a vulnerable sweetness she didn't usually see at work.

"What's up?" Lizzy asked.

"Oh, it's just Delilah. She's…" Tenika laughed and shook her head. "She's got something planned for later, and she's not telling me what it is. These wives, they get up to things. And you know how that goes."

"Well, this whole married thing's still pretty new, so I guess I wouldn't."

"Lizzy. You're just as married I am."

"Okay, yes. We're married. But we're not married married, you know what I'm saying?"

Tenika nodded. Lizzy's wife Kate, an Irish immigrant, had been locked up in Sanctuary in the local Unitarian church since their wedding ten months earlier. This was how she avoided being deported back to Ireland, given her lack of legal immigration status. But now, even their lawyer said it was finally safe to come out and live together. Any day she'd be home—just as they'd been hoping for more than a year now.

"I feel you," Tenika said. "But this is it, sister. You are about to be extremely married."

Lizzy let out a sharp exhale. "I know! I know. I'm so used to just seeing Kate for an hour or two a day at the church. I won't even know what to do. Like…we get to actually have sex and sleep together and everything."

"I'll drink to that." Tenika chuckled. She raised her beer

bottle and touched Lizzy's glass. "Anyway, I never thought you'd hear me saying this, but here's to the institution of marriage. And these two fine women we managed to bring home."

Lizzy and Tenika toasted and drank. Then they each settled back reflectively. "So, T...tell me," said Lizzy after a moment. "What's the one big lesson you've learned from being married so far?"

Tenika folded her arms and pondered the question. "You know that thing people say? 'Happy wife, happy life?'"

"Yeah?"

"Fucker's true," she chuckled. "Things go *way* better when Delilah's feeling good. So I just make that my priority now."

"But what if you disagree about stuff? What do you do then?"

Tenika put down her bottle of beer and gave her business partner a look. "Lizzy, I'm not saying you lay down on your back and put your paws in the air like some damn dog. I'm saying you keep it real, but you do it with respect. You think about her feelings—and you double check yourself. Are you just being selfish or grumpy or...you know what I'm saying?"

Lizzy nodded and took another pull of her Guinness. "Okay, I can do that," she said.

"Don't worry about it, sis. You've got this. Anyway, Delilah and I want to have a party for you two. Since you didn't really get to have one after the wedding."

Lizzy lit up. "Seriously? That would be excellent." Unlike Lizzy and Kate, Tenika and Delilah lived in an actual house—one that Tenika had owned for some years. They were known for their parties.

Lizzy and Kate's 'reception' at the church had been tacos from a nearby taco truck and some bottles of soda from Costco. But then the entire wedding had somehow been pulled together in just twenty-four hours, on the advice of Kate's lawyer.

"We'll get the grill going, call all the girls, bring in some wine. Maybe your band can play. It'll be great."

Leaning over, Lizzy gave Tenika a slightly awkward hug. "You are a very good friend, T. Seriously."

Tenika blew off her friend's sudden outpouring of mushiness. "No biggie," she said. "Anyway, we'll pick a date. Let's do it soon, okay?"

"I'll call the band tonight. And Kate's going to be thrilled." Lizzy took another sip of beer and drank happily. But then a shadow passed over her face.

"What?" Tenika asked.

"Oh…it's nothing."

"Lizzy." Tenika shook her head. "You think I can't read your mind? How many years do I have to spend every frigging waking hour with you? What the hell is it?"

Lizzy looked down guiltily. "I guess I didn't tell you the rest," Lizzy admitted.

Her business partner just gave her a look. "I'm waiting."

Lizzy took a long breath. "Kate's coming home and that's all wonderful and everything. But we only have eighteen months basically, before we're back in the unloving arms of ICE."

Tenika put her beer down on the bar. "What are you talking about?"

"We're going to have to meet with Immigration in eighteen months and convince them that our marriage is legit. That we didn't just marry for a green card. There's like this big test. You have to answer questions in separate rooms about what kind of toothpaste you use, what side of the bed you sleep on, and shit like that."

"No sweat. You're about to start living together. Anyway, it is legit. You guys love each other. You're a match made in heaven."

"Sometimes," said Lizzy uneasily.

"Oh, Jesus. Not this again! Listen, sister, you really need to let go of the drama. In fact, I'm telling you to. Where's the gratitude, huh? You've got a damn rock star of a wife and you know it."

Lizzy put up her hand. "She's not the problem! I mean…I don't know what I mean…I…" Lizzy's voice faltered. "Never mind," she muttered.

"Yeah, I'm not," said Tenika finishing her beer. Then she got up, and patted Lizzy on the shoulder. "You're just nervous. Happens to the best of us."

"I guess."

"Well, don't worry about it," Tenika said, pulling out her truck keys. "I'm going home to make my wife happy, and I suggest you go home and start working on the same. 'Cause it's countdown time, sis. Less than twenty-four hours, right?"

"Yep," Lizzy said as she watched her partner turn and go. Then she smiled.

Somehow, in spite of everything, her dream was finally coming true.

Chapter Three

Monroe walked through the silence of the church sanctuary. It was a gloomy day, perfect for losing the love of your life. Or so it seemed.

Monroe approached Kate's bedroom door and listened. Her voice spilled through the cracks around the edges of the closed door. Her tone was low and intimate, and Monroe guessed she was talking to her wife, Lizzy, on the phone.

"Yes, yes, love… Okay. See you in a minute." Monroe heard her say. "Me, too," she said with a little laugh. Then Kate hung up.

There was no time to lose.

Hands on hips, Monroe glanced around, a little mournfully. None of this was easy. Not one single bit. But then, that was life when you were a half-broke queer musician who identified as a 'they.'

And that was another thing that galled Monroe. Few people ever got that critical detail right. It was always, 'Excuse me, ma'am,' and 'Yes, miss?' This was the shit that drove Monroe wild.

But Kate, on the other hand, had never once made that mistake. And she soundly cuffed those who did. Monroe had heard it with their own ears.

"Monroe's non-binary, you know," was Kate's exact phrase. Monroe was not a woman or a man. Instead, they were just not making the distinction. *Kate got it.* That, alone, had put Monroe on a fluffy pink cloud of unrequited love for Kate for…well…as long as she'd been at the church, which had been nearly a year.

And now, in less than an hour, Kate was leaving Monroe's world, possibly forever. Even worse, she was heading straight into the arms of her new wife, a woman she clearly adored.

Monroe cleared their throat and knocked gently on the door. The playlist Monroe had put together on a stick drive for Kate was soundly tucked into the pocket of their jeans, along with a note thanking Kate for everything she had done. Monroe just hoped it wasn't too gushy.

For the fact was, Monroe would miss Kate like hell. Ten months earlier, right here at Unitarian Universalists for Peace and Justice, they'd watched Kate marry Lizzy. And now finally, her green card status was kicking in and she could leave the church.

ICE was no longer standing at the door, threatening to deport her. Kate could actually get on with her life in Oakland.

Suddenly the door swung open and there she was. Monroe blinked, as if the lights had suddenly been turned on a little too brightly. Kate was stunning in a gray, rough knit turtleneck sweater that belied the September warmth outside. Her long strawberry red hair spilled over her shoulders, and she smiled broadly at Monroe.

"I'm so glad you came by," she said, in her lilting Irish accent. "Would've been wrong to slip away without a proper good-bye, wouldn't it?"

Kate held open her arms, and Monroe went to her, burying her in a massive hug.

"Yeah," said Monroe tightly into the wool of Kate's shoulder. Steadfastly, they tried to ignore the lump forming in their throat. Regardless, tears popped into Monroe's eyes. Stepping back, they wiped at them with an embarrassed laugh. "Sorry."

Kate smiled, giving Monroe a sympathetic pat on the arm. "What ever could you be sorry about, love?"

"That I'm…you know." Monroe faltered.

"Sad? It feels like the end of an era, for Lord's sweet sake, Monroe. It was epic, all we've been through."

It was true, of course. Not even a year earlier, their friend Catalina, the other woman who'd been in Sanctuary at the church, suddenly dropped dead from a massive heart attack. Monroe had been the one who found her that day, collapsed on the floor of her bedroom. The two of them had grieved her death together for months.

Then there was Kate's near breakup with Lizzy—and the wedding that had unexpectedly followed. And Lizzy's dedicated visits to the church, nearly every day of the past ten months, even though it was strictly forbidden in the church's rules for them to spend the night together. It had something to do with the city's strict Sanctuary zoning rules.

The momentum of their relationship was hard to ignore. Everything was Kate and Lizzy, Lizzy and Kate. Meanwhile, Monroe silently observed all of it at a respectful distance. Then every night, as their job as Grounds Superintendent and Music Director ended, Monroe went home, utterly and inexplicably alone.

But of course, there was an explanation.

Monroe was alone because Monroe was terrified, mostly of people in general. But also of being seen, and even of life itself. But then, maybe that's what made Monroe such a good musician. At least, that's what Kate thought. Monroe's sensitivity produced music that was "breathtaking." (A direct quote from Kate.)

How in God's name were they going to get along without Kate?

"Lizzy's on her way?"

"Mm-hmm," Kate nodded. Monroe glanced around the storage room turned bedroom. Kate's suitcase was packed and placed by the door, and her bed stripped. A large bag with her comforter and pillows, a computer case and a backpack sat by the door as well, along with a shopping bag full of groceries.

She'd even cleared out the refrigerator.

"I wonder who our next Sanctuary guest will be," Monroe ventured.

"Well whoever it is, they will be very fortunate," Kate said.

They gazed at each other for a moment. Then Kate looked away.

"Oh! Here…" Monroe dug out the stick drive and the card, and handed them to Kate. "I…uh…" Words failed Monroe now, and they studied the floor in agitation.

Kate took the items and smiled once again. "Is this more of your music?"

"It's all of it, basically. Everything that's decent."

Kate shook her head in appreciation. "Wow," she said softly. "This is going to be very valuable someday, Monroe. Mark my words."

Monroe gave a sniff. "Well, I don't know about that."

"No, but I do. You're going to be famous. I can feel it."

Monroe glanced up at their friend. "Oh, Kate, come on…"

"I'm deadly serious," Kate remarked. "Anyway, thank you. And Monroe, Lizzy's business partner Tenika is having a party for us. I hope you'll come."

Monroe stuck their hands in their pockets. Seeing Kate in newly wedded bliss with Lizzy was about the last thing they needed to witness. "Sounds great," Monroe said, attempting to sound upbeat.

"Her band is playing," Kate continued. "Have you heard The Breakdowns?"

Monroe said they hadn't, just as a car horn sounded outside. Kate pulled open the big door. A few seconds later, Lizzy appeared and leaning in, kissed Kate lightly on the mouth. "This is it!" she cried jubilantly. "Time to go be married."

Glancing around Lizzy saw Monroe now. "Oh…hey, Monroe," she said easily.

"Lizzy."

There was an awkward pause. "Monroe's going to come to Tenika's party for us," Kate explained.

"Oh yeah? Great! This everything, babe?" Lizzy picked up Kate's bag and grabbed the armful of groceries.

Suddenly, Monroe was spurred into action. "Let me help."

"We've got this, but thanks," Lizzy said, turning back toward her truck.

Kate turned back to Monroe. "Don't forget what Catalina said," she remarked. "Everyone's got someone. Right? Even if you don't know her yet." She gave Monroe's arm a reassuring pat. "Who knows...you might just have to go to a party and meet someone..." Kate smiled as her voice drifted off.

"I'll be there," Monroe said, trying to ignore the stab of grief that was rapidly filling their body.

"Okay, this is the last of it!" exulted Lizzy as she picked up Kate's last bag. She stopped and glanced at Monroe. "You okay?"

Monroe just rocked on their heels, hands in pockets, watching the scene unfold in front of them. "Me, oh I'm fine."

"Well, bye then," Lizzy said, passing through the door with Kate's suitcase. Kate paused at the door and looked at Monroe.

"We'll text. Right?" she said. "And stay in touch?" She sounded genuinely hopeful.

"Sure." Of course, Monroe wasn't certain they would do that at all. It was the kind of thing people always said, just as they were leaving forever.

Leaning over, Kate kissed Monroe's cheek. "Bye," she said gently. "And thanks for everything. If it wasn't for you, I'd be back in Dublin right now. You know you made it all possible."

Monroe was silent. Monroe had indeed made it possible. Monroe had been the one who talked the minister into reclaiming the storage room as an extra Sanctuary space. And it was Monroe who'd gotten the small bathroom working again, and cleaned it out.

In return, they received Kate, a gift from the heavens, albeit a temporary one.

Silently, Monroe watched Lizzy and Kate move toward the truck with the last of her things. Kate turned and gave one last smile, and then they were gone. The church door slammed shut behind them, a nod toward finality.

Shit.

Turning away, Monroe pulled out the large ring of keys on their belt and locked the storage room door. How the fuck was Monroe going to cope with losing Kate? Not that Monroe ever actually had Kate to begin with.

There had been a few fumbled hugs, and some devoted gazes, and that was about it. Really, living in fantasy was unsustainable. Monroe knew that.

It was like Kate said. There had to be someone, somewhere, who was right for Monroe. Catalina had said so.

Who knew? Maybe they actually would show up at Kate and Lizzy's party after all.

At the very least, it was worth a shot.

Chapter Four

Frankie hated situations like this. But then this was life as a cop, even when you were undercover. Somehow you were always on duty, even without the protection of a uniform and a badge.

At this moment, she worked her way along the side of the rush hour traffic crossing the Golden Gate Bridge, her head tucked in against the cold push of wind off the Pacific. A moment earlier, she'd abandoned her car to help a young woman she'd just spotted as she was heading over the bridge to Marin after work.

Jamming on her brakes, Frankie had put on her warning lights, left the car parked in the far right lane and picked her way through traffic to the other side. All the while cars trying to get across the bridge leaned on their horns impatiently. Of course, they didn't realize she was a police officer, or that she was trying to save a potential jumper. To them, Frankie just looked like just another dumb ass trying to do God knows what.

The Gate at any time of the year was not a place to be messed with, which is why it was especially urgent she reach the girl just up ahead. The evening fog was already rolling in and it was bone-deep cold.

Frankie jammed her hands into the pockets of her jacket as she walked toward the railing where the jumper was, trying to keep her approach cool and measured.

The girl was standing on a narrow, unprotected lip just beyond the railing. Seven hundred fifty feet below her was the heaving, churning, black and white surface of the bay, and there was nothing to block her fall. The girl didn't appear to be more than thirteen or fourteen, but somehow, she'd managed to get herself out there. With one shaking hand, she clung to the orange metal strut beside her. The girl looked terrified.

Frankie tried to put aside her striking resemblance to Tiffani as she approached. Tiffani, whose lifeless body on Ocean Beach had challenged everything Frankie once knew about herself. She'd been with the SFPD for decades now, but that didn't mean she'd kicked her PTSD. If anything it had gotten worse.

Take it easy, Frankie reminded herself once more. *Easy.*

Her mind had already run through the suicide prevention protocol twice in the last moment, and her request for a negotiator had been radioed in. All she had to do was keep the girl there and keep her talking. Perhaps even get her to climb back over the railing and return to safety.

"Hi," Frankie said, pausing at the railing just beyond the girl's reach. "How's it going?" It was a lame opening line to a jumper, she knew, but in all her years on the force, Frankie had never done this before.

The girl ignored her and said nothing.

"What's your name?" Frankie ventured, but still the girl didn't respond. She just focused on the black, heaving bay in front of her.

Frankie took a small step closer. "I'm sure you've got your reasons for being out there, but maybe I can help," she began. "If you want to talk about it, I'm here."

Now the girl glanced at Frankie anxiously, as if perhaps she did want to talk. She was heartbreakingly young, barely a teenager.

Now Frankie leaned against the railing as casually as she could, keeping a relaxed posture. Meanwhile she had to keep just enough distance, so she wouldn't get pulled over should the girl grab for her as she jumped.

"I know you don't know me," Frankie continued, keeping her tone as relaxed as possible, "but I'm a really good listener…and I'd really like to help. Honestly."

The girl turned her head now and looked directly at Frankie, and a pang of grief shot through her body.

This girl looked too much like Tiffani—what the fuck was this?

Frankie swallowed and continued, pushing that thought from her mind. "Things must be pretty hard, huh?"

The girl gave the slightest nod. "Yeah," she said softly.

"You want to tell me about it? Maybe we could figure out some other options."

"There aren't any," the girl said. Tears were running down her cheeks now. "There really aren't."

Frankie's mind spun along, grasping wildly for the right thing to say. She'd gotten this far, and that was a good thing. The patrol car would be along any moment. Urgently, she tried to recreate the script for suicide prevention, but it was something she hadn't thought about for years. Then a thought struck her.

Use the word 'safe'. Safe. A positive reinforcement word.

"Well…how about this? Is there someone I can get on the phone for you? Someone you'd feel safe with?"

The word 'safe' lingered in the air between them for a moment. But the girl looked away. Once again, she fixed her gaze out at the blackening sea before her.

"Okay…" Frankie continued uneasily.

If she could just get the girl in her car, Frankie could take her back to the station, regroup and figure out what to do next. All of her instincts lurched along, looking for the magic combination of words that would bring the girl back over the railing. Or at least make her wait just a little longer.

Say 'safe' again.

33

"Well, is there somewhere I could take you? Some place you'd feel safe? I'll give you a ride anywhere you want to go. I mean…it's pretty cold out here."

Cars were stopping now to watch the scene as it unfolded between them, which led to a lot more cars honking behind them.

"No," the girl said. Turning her head, she gave Frankie a penetrating stare, as if she were challenging Frankie to say the right thing.

"What is it?" Frankie asked. "You can tell me. I'm really here just to listen."

In the distance now, beyond all the honking. Frankie could hear a siren. It was coming from Marin, probably from the station in Sausalito. The girl heard it too, and she looked up. Tears were still running down her face.

"Come on now," Frankie soothed. "Just tell me your name. I can help you. Really…we can do this."

She pulled out the badge that hung from a chain beneath her shirt. "See? I'm a cop," Frankie said, showing the girl her badge. "You really can trust me."

Behind her, Frankie could feel the scattered movement of traffic as the siren's approach became louder. "I know things are hard or you wouldn't be out there," Frankie began again.

She heard the sound of running footsteps, then a beam of light passed over the girl's face, turning it white. Support had arrived.

At that moment, the girl gave a sigh. Looking at Frankie, she let go of her grip on the steel beam beside her. Then silently, she jumped. Frankie watched in shocked horror as her body hurtled toward the water.

Seconds later the bay swallowed the girl with only the slightest splash. Adrenaline surged up through Frankie's body and her mind momentarily went white. Calls behind her forced Frankie to turn around. It was the negotiator and two other officers.

For a moment, she was too stunned to say anything. Opening her mouth, no words came out. The negotiator reached her first. "What?" he asked, but Frankie just shook her head.

"I…I…" Frankie literally could not find the words to say what had just happened. She stared blankly at the man. Then finally, she pulled her badge on the chain from inside her shirt. Wordlessly she showed it to him.

The negotiator peered over the edge, sighed and turned back to the other two men. "It's over," he said quietly.

Moments later, Frankie was driving the rest of the way to Marin, methodically ticking mile after mile toward the Sausalito Police Station to file an eyewitness report.

Wild, cold fear filled her as she passed into the entrance of the Robin Williams Tunnel, a rainbow randomly painted around its gaping black entrance. Her heart pounded faster and faster as she drove toward the fading light on the other side. Frankie's breathing contracted into ragged gasps as her heart threatened to beat right out of her chest. As she got to the other side, she realized she was having a panic attack.

Clutching the wheel more tightly and she slowed the car as she willed herself to calm down. There was an exit right ahead. She could get off there. She could get hold of herself.

But Frankie was already gone. Something had split off in the moment the girl had jumped. Something she would have a very, very hard time retrieving.

Finally, Frankie pulled off at the Spencer Avenue exit, and stopped the car as a wave of nausea overtook her. Retching, she scrambled out of the driver's seat and fell to her knees at the edge of the pull over. She vomited and retched repeatedly in the grass. Then she remained there on her hands and knees for another moment, still panting.

A voice sounded behind her. She prayed it wasn't the other officers—they couldn't see her like this. But it was just another motorist, a man, who'd seen her and gotten out of his car. "Are you all right?" he asked.

Standing up, Frankie wiped her mouth, put her hands on her hips and shook her head helplessly. "Yeah…" she said. "Yeah. It's okay. Thank you."

What the hell was she going to do now?

*

Sally held the phone to her ear and paced. Yet again, her call went straight to voicemail. Either Frankie was on the phone for a very long time—it was now going on three hours—or she had turned her phone off. Which was just plain weird.

Usually Sally could get her girlfriend on the first ring or text. Putting down the phone once again, Sally resisted the natural urge to worry. This was her life, she reminded herself. This was what she signed up for when she decided to date a cop.

Standing up, Sally considered her options. She'd go for a walk, because walks usually helped. Anyway, what else was she going to do? Frankie undoubtedly had some very good reason, a professional reason even, for not taking her call. Really, she told herself, there was no reason to worry.

And yet…there was. Sally could feel it deep in her gut, and generally her intuition was never, ever wrong. Sighing, she glanced around for her deck of goddess cards. It was the first place she turned at moments like this.

Frankie needed her. She was almost sure of it. And of course, Frankie would not immediately let her know, for she was reticent about such things. That was her girlfriend in a nutshell.

A moment later, Sally located the deck sitting on the coffee table in Tenika's and Delilah's living room. It was beside the couch that had served as Sally's temporary bed for the last year. Sitting down, she gently pulled the worn, gilded cards from their box and gave them a tap. Then she shuffled them and laid them out on the coffee table in front of her.

Sally pulled a card and placed it on the table. It was the card for the Irish princess Isolt, and not surprisingly it was reversed. 'Eternal Love' said the card. Isolt was the card that always showed up when you were doubting your connection to another person, or you needed some kind of reassurance that your relationship was right and true. The fact that it was reversed was just Spirit's way of waving a red flag that something was wrong.

As she'd suspected, Sally was right. *Don't doubt your connection*, Isolt seemed to say. *Trust it.*

Which meant something was definitely wrong.

This was the very nature of her relationship with Frankie, one so unlikely and yet so certain, both at the same time. It had taken Frankie the better part of six months just to come to terms with the fact that Sally was a psychic. But even Frankie knew that their path was strong and eternal, and for that matter, destined. Sally had even been thinking it might be time for them to live together.

Rising, she walked into the bedroom and pulled a soft gray hoodie from her closet shelf. There was only one thing to do right now.

She needed to go over to Frankie's house immediately. Somehow, she had to help.

*

Sally pressed Frankie's doorbell a second time. She heard it buzz faintly inside the house, but still no footsteps were forthcoming. She paused and regarded the open shutters in the plate glass windows beside her. Which was weird.

Frankie, being hyper-vigilant, was always one to close the shutters promptly the minute the sun set. The obvious assumption was that Frankie was still out, hours after she was due home. And yet…her car was parked right in front of the house.

Furthermore, they had a date in less than an hour. It was not like Frankie to disappear on her.

Sally cupped her hands around her eyes and peered into the darkness of Frankie's house. It was hard to see anything, but she tried. Faintly, she could make out the image of the living room rocker, and the television, and Frankie's old upright piano that she never played.

Sally hesitated. Something was off. But what, exactly?

As she continued to look inside, she saw something move in the shadows by Frankie's dining room table. Peering even more closely, Sally strained to see what it was. With a sickening feeling, she realized it was Frankie, sitting there in the dark at her dining room table, her head in her hands. Sally's heart felt a stab of pain.

Something really was seriously wrong.

Knocking lightly on the window, Sally tried to get Frankie to respond. "Honey?" she called through the glass. "Is everything all right?" There was no movement from the table, so Sally rapped at the window more insistently.

Sally could see Frankie slowly swivel her head in her direction. She watched Frankie hesitate. Then so slowly, as if she could barely move, Frankie rose and walked to the door. It was almost as if she were in a stupor.

Some moments later, Frankie unlocked the door. Finally, she opened it.

Frankie stood before Sally, ashen, still in her clothing from work. Sally could see she still hadn't taken her body armor off.

Gently, she touched Frankie's arm. "Honey, are you okay? What is it?"

Frankie didn't say a word.

"Honey?" Still Frankie didn't answer. Instead, she just left the door open, then she drifted away. Sally followed and watched as her girlfriend lay down in fetal position on the couch in her darkened living room and closed her eyes.

"What is it? What happened?" Sally asked, but Frankie did not reply. Finally, Sally went to her in the dark. Sitting on the living room floor beside the couch, she began to stroke Frankie's arm.

"I'm here, baby," she said, the words coming from somewhere in the back of her mind. "And I'm always going to be."

"Okay," Frankie said in a small voice.

"Something happened at work?" she asked after a minute. Frankie nodded.

"Can you talk about it?"

"No," Frankie said in a small voice.

Sally took a deep breath. She'd never seen her lover like this —not even close. If anything, Frankie was one to tough it out, cracking dark jokes and shrugging off the daily grind of being on the force. Regardless, Sally knew Frankie's PTSD was real. She's been in therapy for it ever since they'd met. It was something Frankie almost never talked about.

Gently Sally removed her hand. "Shall we call your therapist?" she asked, but Frankie did not answer. Instead, she rolled over and pressed her face into the couch cushions.

"Okay," Sally said, sitting back on her heels. "I'm going to leave you alone for about a half hour, honey, while I go get my stuff at home. I'll be back, and I'm taking a key so I can let myself back in. And then I'm not leaving. I'll stay here as long as you need me."

Frankie did not respond.

It didn't matter that Sally had a roster full of readings the next day, and the day after that. *Work be damned*, she thought, as she moved toward the door with new determination. Clearly, there was a crisis at hand and she was needed.

This was what lovers did for each other.

Chapter Five

Delilah squinted and studied the screen on her phone. Then she swallowed hard. This had to be wrong. Unlike the page she'd just been looking at, this website said the cost of In Vitro Fertilization was $20,000. Which was about $15,000 more than she and Tenika had in the bank at any given time. Once more, Delilah looked at the number curiously. *That just had to be wrong.*

Delilah peered at the chart, breaking down the costs. There seemed to be voluminous amounts of information online about 'TTC', or 'trying to conceive' as it was known on the web. And there was an equally huge number of things to spend money on in the process. This included everything from temporary sperm freezers to wildly expensive shots a friend or family member had to learn how to give you.

Delilah sat back and sighed. Then getting up, she began to pace. Unable to stop herself, she looked at her phone once more. This was way more complicated than she thought it would be.

You could shop for an anonymous donor from a sperm bank. You could canvass your male friends for a shot of sperm. One of you could donate eggs to the other, so the baby shared your DNA. The list of ways for a lesbian couple to conceive went on and on.

Putting down her phone, Delilah rose and stretched. Her next client was due to walk into the studio at any moment. He was a nice guy, a gay man named Gerome who was getting his second sleeve tattoo of Japanese cranes.

For a moment Delilah flashed on the idea of asking Gerome to father their child. Then she laughed out loud at herself. What in God's name was she thinking? She barely even knew the man. Having a baby was starting to become an obsession.

Even if Tenika agreed to raise a child with her, she'd never go for a dude like Gerome as the father. First of all, she'd probably want sperm from an African-American guy, so they could at least have a representative racial mix. Which was perfect, of course... but what was Delilah thinking, trying to do this all alone?

The cold truth remained. She still hadn't told Tenika about any of this—or even that she wanted a baby in the first place.

Guiltily, Delilah glanced around the break room. There was absolutely no good reason to go looking at websites and getting all cranked up without her wife. Tenika needed to be part of the conversation, starting now. That really was the first order of business, and Delilah knew it.

She pulled open the mini-fridge and studied its random contents—a container of kim chee-flavored sauerkraut, two blueberry yogurts and a bag of THC gummies. Shaking her head, she closed it again.

Yes, she would tell T. She would do it tonight, when she got home. *For real.*

Delilah tried to imagine what Tenika would say when she told her she wanted to have a baby. Truthfully, she had no idea. Over the course of their eight years together, Tenika had been incredibly reluctant to marry, until suddenly one day she wasn't.

That was after Delilah's health scare last year, when they both thought a sudden tremor she had meant she was getting MS or early onset Parkinson's Disease. Then suddenly, there was T, presenting her with an engagement ring and setting a date.

Her responses had been less than predictable so far. So it's possible, Delilah reasoned, that Tenika was now so happily married she'd be an auto-yes to having kids. Maybe she, too, had been thinking of it.

On the other hand…maybe all this fretting she was doing was for naught, because they could never afford it.

But so far, when it came to bringing it up. Delilah had choked. Twice.

It wasn't that Delilah thought Tenika would give her a flat no. It's that she was afraid to find out the truth. For as long as Delilah stayed in her head, floating along on a pink and blue cloud of fantasies, she didn't have to confront reality.

Maybe the ever practical Tenika would look at her like she was crazy when she asked her. Delilah could just hear her now: *What are you, nuts? That's like thousands of dollars! How are we even going to pay for it? Anyway, I never said I wanted kids…*

A sudden solitary tear slid down Delilah's cheek, betraying her anxiety. She wiped it away with the back of her hand. The door to the shop jingled as her next appointment arrived, and Delilah stood up abruptly, shaking off her worries.

She really had to talk to her wife.

Tonight.

*

Rosalind stood up and stretched, eager to break the seal between herself and her desk. Lately, she'd been working way too hard. But then, that's what usually happened when she was trying to avoid something.

Like the fact that she'd heard exactly nothing from Tasha since she slept with her up at Harbin ten days earlier. But then… what did she expect? She met her at a clothing optional hot spring. That alone should have set off a cascade of red flags in her head.

But no, she'd been swept away by their apparent chemistry, and remarkable similarities. The inner dialogue of delusion went on and on in Rosalind's head. *(Tasha's an activist! She starts things and stands up for things! Just like me!)*

Yet, the last ten days of silence was…well, definitive.

Now Rosalind was just mad at herself. Yet again, the steely pragmatist had gone soft. Here she was, a woman capable of breaking down the numbers and calling out any bro-steeped start up running scams in the Bay Area. What the hell had she been thinking?

Rosalind didn't know, nor at this point did she care. She just knew that she was damn tired of being alone, and that it was time to find a girlfriend. Ideally one who would actually show up and have an honest to God relationship with her. She could definitely do better than Tasha. She had to.

Wearily, Rosalind plunked down her mug, opened the coffee maker and put a plastic Dark French Roast pod in its coffee tray. Closing it, she snapped on the machine, and waited for the reliable trickle of coffee in her cup. As usual, her response was Pavlovian.

God, she needed this buzz. Just like she needed love. The question now was where to find it.

There were nearly eight million people in the Bay Area, a remarkably high percentage of whom were lesbians. Somewhere, one of them had to be a good fit for her. She just knew it.

Rosalind sighed as she extracted the steaming mug from the coffee maker. She would find her woman, she reassured herself. It was just a matter of putting herself out there.

Taking a bracing sip of the hot coffee, she closed her eyes for a moment, imagining what was possible. This time, her feet would stay securely on the ground. She would be critical, observant, and sharp. She would be on her game.

At least she was going to damn well try.

Sighing, Rosalind went back to her desk. One way or another, love would arrive.

She hoped.

*

Gently, Tenika knocked on the door one more time. There was no sound coming from inside, and it seemed like the lights were mostly off in Frankie's house. Sally had given no indication what was up. But something was, that was for damn sure.

Tenika hadn't even waited for Delilah to get home from work. She'd hurried over as soon as she got Sally's text.

After a moment, Sally appeared. "Sorry," she said. Opening the door slightly, she stepped outside and joined Tenika on the front stoop. "Thanks for coming, T."

"What the hell's going on, girlfriend? You've got me worried."

Sally sighed. She looked exhausted. "It's a worrisome situation," she said. "Frankie had to deal with a suicide—a jumper on the GG a few days ago. Now she's in bad shape." Sally paused. "I've never seen her like this. That's why you guys haven't seen me in days."

Tenika nodded. Sally had been sleeping over at Frankie's more and more since. But to be gone for four days in a row was a whole new kind of serious. "So how bad is she?" Tenika asked. "Is she functional?"

Sally shrugged. "Kind of. I mean, she gets up, but then she just lies on the couch all day. Barely even talks. It took me 24 hours just to find out what happened. She's been calling in sick to work. I mean…she's a mess. I'm afraid to leave her alone."

"Wow," Tenika said, shaking her head. "So the jumper jumped, I take it?"

Sally nodded. "Fourteen years old. Frankie couldn't save her. That's why I finally texted you guys."

Tenika studied her friend. "I'm glad you did. So…what do you need exactly? What can we do?"

Sally looked perplexed. "I have no idea, T. I mean, I keep thinking she's going to feel better and kind of rise up and snap out of it…but she's not. The thing is she already has PTSD to begin with. I guess it got triggered. Basically, I'm out of my league here."

"I'm sorry to hear that," Tenika said quietly. Frankie had been a steady, solid presence in their lives for the past year or two, ever since she helped Lizzy and Tenika save Driven Garage.

Then Frankie had shown up at just the right time, and helped the two of them get a restraining order on a competitor who was trying to run them out of business. Since then, she'd become a regular presence in the garage's conversation corner—which is where she ultimately got together with Sally.

Never once had Frankie shown any signs that she was even under stress. But then…look at what she did all day long. She had to hit some kind of bottom sooner or later.

"Does she have a therapist?" Tenika asked.

"Yeah, I've called her twice, but Frankie won't get on the phone with her or even go in for an appointment." Sally paused. "You know how she is."

"I can imagine," said Tenika quietly. Frankie was the strong, silent type. She was the last person to ever ask for help.

"Anyway," Sally said, "that's why you haven't seen me back at the house lately. I kept thinking I would be home…" Her voice drifted off.

"Don't worry about it," Tenika said. "Come back when you can, or when you want to. Anyway, let us know if you're moving in with Frankie," she added with a little smile.

Now Sally gave a laugh. "Oh, T, believe me—you'll know. That would be big news around here. For now, we just have to get through this."

Tenika opened up her arms. "Come here, sis," she said as she wrapped her friend in a long, warm embrace.

"Thanks," Sally said into Tenika's t-shirt-covered shoulder. After a moment, she pulled back and smiled up at her friend. "I needed that."

"You've got to call me if we can do anything," Tenika said. But just then the door swung open, and suddenly there was the rumpled figure of Frankie, blinking in the sunlight.

"Hey, T," she said softly.

"Need a hug?" Tenika asked, and wordlessly, Frankie nodded. Tenika put out her arms and Frankie came into them for an embrace.

"You're going to get through this," she murmured into Frankie's ear. "We've got you, girl."

Frankie gave a sniff as tears began to pour down her face, and a small sob escaped her throat. Against all odds, she began to cry, right there in the autumn sunlight in front of her house. It was the first time Sally had seen her lover cry.

Meanwhile, Tenika just quietly patted her back as Frankie sobbed more and more intensely. After several minutes, Tenika took a bandana from her pocket and offered it to Frankie, who blew her nose. She shook her head, as if trying to fling the bad thoughts away. Then she wiped her face on the cloth in her hand, her eyes on the ground.

"Okay," Frankie said as if she was trying to calm somebody down. "It's okay." She handed the bandana back to her friend.

"Look, Frankie, shit happens," Tenika reasoned. "But you got this. I know you do. You're a hella strong woman."

"Yeah…well…not now…" Frankie's voice drifted off. Then without another word she headed back toward the doorway. Turning, she paused and looked at her friend. "Thanks," she said.

Then slipping inside, Frankie disappeared into the darkness once more.

Tenika shook her head and looked at Sally with a sigh. "That's some serious shit."

"Yep." Sally paused and looked at her friend. "I thought you'd want to know. Anyway, thank you for coming, T. That's the first time she's even been able to cry."

Tenika shrugged and gave a chuckle. "I feel like I didn't do a thing."

"You did," Sally affirmed. "You totally did."

The two women exchanged a knowing smile.

It was clear there would be much more to come.

*

Something was up, that much Tenika knew. It was the second trip she and Delilah had made to the Albany Bulb in ten days. It wasn't that Tenika objected.

She loved the place with sweeping views of the bay, and its ragged shoreline with the weird scrap metal sculptures and the technicolor graffiti. It's just that this was their special place. And going there twice in less than a month made it a whole lot less special.

The first time they went there was the night that Lizzy moved Kate back into their place. Delilah had really been ramped up that night—a little too animated, it seemed. And a little too gleeful. She'd even managed to run home after work, and whip up Tenika's favorite double fudge brownies to eat on the beach.

Delilah was coy when Tenika asked why. "No reason," she'd said lightly. "Just love."

Which *was* believable. But still…this was Tenika's first warning sign that something was up. And now here they were again. Another trip to the Albany Bulb, yet again complete with more homemade baked goods.

Silently, Tenika watched as her partner pulled a chilled bottle of Sauvignon Blanc from the fridge, and tucked it neatly into the basket beside the wax paper bundle of chocolate chip cookies. "You want help?" she asked.

"No," said Delilah, and she smiled at her partner, her dimples lighting up her face. Today she had on her 'Dorothy' outfit—a blue gingham swing skirt she'd found in a vintage clothing store. She'd topped it off with a prim yellow cardigan, a pair of black ankle socks and pink tee strap heels. Her long black hair was plaited into braids, and woven together at the back of her head, and tiny plastic Corgi dogs adorned her ears.

The pink heels were about the last shoe most women would wear to walk the rough and tumble dirt and gravel trails of the Albany Bulb, but that was Delilah for you. Not only would she wear them, she'd manage just fine and be her fully quirky fashionista self in the process.

As for the earrings, Tenika knew this was Delilah's way of paying homage to their marriage. The engagement ring Tenika had given her—also at the Albany Bulb—was a vintage gold band with an enameled Corgi on it.

Yeah, something was definitely up. Tenika could feel it. She sighed as she sat there, watching her wife bustle around the kitchen. "Honey?" she began, testing the waters.

Delilah looked up brightly. "Hmm?"

Just a few hours earlier, she'd been an ardent and attentive lover to Tenika. Perhaps a little more than usual, Tenika thought, as they lounged in the Saturday sunshine afterwards. She'd even let Tenika go to a few places they didn't usually go. In the words of the sex columnist in their local free paper, Delilah had indeed been 'good, game, and giving.'

Tenika's advice to Lizzy a few weeks earlier now rung in her ears. "Happy wife, happy life," she'd jauntily told her friend. Tenika paused. She knew she had to play this carefully. "So baby…" she began again.

"Yeah, T?" This time Delilah did not look up. Tenika watched her toss the last of the feta cheese into the pasta salad she'd just made, and give it a stir. Delilah snapped the Tupperware lid into place, and turned to her partner. Then she paused, hand on hip. "What, honey?"

Tenika said nothing, because what was she going to say? *I think something's up because you're being so loving, sweet and attentive?* No, Delilah was just being happily married.

That was all that was supposedly wrong…right?

Get over yourself, Tenika thought grimly as a pang of shame oozed through her.

"No, tell me. What were you going to say, sweetie?" Delilah repeated, but Tenika didn't answer immediately. Moving on, Delilah plucked a few leaves from their counter top basil plant, and rinsed them off at the sink.

"Nothing," Tenika finally said. Then she paused.

Oh, get over yourself. Rising, Tenika shook the last of her doubts away. Moving toward her lover, she kissed the back of her neck. "Love you, baby."

"I love you, too," Delilah said, her eyes on the basil in her hands.

No, nothing was up. Nothing at all, Tenika decided. It was just her usual wrong-headed struggle to be happy.

Who knew happiness could be so hard?

Chapter Six

Kate walked into Driven with the air of the newly liberated. She was carrying a large bakery box. "Hello, women!"

"Hey!" Tenika looked around the hood of the Audi she was working on, her face lit up. She put down her tools, peeled off her gloves and gave Kate a long hug. "I was wondering when you were finally going to make it back here."

Then she gave her business partner a knowing look. "Or were you two just a little too busy the last few days?"

Kate laughed out loud. "Oh, please!" Lizzy protested, giving Tenika a sidelong glance. She placed a gentle kiss on her lover's forehead. "Hey, there."

Putting down the box, Kate leaned up on tip toes for one more kiss, this time on the mouth. "Hi." The two women smiled at each other for a lingering moment. "I made it," Kate said.

"Yup." Lizzy nodded. They continued to gaze at each other, unblinking.

"Cut it out, you two, we've got work to do," Tenika chided. Then she turned toward the conversation corner. "Hey, everyone! Kate's in the house!"

The four women seated on the other side of the garage looked up and immediately smiles broke out. An older silver-haired woman with a rounded face stood up, her arms wide open. "We've missed you, honey!"

"Alice," Kate said warmly, striding over for a hug. At this point, Alice was more of a regular than an actual customer. Her retirement gig had apparently evolved into hanging in Driven's conversation corner, doing jigsaw puzzles, drinking the free coffee and ardently searching for a new girlfriend.

But then, that's exactly what the conversation corner was for. It had been Kate's idea.

They'd created it more than a year earlier, back when Kate and Lizzy met. At the time, Driven was hanging on by the skimpiest of threads, but as Kate predicted, once there was coffee, comfort and the vague promise of romance, the single lesbians could not stay away. And after a paint job and the purchase of couches, tables, puzzles and a decent coffee maker, in they came.

This little corner of Oakland had since become the de facto hang out for any woman wanting to find her next queer love. Which was a beautiful thing, given that most of the lesbian bars in the Bay had disappeared over the years. It was the perfect blend of convenience and pleasure. Mainly because it was so easy to relax here while your oil was being changed, or your check engine light was being investigated.

When Kate was around, she kept the place stocked with freshly brewed coffee, rich cream and the occasional, overflowing box of donuts. Not one of their loyal patrons had forgotten this. And now Kate was back once more, donuts in hand.

To Alice's delight, she now approached carrying a large box of Maple-Bacon cronuts. "It's like a croissant, but it's a donut," Kate explained. "I figured it was time to celebrate."

At that moment, Rosalind suddenly popped her head in the doorway of the garage. "Kate? Is that you?"

"Damn, it's like old home week today," Lizzy said and her business partner smiled.

Soon Rosalind was ensconced with Kate on the couch, coffees in hand, while Alice was on high alert over by the puzzle table.

Discreetly, she was taking in every word of their conversation, for Alice had carried a small flame for Rosalind ever since they'd met here months earlier. Who cared if they had a thirty-year age difference?

"I read every last word of *The Chronicle* article, repeatedly!" Kate said. "I was so impressed."

Rosalind looked down, shyly. "I was pretty shocked myself, to tell you the truth. But…yeah. I guess some things happened while you were gone."

"And now? Let's get down to business, Rosalind. What about love?" Kate asked. At this, Alice looked over encouragingly, though Rosalind ignored her gaze.

"I'm…well…"Rosalind faltered.

"Looking, perhaps?" asked Kate with a smile.

Rosalind studied her hands. "Well, okay. I mean…*maybe.*"

"Why maybe? It's a short life, Rosalind—shorter than it looks. And if you're not properly looking for a love, it may never happen, dear."

"It will—well, it may. I mean, it's complicated, Kate."

"Ah," Kate smiled knowingly. "I could have guessed."

"There was this woman, but she's…" A bleak look came over Rosalind's face for just a moment. Then she remembered where she was, and why she had come there.

She sat up a little straighter. "Yes," Rosalind suddenly said. "I actually am looking."

Over at the puzzle table, Alice leaned toward the two women just a titch more closely, determined to catch every word.

"And for what in particular?" Kate continued.

Rosalind hesitated. "Someone interesting, I guess. And definitely someone my age." Pointedly, she did not look at Alice, whose hopeful expression now disappeared once and for all. "Just…you know…someone nice."

Kate patted her knee. "My dear, we can do much, much better than 'nice.' There's going to be a party soon at Tenika's, from what I understand. I'll make sure you are included," Kate said. "You too, Alice," she added, without looking up.

Alice smiled and took a bite of her cronut.

"Well, then, that's all settled then," Kate said, rising. She gave Rosalind an encouraging smile. "You'll get snapped up in no time, I am sure of it."

Watching Kate walk away, Rosalind suddenly felt reassured. This might actually be easier than she thought.

"See ya," she said easily to Alice, as she moved toward the exit. Her business here was done.

For now.

*

Frankie sat up wearily in the bed. She couldn't lie here for one more moment. Beside her, the sleeping figure of Sally was oblivious, lost in her cocoon of sleep and dreams.

Damn it. You'd think she'd finally get to sleep after all these nights of insomnia. But no. That's how insomnia was. Relentless. Once it took hold, you might as well just surrender.

Restlessly, Frankie put on a sweatshirt and padded into the living room. She plopped down on the couch and yawned. Really, she should read a book. A boring book. The most boring book she could find. That might do the trick.

But instead, she just sat there, her thoughts still going around and around in a manic circle. It was hard not to keep replaying the scene on the bridge, though Frankie knew that it did her no good. That single, indelible moment of shock, and the high grade panic that coursed through her body played on in a steady loop in her brain.

Frankie was in full-blown PTSD, and she knew it. *Why the hell did that kid have to look so much like Tiffani?* The world, she decided, was grossly unfair.

She thought of her father and his relentless pep talks, essentially telling her to 'man up' even as a kid. But then, being raised by a single dad tended to do that to a girl. Especially since he was in law enforcement as well. She shook her head, realizing she was in no rush to share her current dilemma with her father, or the fact that she was now on leave. Her father was as old school as they came. He'd be anything but supportive now.

Walking over to the china cabinet where she kept her mother's silver and her grandmother's dishes, Frankie pulled open a small drawer and pulled out the cannabis cigarette Tenika had recently brought by for her. Frankie held the pre-roll in her hand and studied it cautiously.

It wasn't like cannabis was illegal or anything. Not in California, at least. And it wasn't even like she was working. Frankie couldn't work, even her Lieutenant agreed. He'd given her the rest of the month off on sick leave, and a referral to a staff psychiatrist from the Behavioral Sciences Unit.

Still, this break didn't sit well with Frankie. If she was going to miss a bunch of work days, she wanted to at least have a broken leg or something justifiable. The idea that she was merely depressed, or grieving, or stricken, or whatever you wanted to call it, was a huge source of personal embarrassment to Frankie.

So, in the end, she might as well get stoned.

Frankie pulled open the drawer again, looking for matches. She didn't think Sally would mind if she lit the joint. The worst that could happen was that she'd take a few puffs and stink the house up.

If anything, Sally was incredibly supportive. Too supportive, perhaps. For Frankie also worried that Sally would one day just leave, especially if Frankie couldn't get her ass in gear and get back to work. She kept telling Sally to get back to the shop and do her readings, but she just stayed and stayed, insisting she didn't want to leave Frankie alone.

Sally *seemed* engaged, the perfect picture of the perfect partner. But...what if she wasn't?

What if she was actually silently resentful of all the laundry she'd been folding and the meals she'd been cooking for Frankie? What if Sally was running out of money? Frankie honestly didn't know how long Sally could afford to hole up with her like this. She hadn't seen a client in weeks.

Still, so far, Sally remained the picture of quiet patience, not pushing Frankie to do more than she could handle. She even drove Frankie to her therapy appointments. No, Sally had been pretty perfect, when you came right down to it. Suspiciously perfect.

Frankie wondered how long it would last.

Lighting the joint, she took a long inhale, then coughed several times as the harsh smoke invaded her lungs. Peering at the joint, she wondered what she was doing wrong. The pot smoke burned in her lungs and irritated the back of her throat. *Damn*, she thought, *what's the big appeal here?*

Then Frankie took another toke, more out of curiosity than anything else. The smoke stayed in the top of her head this time, and immediately, she began to feel her thoughts slow and melt into nothingness. A sensation of complete and total ease poured through her body.

Frankie wandered over to the couch and lay back against the cushions as she took another draw from the joint. Closing her eyes, this time she savored the slow crawl of the smoke up into the upper reaches of her brain. A deeper sense of peace poured through her body now, and she surrendered to it. Taking one final draw, she kept the smoke locked in her mouth, pulling it up toward all of the toxic, troubling panicked thoughts that had cranked through her exhausted nervous system for the last nine days.

What would it take to finally let go?

Frankie meandered into the kitchen now, and stubbed what was left of the pre-roll out on a dirty plate on the counter. Sitting down in a nearby chair, she sat back, studied the kitchen's aging paint job and assessed how she felt.

She felt…reasonable. Actually, she felt languid, and some-what free, as well. It was an incredible relief. Frankie smiled now, for the first time since the incident on the bridge. Then she chuckled, shaking her head at the absurdity of the mental cage she'd been occupying for the last few weeks.

Suddenly it was all so obvious. Frankie had work to do—that much was clear. But it was inner work that could come with time. For now, she needed to sleep. Then she needed to get up, put on her body armor and go back to work.

Frankie smiled once more, grateful to whatever force had brought Tenika and her pre-roll over to her house. This time their roles had reversed, and it was Tenika saving her ass. Standing up, Frankie yawned and slowly made her way back to her bed.

The world really was kind of perfect, when you got right down to it.

*

This was it. Delilah checked the time on the Felix the Cat wall clock behind her. Then she glanced back at the recipe on the phone propped up in front of her. She was up to her elbows in greased kale, at the moment, as she hand-tossed the kale salad that was the nutritional star of the dinner she was making tonight.

The chicken pot pie in the oven was browning nicely. Tenika's favorite after-work beer, Obsidian, had been chilling for hours. And the apple brown betty she'd put together from local apples made the entire house smell like cinnamon.

She'd had to cancel her four o'clock client to pull it off. But now, two hours later, Delilah was glad she had. Tenika was going to be blown away.

She heard the front door open as her wife arrived. "Hey there…wow! What do I smell?"

"Hi, honey," Delilah called.

"Whoa," Tenika said in a low voice as she walked into the

kitchen. "Now you're making…what? Is that apple brown betty?"

She leaned over and kissed Delilah on the mouth. "What's all this?"

Delilah shrugged lightly. "Just—"

"Wait a minute here…" Delilah was now peering in the oven at the chicken pot pie. "You've made this yourself?"

Delilah didn't look at her, but kept her eyes on the salad in front of her as she added slices of tangerine. "Mm-hmm."

Tenika studied her wife, hard at work on her salad. "I'm sorry," she said, not even sitting down, "but I just gotta ask. Do you want something? Is there something you're not getting from me?"

For a moment, Delilah froze. *Shit.* It hadn't occurred to her that Tenika was going to beat her to the point. "No, not at all, I—" she began. But then she stopped. Her wife was not stupid.

Turning, Delilah began a new tack. "We're celebrating," she announced, her voice lit with false cheer.

"Oh?" Tenika folded her arms suspiciously and waited for the explanation.

"I found out about something…amazing," Delilah said. A sudden cold chill of fear crept down her spine as the entire evening began to dissolve around her. Gone were her carefully laid plans, complete with seduction. This was definitely not going as planned.

"I mean, I've known about it. And maybe you have, too, T, but the thing is we haven't even begun to talk about it, and I just think that—"

Tenika looked at her. "Wait a minute. What are we talking about?"

Delilah paused, hesitating. This is so not how she wanted this conversation to go. Behind her, the chicken pot pie suddenly became more fragrant. She took a long breath.

"Babies," she said. "Or at least one."

Tenika blinked. "You want to have a baby?"

The two women looked at each other in silence. Delilah's throat was dry. "Yeah."

"Is this why you've been baking all those cookies and shit?"

"No! No...I..." Delilah's words failed her. Miserably, she sat down. "Yes," she said in a small voice.

A look of annoyance crossed Tenika's face. "Then why the fuck didn't you just ask me?" Tenika began to pace in front of Delilah, a mute look of fury on her face. "I'm not some man you have to manipulate into getting what you want, you know."

"I didn't mean to...I just..."Tears sprung up in Delilah's eyes.

"For Christ's sake! I'll talk to you about this any time, and you know that, Delilah." Tenika stopped now and faced her wife, seated in front of her. "Make me a pie because you want to make me a pie. But don't play me, sister. Don't do that shit to me. That is not okay."

"Okay," Delilah muttered.

Silently, Tenika opened the refrigerator, extracted a bottle of beer, and opened it at the counter. Then turning, she did what she always did at such moments. She left.

A moment later, Delilah heard the front door quietly close. Putting her head down in her arms, she began to weep. Once again, she'd been victim to her need to control the situation. She'd forgotten her own golden rule, one she seemed to keep learning and relearning again and again.

In no way was it ever okay to push Tenika. The woman simply wouldn't put up with it. And now...here she was, alone on a ruined evening. Rising wearily, Delilah pulled the now steaming chicken pot pie from the oven and tested the crust. It was perfect. She left it sitting on the stovetop.

Walking away, Delilah untied her apron in a few quick moves. Then balling it up, she threw it on the floor in frustration.

She still had no idea what Tenika thought about having a baby.

Chapter Seven

Soft light filtered through a crack in the curtains in the small back room at Desire's Magical Garden. Rosalind was supposed to be preparing a massive fund-raising mailing right now, but she didn't care. She was just glad she'd managed to wrangle an appointment on Sally's jam-packed schedule.

For days, Rosalind had been waiting impatiently for her reading with Sally, and now it was here. If she was going to find real love at this exact moment in her life, Sally was sure to see it.

Or she'd gently tell Rosalind why it wasn't meant to be.

So far, Sally's readings had been a hundred percent right, and Rosalind was in no mood to doubt. Nervously, she kneaded her hands, politely folded in her lap.

Sally laid down the last of the initial twelve-card spread. Then she shook her head in amazement. She looked up in wonder at Rosalind. "Wow…what's up with your parents?"

Rosalind swallowed hard. "My parents?" she asked. Visions of sudden strokes and aneurysms swam into her consciousness. After all, they were nearly in their seventies.

Sally cocked her head curiously and smiled at her client. "Well, something's brewing. They're all over this spread." Pausing, she closed her eyes, then she opened them and looked directly at Rosalind.

"I think it's something you're not telling them."

Rosalind immediately flushed hot with embarrassment. She knew just what Sally was referring to, of course. She knew *exactly* what.

The fact that she still hadn't come out to her aging Chinese evangelical Christian parents was heavy on her mind, as it had been for more than a year. Delaying the announcement was part of a tactical strategy, driven primarily by fear.

Rosalind had publicly humiliated the family when she turned her former company, True Wire, over to the FBI, and the story broke on the front page of *The San Francisco Chronicle*. It galled them that she'd lost her 'good job,' and all the benefits that came with it, only to start a much riskier foundation that forced her to live paycheck to paycheck.

Furthermore, her foundation fought for women's rights in the tech workspace. That, alone, baffled her traditional parents. They didn't even seem to care that her new work made her the national face of feminist resistance in tech.

So…yeah. They were *really* going to hate it when she told them she was a lesbian, on top of everything else.

"Oh, wow," Rosalind muttered grimly. Surely her parents didn't need to know this, too. Did they?

Sally looked up. "You know what I'm talking about then?"

Rosalind nodded. "Basically I'm trying to spare them. I haven't come out to them, yet, Sally. Or anyone else, really. Except you, more or less." She wasn't going to mention her fling with Tasha.

Rosalind paused and sighed. "You have no idea how rough the last six months have been for them. They're barely speaking to me as it is."

Sally gave her a sympathetic look. "I can only imagine."

"The nightmare of most Chinese immigrant parents who've sacrificed every last thing so their kid could go to Harvard *and* MIT is to watch all that education, tuition and scholarships go to hell. Which is basically what they think I've done with my career. Being a feminist spokeswoman is…like…the cherry on top. It might only be worse if I'd died. And that's *before* we get to the part about my love life."

"I see," said Sally. She focused on the cards in her hand, and gave them a quick shuffle. "Draw three," she said, proffering the deck to Rosalind.

Carefully, Rosalind pulled out three cards and laid them down on the table. Maat, the Egyptian goddess of justice, was followed by Damara, a Celtic deity who was all about protecting children and their innocence, and Coventina, the ancient goddess of water, pools and purification.

Sally smiled. "Have you been up to Harbin yet?" she asked. It was Sally who'd originally told Rosalind about the place.

Rosalind nodded, feeling her face redden. "Yeah."

"And?"

Rosalind folded her arms and didn't answer for a moment as she studied the cards before her in the lamp-lit gloom of the salon. A small tear began to trickle down her cheek. Sally put a hand on hers and gave it a consoling pat. "You don't have to answer me, you know."

"No…I want to." Rosalind wiped at her tears with the back of her hand as her voice shook. Then she laughed self-consciously. "I mean, it was nothing. Just a fling. I mean…it totally doesn't count. Except that it does, I guess? In terms of being gay or… whatever. I'd never…" Rosalind's voice drifted away.

Sally nodded. "I get it." She turned her attention back to the cards. "There's a lot going on here, Rosalind. But the main message is that your parents don't quite see how you are serving justice. That is their own blindness, but listen—it's all good, because you are here to wake them up. To help them become sympathetic to others whose ways are different."

"But what if I tell them and they tell me to leave? To just get out and leave the family?" She paused, a stricken look on her face.

"They could, you know. I feel like I'm already on incredibly thin ice."

The two women were quiet for a moment.

"I love them," Rosalind added in a soft voice.

"Yes, of course you do, but this is your karma, Rosalind. It's your sacred duty, and you have no choice but to comply. But I'd also say the water is calling you again. Why not go back to Harbin? Ask the statue of Kwan Yin to guide you. Leave her a little something. Then say your prayers, and ask her for help."

Sally paused and smiled at her. "Just soak in the pools to your heart's delight. Revel in the healing power of that water, because you will need it, Rosalind. Coming out is always a big task, but honestly? This really is what's next for you."

Rosalind looked doubtful. "You're sure it's not...say...finding a new lover?"

Sally looked askance. "Anything is possible. But I'd say this time is really about parenting. Not you being a parent, but you being a daughter. And being open to their comments. Your mother and father may surprise you, you know."

Rosalind shook her head. "I don't know..."

"One thing is clear," Sally added. "If you don't tell them, and truly own who you are, you'll never attract the love that is patiently waiting for you. This is what is waiting for us all, but only when we truly open up to it. And some of us never do, of course. There are often tests along the way. It's kind of like...you're on notice to get with the program."

Rosalind closed her eyes. This was not the news she wanted or even expected to hear. Still, there was the ring of truth to Sally's words. Rosalind could feel it in her gut. "Okay," she said uncertainly.

Rosalind sank back against her chair and grimacing, she slowly shook her head.

She couldn't believe that *this* was the path forward.

*

Tenika pulled on to the highway going south to San Leandro. Immediately, they hit traffic.

"Saturday," Delilah said, shaking her head.

Tenika didn't say much. She just slung a bony wrist over the top of the steering wheel, and regarded the crawling sea of cars before her.

Delilah shifted uncomfortably in the seat beside her. "T?"

Tenika looked straight ahead. "What?"

There wasn't hostility in her voice, exactly. It was more of a coolness, as if a strange new lack of trust had invaded their landscape. Ever since Delilah brought up having a baby, Tenika had been all one word answers and avoided glances. And needless to say, an iceberg of tension had lodged itself firmly between them in bed.

"Oh, come on honey…please." Delilah regarded her lover plaintively. "Don't be all like that. Just…talk to me. Please."

Tenika looked at her. "What do you want me to say, Delilah? I told you how I feel. You know what's on my mind."

"And I apologized—"

"Delilah, we are not getting into this again. Let's just go to Costco, buy the damn groceries for the party, and get on with having people over. Can we just do that?"

"Okay. But not like this, honey. Please. This is…*wrong.*"

Tenika knew it was wrong, of course. The tension was palpable. She also knew that all they had to do was talk it through. The problem was the problem, itself. She *so* didn't want to talk about it with Delilah—the very subject stopped her in her tracks.

Now, as they were about to throw a party for forty people, was hardly the time to get into it.

Tenika continued smoothly, eyes still on the traffic ahead. "Did you put ice on the list?"

"Come on, T, don't pull the distraction thing."

Tenika's voice lowered fiercely. "I'm thinking about our guests."

"And I'm telling you to talk to me. All I know is that you won't even get into it with me. I mean, don't I deserve to know how you feel? What's so bad about having a baby?"

Tenika took a long, shaky inhale and studied the sea of cars ahead. Delilah was crafty, all right. She knew the traffic would suck—and this time there would be no walking out. How the fuck was she supposed to get into all of this? And now, of all times. Just as her cousin Keisha was about to show up at their house?

"Look, all right. Fine. Let's talk about it. But I'm just going to flat out tell you, Delilah, I'm pissed. I feel used and manipulated."

Delilah's voice ratcheted up in frustration. "I'm sorry! I told you I'm sorry. Repeatedly, T. What more can I do?"

Tenika hit the brakes as they slowed to another stop. Then she looked at her wife intently. "You can promise to not fucking manipulate me ever again," she said, her voice hissing with intensity. "Just put it to me straight when you want something. Have you got that?"

Delilah shrank back. "Okay," she half whispered. "Fine. All right. Just...*Jesus.*"

Now the silence between them grew. And it grew some more. They barely crept along in the traffic. Still, neither of them moved a muscle. As if doing so would somehow set off another reaction.

Finally, Delilah spoke up. She cleared her throat. "So it's a 'no' then."

"I didn't say that. I just...it's complicated. That's all I'm going to say right now. We're about to have a party, for Christsakes. But I heard you. I know you want to have a baby, okay?"

"Okay..." Delilah's said meekly.

"Anyway, this is not like a quick, easy thing for me, okay? I need to think about it."

Delilah kept her eyes on the road now, as if she wasn't even hearing her.

"Honey?" Tenika ventured.

"I heard you. You'll talk to me about it later. Which is weird because we'll be sitting here for God knows how long. Could be another hour."

"Yeah, and I got shit to think about. I mean...it's..." Tenika stopped, aware she was getting triggered again. "Look, I'm sorry. There's some stuff about raising kids, it's just really hard for me. Let me process it, and I'll tell you when I'm ready to talk."

Tenika gave a long sigh, and looked ahead sadly. "I'm...sorry," she murmured after a moment.

Delilah reached out her hand, and Tenika took it. "It's okay," Delilah said. "I just didn't know that it was hard for you."

"Can we drop it for now?"

"All right."

Tenika snapped on the radio and *The Soul of the Bay* came soaring in. Whitney Houston was singing, "You Give Good Love."

Tenika looked over at her wife with a tinge of shame. *Why couldn't she just shake off the past? All of that shit happened about a thousand years ago.* "I love you baby," she said.

Delilah glanced over at her and squeezed her hand. "Yeah, love you, too."

"You got ice on the list, right?"

"Got it," Delilah replied.

Miraculously the traffic picked up and, once again, they began to move. The tension was broken, and Keisha was coming over tonight. That alone would be a step toward clarity.

If Tenika could bring herself to talk about it.

*

Frankie yawned and shook her head, sitting up a little straighter in the driver's seat. *Damn insomnia.*

She cleared her throat, determined not to let sleepiness overtake her. She'd already had a black coffee and two caffeine tablets today. Technically, she was locked and loaded as far as her central nervous system was concerned. She'd even talked her boss into letting her come back two weeks early.

But still, sitting there motionless for hours in the warmth of the car, on a sunny fall afternoon in the Bay, it was hard not to fall asleep. Especially since absolutely nothing was happening at Frankie's stake out. There hadn't even been a light on in the house she was watching for the past four hours.

She slunk a bit down in her seat as two young men walked down the sidewalk on the other side. They eyed her with curiosity.

Yeah, why was she sitting here anyway? She had to wonder, herself, as this wasn't the kind of status assignment she'd been used to. But then…that was life when you came crawling back to the SFPD on your knees after medical leave. Especially one that was funneled through the Behavioral Sciences Unit.

Frankie cleared her throat and swiveled her head right and left. The two men had stopped and were still looking at her. She fiddled with her phone in an attempt to look less like an undercover cop on a stake out.

Closing her eyes, Frankie put her head back against the headrest and feigned sleep. That was always a reliable cover move. Her breathing slowed as her body relaxed. She tried to keep her attention focused, counting backwards from fifty.

Because no way, under any circumstances, could she actually fall asleep. Not here, not now. Not in this cocoon of this warm, cozy, comfortable car. No way in hell. Falling asleep would be nothing less than a mortal sin.

It could get her fired from the force. It could even make her pension disappear.

Frankie was being paid to watch everything coming in and going out of 1477 Loretta Avenue, and that is just what she intended to do. And she'd do it just as soon as those two yahoos finally took off and left her alone.

Frankie cracked one eye slightly. The two of them were still there, deep in discussion. One of them glanced in her direction again. She closed her eyes once more.

Frankie had been asleep for several moments when she felt the sudden rush of a passing car. Immediately, a sting of adrenaline buzzed through her brain as she woke up and looked.

Shit. She'd been asleep.

A patrol car from her station was now retreating in the distance. It could definitely have been driven by the Lieutenant. Especially if her boss was checking up on her.

"*Fuck*," Frankie murmured under her breath. That was all she needed, for the Lieutenant to catch her sleeping on the job. It was grounds for disciplinary action at least.

She could see it now. *Officer Kennedy is no longer fit for duty.*

The two men were long gone now, and a new sense of dread and apprehension filled Frankie's head as she studied the house she'd been staking out. Nothing apparently had changed. But of course, she couldn't know for sure.

Frankie had been back at work for exactly twenty-four hours. And now this.

She could feel it. Things were about to get seriously difficult.

*

Tenika sat in the Costco gas line, waiting the eternal wait for cheap gas. But she figured it was worth it, even if there *was* a party happening at their house in less than four hours. She inched the truck forward. Only two more cars ahead of her.

Keisha.

Tenika sighed. She hadn't seen her cousin in a very long time. Maybe even a year? Which was weird, given that she just lived on the other side of the city. Or at least Tenika hoped she still did. Everyone was getting squeezed these days in the old neighborhood. But then, that was gentrification for you. It tended to eat people alive, even if they'd been there all their lives.

She slid a sidelong glance out the window at the cars stacked up around her, and tried not to think about the subject at hand. Namely, Walter and that thing that Tenika seldom let her mind rest on. He was three years old when it happened.

Walter was a typical toddler, half hyper and all over the place all the time. Except when he was raising hell because his three-year-old plans got derailed. But maybe that was all kids that age. Tenika didn't know. She tended to avoid all small children after Walter moved away.

Which he probably wouldn't have if she and Keisha hadn't been left in charge that day.

Given how her mother was, there was always too much to do when Tenika was fourteen. That was the damn shame of it. First there was school followed by all kinds of housework, the usual homework, and then getting dinner for the two of them. Then Keisha decided they should have a babysitting business, just to make some money.

Hell, at that point in her life, Tenika was doing well if she could just keep her clothes on right side out.

Which is why she'd invited Keisha over after school in the first place, 'cause Keisha always liked to help. And she always had good ideas. On that particular day, Tenika had an Algebra test, which Keisha was also pretty good at. When push came to shove, Keisha was a rock star on many fronts. Just not child care as it turned out.

Tenika shoved aside the barrage of thoughts that were now barreling toward her loud and fast, just as they always did when she opened this particular can of worms. She glanced at her watch and inched forward in the gas line. This was totally not the time to get into all of this.

She'd save such ruminations for another time, just like she always did.

Delilah had only met Keisha a few times, and she always asked Tenika why she didn't have her over more often, given that they'd practically been like sisters growing up.

Until now, Tenika had been vague. Mainly because there were some things better left alone.

But now Delilah wanted a baby.

Which meant everything was seriously about to change.

Chapter Eight

Delilah pulled a lavender tulip from the stiff cellophane wrapper that held it in place. Expertly, she snipped the end and shoved it into an appropriate spot among the flowers already in place in the glass vase before her. Then pausing, she scanned the remaining flowers strewn across her counter.

The party was in less than an hour, so she had to keep moving. There was still a lot to do. She could hear Tenika cleaning the grill in the backyard. She was humming in her low, off-key rasp. It made Delilah smile.

Finally, all was well. Or pretty well at least. Somehow there was still a tiny edge of tension left. The merest residue of annoyance still lingered in the air. Which meant it was something Delilah couldn't ignore.

She pulled a white Asian Lily from its wrapper, trimmed it and stuck it in an open spot on the right side of the arrangement.

Whatever, she thought with a shrug. Tenika had been annoyed before, and she'd be annoyed again. That was how marriage worked, right? The goal was to have nice long stretches of love, peace and happiness between the occasional rough spots.

Either way, Delilah was left wondering. The idea that having a baby was "complicated" for her wife was something she could never have anticipated. Really, she'd figured Tenika would either be a solid Yes or No on the subject. And now here they were, parked in this uncomfortable straddle in between. Especially since Tenika apparently couldn't even talk about what was bothering her.

Delilah couldn't imagine what the problem was in the first place.

Somehow there would have to be more discussion and more resolution. And more waiting for the right time to bring it up again. That was before they even got into the complexity and expense of a lesbian pregnancy. In other words, nothing was going to happen fast on the baby front.

Delilah sighed as she poked flowers into the arrangement in front of her. So maybe none of this was worth it. Maybe she should just drop the matter now, rather than make a big fuss.

After all, she could get along without raising kids, couldn't she?

A wave of defeat came over Delilah, and she stopped, a hot pink Shasta daisy hanging limply from her hand. *No, actually.* She couldn't. Inserting the daisy into the center of the arrangement with an authoritative move, she stepped back and surveyed her work.

"Hey…that looks great!" Tenika came striding through the kitchen. Delilah spun to look at her. "So do you," Tenika said, pausing to give her wife a tender kiss on the throat.

Delilah smiled. "Thanks," she said lightly. She kept that smile working, pushing hard against the pang of sadness now working its way through her gut. She wanted a baby so badly she could taste it. *No tears*, she chided herself. *Not now. Not here.*

Tenika frowned. "You okay?"

"Never better." Delilah tried to keep her tone light as she turned back to her work, giving the flowers a final shake into place.

"Huh." Tenika looked at her for one more moment, then she turned and went about her business.

There goes my life, Delilah thought to herself. Her happiness, her sorrow, her family, her heart, her soul…all of it rested with Tenika. *Whither though goes, I will go.* Those were the words they said to each other at the wedding, and still they rung true. Even in matters where they didn't necessarily agree.

But then, perhaps that was the point.

*

Kate snaked her way around the pile of monitors and gear that was now piling up outside Tenika and Delilah's home. Then she knocked on the front door as Lizzy unloaded the final speaker from the back of her truck. Lizzy's band, The Breakdowns, would be arriving shortly to set up and sound check before the party started.

"Aren't they answering? I hear a radio," Lizzy said.

Leaning in toward an open window, Kate gave a loud call. "Anyone home?" Footsteps quickly responded, and a moment later they were being welcomed in by Tenika.

"Just put it all over in that corner," Tenika directed as she helped Lizzy load the equipment in through the door.

"Wow!" said Kate, glancing around the house at the party preparations. A large table had been spread with an array of salads, freshly baked bread, flowers, and a large empty platter in the center. "That's for the ribs," Tenika announced.

Lizzy looked up and gave a hoot. "Come on…ribs? *Your* ribs? Really?"

"I told you we were throwing a party. You thought I was making it up? Yes, my ribs. Yes, champagne. Yes, a gorgeous wedding cake that Delilah baked and decorated herself. I always say get a tattoo artist when you want great filigree. We've got you girls set up, and I do mean *set up.*" Tenika's voice spiraled up in enthusiasm. "This is a wedding party you two are going to remember, if it's the last damn thing we do."

Kate beamed at her friend. Walking over to Tenika, she gave her a big hug. "This is all…well, it's just amazing. We are so lucky you two are in our lives."

Meanwhile, Lizzy pressed forward into the kitchen, heading

straight for the large sheet cake on a platter by the laundry. Lizzy let out a low, awestruck whistle. "Whoa," she said softly.

The pale butter cream frosting held a rambling tumble of precisely crafted flowers in a splash of colors, complete with tiny frosting leaves. The words 'Kate and Lizzie, Together Forever!' spread triumphantly across the top in ornate chocolate script as chocolate filigree spread over the edges of the cake.

"Kate—honey. Come here! You've got to look at this."

Tenika came up behind Lizzy. "Isn't that something? She was up for hours last night working on it."

"I'm blown away by all of this, T. And the party hasn't even started yet." Lizzy gazed over at her business partner and shook her head in amazement as Kate joined them from the other room.

"Oh…my," she said with a small gasp as she eyed the cake. "Delilah did this?"

Delilah appeared from the bedroom. "You like it?" she asked. She was wearing a pink dress adorned with black and white dominoes, a pair of hot pink stockings and some vintage black and white spectator pumps.

"It's incredible," said Kate. "Hail to the chef!"

Delilah smiled shyly as the three others burst into applause, and she curtsied and beamed. Then she returned to the loaves of freshly baked sourdough she'd been slicing at the counter.

"I always tell her she could start a bakery if she ever gets tired of inking people," Tenika remarked.

"Got that right," Lizzy concurred. "Just…wow." She turned to her love. "Well, I guess we're married now, huh? Sure feels like it at least." Leaning in, Lizzy gave her new wife a deep kiss.

The party had, indeed, begun.

*

Monroe really, really didn't want to be the first guest, but somehow that was how it always worked out. Which is why Monroe went to so few parties to begin with. They attributed it to their rampant social anxiety, which was always screwing things up.

Here Monroe sat, alone at their own kitchen table, as they often were when not seated at a piano. As Monroe waited for time to pass, they scanned their phone once more, looking futilely for messages, or emails, or distractions of any kind. Anything to stop thinking about the looming social test of Tenika and Delilah's party, which would begin in less than twenty minutes.

The phone was silent as usual. The moments ticked by, painfully slow.

Monroe hadn't actually been invited anywhere in a long time, not since before Kate came to the church for Sanctuary. And now, here was Kate, trying gamely to fix Monroe up with someone. Anyone. Presumably, it was safe to assume that tonight might actually be the night.

Monroe tried on that jaunty thought and immediately rejected it. *Who the hell knew?* The prospect of walking into a party filled with strangers, and actually connecting with even one of them, seemed incredibly unlikely. Of course, Kate had gone on about all of them at one time or another to Monroe—especially someone named Rosalind who was apparently this militant tech crusader.

Idly, Monroe wondered how Rosalind felt about gender queer people in general. Was she open enough to actually date one? Because maybe she wasn't. God knew a whole lot of other people still weren't. Which made the prospect of trying to have a serious relationship damn near impossible.

Really, finding the 'one' was a complete and total crap shoot—a needle in a haystack in the best of circumstances. Especially when you are truly trying to get over your crush on the newly married guest of honor. Monroe suspected Kate would be radiant, glowing, and parked on Lizzy's arm all night long.

Monroe glanced at their watch and stood up, straightening their tie. They took a deep breath, squared their shoulders, and picked up their jacket.

Party time had indeed arrived.

*

"Come on, sweetheart…I know you can do this." Sally stood over the reclining figure of Frankie, who was still stationed in her regular spot on the couch.

"Yeah. Sure, I could. But why, Sally?" Frankie paused and studied her girlfriend. "Why, honey?"

Sally threw up her hands in exasperation. "Because it's a party! It's *fun*. It's people talking and dancing. It's barbecue, and music, and drinks. You love these things, baby. At least you used to. Maybe you'll go and get into it again."

Frankie was silent. She eyed Sally uncertainly.

"Frankie, please. The therapist said you have to get out of here. Get back into the flow of life."

"Yeah, well I got into the flow of life and look what it got me. A desk job and a whole lot of time with Behavioral Sciences." Frankie's asleep at the wheel moment had, indeed, been observed by her boss, and she was now, once again, being disciplined. This time she had been relegated to the department's Video Library, a virtual No Man's Land for cops. "How the fuck am I going to explain that to everyone, huh?"

A cloud of fury passed over Frankie's face and she sat up, angrily. "This is so fucked. *I'm* so fucked. I mean…Sally—I could lose my pension. I've worked for it for years. Years! I could be fired any day now. You realize that, don't you?"

Sally threw up her hands in exasperation. "Would you please stop saying this again and again, Frankie. The fact is you haven't been fired. You just got moved…sideways, really. You'll get back on the beat again."

She sat down next to Frankie, and put her hand on her knee. "Honey, this is temporary. You're an excellent cop and everyone knows it. You're just dealing with something. Anyway, what's so bad about Behavioral Sciences?"

Frankie looked at her in horror. "It's where the nut jobs go! And I'm not nuts."

"No," said Sally, "but apparently you're crazy enough to blow off the party of the year." She stood up. "Anyway, I'm going, whether you decide to join me or not."

"Fine," said Frankie, snapping on the television remote. The sound of a news reporter filled the living room as Sally went to find the dress she'd brought for the occasion.

Ten minutes later, Sally checked herself in the mirror. Turning slightly, she examined her profile and smiled at what she saw. If this didn't get Frankie off the couch, nothing would.

"Et voila," she said as she entered the living room. Sally stood before Frankie and presented herself. The sleeveless red dress was new, and its tight, scooped bodice set off her best feature, her beautifully pale, overflowing bosom. The dress flared gently below the waist, accenting her hips in a soft swirl around her as she moved. Sally had completed the look with some pretty gold sandals and simple jewelry.

Frankie sat up suddenly. "Wow," she said. "Wait…you're wearing *that?*"

Sally crossed her arms. "No, I'm going to take it off and go nude. What do you think, dear?"

"Oh—well, gee." Frankie hesitated for a moment. "I mean, you're a knockout." She shook her head. "And if I'm not there… Jesus. I hate to think who's going to be hitting on you," she muttered half to herself.

Sally gave a bemused smile. "So you're jealous now?" she asked as she looked around for her purse and her car keys. "There are some leftovers in the fridge, honey, and I guess I'll be back about—"

Frankie stood up and cut her off. "Forget it, Sally. I'm going." She headed off to the bedroom to change her clothes.

"Oh. Great," Sally said lightly, suppressing a smile. "Glad you changed your mind."

She really could read her lover like a book. And at times like this, that was pretty convenient.

*

Rosalind pulled up to a stoplight and braked. As she did, her heart gave an uncomfortable flutter. There were butterflies in her stomach and anxious thoughts prowling her mind. Once again, she glanced in her rear view mirror to make sure her lipstick wasn't smudged.

God, I am nervous.

Rosalind took three deep breaths as she waited for the light to change, and she reasoned with herself. It was just a party. A party she could leave any time, even five minutes after she got there. And Lizzy, Tenika and Kate would all be there. They were nice people. She even liked them.

The only problem was her own anxiety, really. It was Rosalind's first lesbian party, and basically, she was a basket case.

Nervously, she glanced in the back seat, checking on the bottle of wine and the bouquet of flowers she'd brought for Lizzy and Kate. Taking one more deep breath, she impatiently tapped her fingers on the steering wheel. The traffic light was taking forever.

If truth be told, Rosalind was both nervous and excited. The idea of entering a scene she'd held at arm's length for so long was exhilarating. She was finally giving herself a chance to check it all out. It felt remarkably right, if terrifying. That much she knew.

The light changed and Rosalind drove on, humming along with the radio as she went. There would be lesbians there. Lots and lots of lesbians, and nice ones, apparently. Even young ones, like herself. There would be butch dykes, and casually non-committal androgynous types in their plaid shirts and their cute haircuts, and femme women with tight skirts and cascades of curls. There would be all this and more and... Rosalind stopped herself. *Shit.*

Yet again, she'd forgotten a key component of her new life.

Rosalind was now an official 'personality,' which meant that her life no longer belonged entirely to her. People might recognize her from all the media she'd gotten. They'd figure out soon enough that she was the Anti-Tech-Bro Crusader. And here she was, an arm's length away, having a drink and looking for a lover. A lesbian lover.

Someone might tell the media.

Or they might take a picture of her and share it on Instagram. It could be a picture of her dancing with another woman, or somehow looking romantically entangled and very, very queer. And once that hit Twitter, well forget it.

The San Francisco Chronicle, The New York Times, Buzzfeed, The L.A. Times and everyone else would jump on the bandwagon, and now her sex life would be posted from coast to coast. And that's how her parents would finally find out the truth about their perfect daughter. Via her loyalist brother's Facebook page.

Or worse, they might read it for themselves in a newspaper. Which is how they found out about her first crusade, and the loss of her coveted former job.

Rosalind grimaced as she drove. *How could I have forgotten this simple but critical fact?* It was a true case of denial.

She pulled up to the next stop light and considered her options. She could just turn around right now. Simply punt the party and go home. That would be the prudent thing to do, of course.

Rosalind's heart sank at this option. Here she was in her new never-before-worn elegant summer shift, purchased with scant savings against all of her most frugal instincts. Not to mention the designer make up she'd spent a good half hour putting on.

She had to be hot tonight. She simply *had* to. That had been the first priority. Rosalind's brief fling with Tasha had most certainly whet her appetite for more, and now she was officially on the prowl for a lover. So why not dress the part?

Rosalind shook off her thoughts and drove on grimly as the light changed. She was not backing down. This was her life, she decided, so she might as well get used to it.

And if her parents found out about her lesbianism online, or from one of her aunties or her cousin or…her brother, then…well…

Fuck it.

Rosalind set her jaw and turned onto the street where Tenika and her wife lived. She checked Google Maps, and saw she was less than one minute away from arrival. The fluttering in her body rose up to maximum intensity. A thousand agitated butterflies beat their wings as fast as they could against her ribs, stirring up every iota of her nervous system.

This is it, she told herself. This was what she had come for, and she was going to get it, if it took every ounce of strength she had. After all, Rosalind had already been through worse than being outed in the press. Hadn't she?

She parked. Then stepping up to the door, she clutched her wine and her flowers and rang the bell. Rosalind could hear recorded music and a swell of partyers inside. Footsteps approached and a voice, maybe Tenika's, called out that she was coming.

For one brief, hysterical moment, she considered turning around and simply fleeing, as if she hadn't rung the doorbell at all. She located her car in her site line, and calculated how long it might take to reach it. Could she make it safely back to her car before the door opened?

Yet, at that moment the front door swung wide, and there stood Tenika, smiling at her. "Hey! You made it!" she said, leaning in for a hug.

Rosalind took a deep breath, and found herself at a loss for words as her heart pounded wildly in her chest. All she could do was hug Tenika and allow herself to be led inside. "Here," she finally said, pushing the wine and flowers at Tenika. "Congratulations."

Tenika laughed. "I'll pass that on to Lizzy and Kate."

Rosalind turned crimson. "Oh right. It's for them."

Tenika began explaining where she could get a drink, but Rosalind wasn't listening. Because directly behind Tenika stood a startling, fascinating person. Really one of the more interesting people Rosalind had ever seen. This person seemed to be a woman, but not quite. Neither butch nor femme, their buzz cut hair and dress were entirely androgynous, including a smart turquoise bow tie, no less. Their eyes were piercing blue as they gazed back at her, and they rocked Rosalind to her core.

A phrase came swimming up to Rosalind's mind. *Gender queer.* The entire idea gave her a thrill that ran from her brain straight to her vulva.

"This is Monroe," said Tenika as the very interesting person stepped up to join them. Then, picking up some invisible cue, Tenika turned and headed toward the kitchen, effectively disappearing.

Rosalind stood there uncertainly for a moment, not even sure what to say or where to look. If she were to look at this one extraordinary person in front of her for much longer it would almost definitely cause all of her inner wiring to melt on the spot.

Monroe took a single bold step closer and smiled at Rosalind. "What's your name?"

Now Rosalind lifted her head and gazed directly at Monroe, and as she did pure recognition flooded her body. Words now officially left her, and she faltered for a moment, unsure exactly what to do. "I just... Uh...Do you know where the bathroom is?" Rosalind finally stammered.

But instead of waiting for a reply, she took off, heading down the short corridor to her left. Stepping into the first room she found, she closed the door firmly and began hyperventilating.

Great, she thought. She was having a panic attack. She hadn't had one of these in years. *What excellent timing.*

Sitting down on a nearby bed, Rosalind steadied herself and focused on controlling her ragged, gasping breathing until her frantically beating heart slowed in her chest. It was all too much, too soon. Outside the door, there was a gentle tap.

"Everything okay in there?"

The very interesting Monroe was now on the other side of the bedroom door, picking up on the queue that she needed help. *Score one for Monroe,* Rosalind thought to herself. At least they were attentive.

She did not answer. Instead, Rosalind lay down on the bed, curled into fetal position, and very, very quietly, she began to weep.

Chapter Nine

M onroe watched the rapidly retreating figure of the beautiful dark haired Asian woman and their heart sank.

Here we go again, Monroe thought. *Skunked. As usual.* And this one was so pretty...

This time there had been actual hope. For maybe ten seconds the heavens had opened, the angels sang and all was well in Monroe's world. This was it! Monroe had found exactly what they'd come for, and it hadn't even been difficult. In fact, they'd only been at the party for ten minutes or so when she walked in.

But then the mysterious beauty—whose name Monroe had not yet even learned—disappeared. Furthermore, she'd locked herself into Tenika and Delilah's bedroom. Which had to be some kind of very direct signal, but of what Monroe wasn't quite sure. There had been a spark of connection. Monroe knew that much for sure.

For a moment, Monroe just stood there, uncertain. Perhaps the woman was lost. After all, she'd said she was looking for a bathroom, right? Perhaps Monroe should say something?

After all, the woman in question did look a bit faint. Maybe her retreat wasn't about Monroe at all. Maybe she wasn't feeling well, and genuinely needed help.

Maybe she had collapsed in a heap on the other side of the now locked bedroom door.

Monroe stuck their hands in their pockets and fiddled with some loose change, trying to determine the best course of action. To say nothing and move on just seemed cold and like a massive mistake, not to mention a lost opportunity. This woman was... dazzling. That might be the best description. She also looked vaguely familiar, though Monroe couldn't say exactly why.

Yet, to go rattle the doorknob and knock on the door would be decidedly uncool. Maybe even intrusive. That was something some far pushier person would do, right?

Instead, Monroe could just stand there, waiting as patiently as a sentry, because eventually the beautiful woman would have to emerge and walk by.

Even if it was only to go right out the front door.

Yet, still, there was that scary lingering question. What if the woman in question seriously needed help right now?

In a single, wild impulse, Monroe strode down the hall and paused before the locked bedroom door. Summoning up all of their courage, they tapped gently.

"Everything okay in there?"

There was no reply.

Now a new, scarier thought entered Monroe's head. What if she'd passed out? What if she wasn't even conscious? What if she'd had a seizure...or something even worse?

Fuck it.

Swiftly, Monroe retreated toward the kitchen. It was time to get Kate.

Moments later, Kate cleared her throat and knocked lightly on Delilah and Tenika's bedroom door. "Rosalind? It's Kate. Are you all right, love?"

A muffled sound rose from inside. "Kate?" a small voice asked. It was indeed Rosalind.

"Yes, are you okay?" Monroe had said something about her being in distress, but they didn't seem to know more than that. So

Kate was doing what Kate did best, gently sending Monroe off to get a plate of barbecue while she attended to her guest.

Now Kate addressed the locked door as Monroe loped off to the backyard. "Rosalind?"

"Are you alone?"

"Yes, I am."

A moment later the bedroom door opened, and there stood Rosalind, looking slightly rumpled. Her mascara was smudged from tears and her usually impeccable skirt was now wrinkled in large pleats across her front. Kate slipped into the bedroom and shut the door behind her.

"Hug?" she asked, and Rosalind nodded.

The two women embraced, and Kate noticed that Rosalind's thin body was trembling.

Kate pulled back to look at her friend. "Rosalind—what on earth is the matter?"

"I think I had a panic attack. I…" Rosalind sighed and shook her head. "I mean, maybe it was a panic attack. I'm not sure what it was."

Kate smiled. "Ah. Well, first let's get you a glass of water." She paused. "Do you think you need to go home?"

Rosalind silently shook her head, her look now one of determination.

"Ah, all right. Then once you collect yourself, and you feel ready to rejoin the party, let's get you a drink, shall we? Unless perhaps you need to lie down some more?"

"No—no," Rosalind demurred. "I could definitely use a glass of wine. If you think I should." Her seriousness made Kate break out into a laugh.

"Of course I think you should. Why on earth not? You may have had a panic attack, dear, but it will pass. Meanwhile, you're at an excellent party!"

"Oh, yeah. Right. I just meant—"

"No worries," Kate said, moving toward the bathroom. She returned a moment later, glass of water in hand. She handed it to Rosalind who drank it down.

Kate continued, "You might want to fix your eye make up a bit, as well. Is a bit smudgy is all. Then there are lots of people to meet if you're up for it…" She smiled at Rosalind, sitting on the bed before her.

Rosalind handed the empty glass back to her, and squaring her shoulders, she stood once more. "Thanks," she said, taking a deep breath to calm herself.

"Are you all right now?"

"Me?" Rosalind squeaked. "Oh, yeah. Perfect. I'm fine." Her wan tone did not suggest she was fine at all, but rather highly resistant to being seen as anything less than 'fine.'

A moment later, Kate was standing with Rosalind in the bathroom, watching her reapply the mascara and foundation that was in her purse.

"How'd you know I was in the bedroom?" Rosalind asked as she leaned toward the mirror, mascara wand in hand.

"Monroe told me. They seemed worried about you."

"Oh."

"You met?"

"The very androgynous…person?" Rosalind avoided her friend's gaze in the mirror.

"Exactly. Monroe's a 'they.' Gender queer. Or non-binary, as Monroe puts it," Kate explained.

The very phrase "non-binary" moved into Rosalind's consciousness like a slowly exploding bomb in her brain. *Non-binary. Not choosing male or female.* Monroe was somewhere deliciously in between. Instantly, Rosalind began to blush crimson with the alarming realization that she'd been instantly aroused.

Frantically, she fanned herself with her hand, hoping to offset the heat now radiating from her face.

"Oh. My…" said Kate with a smile.

"No, it's just…my hormones. I think they're out of whack or something. I'm sure that's why I'm so wound up."

"Of course, dear," Kate nodded. "I'll let you get yourself together and go find you a drink. Sauvignon Blanc? Or a sangria?"

"White wine is perfect."

Rosalind watched Kate leave the bathroom as a wave of shyness overtook her. *Why on earth did I even come to this party?*

Still, there was one thing Rosalind now understood. There was no way in hell she was leaving.

It was time to put on her big girl pants and go talk to Monroe. This was exactly what she had come for.

*

Frankie clutched the rapidly warming bottle of beer in her hand, and gazed out over the Oakland landscape of small houses, random billboards and signs, and the dark mansion-covered hills, rising off in the distance. "Basically, my life's on hold," she admitted.

Beside her, Tenika was turning over the chicken on the grill as the smell of sweet, smoky barbecue radiated through their tiny backyard.

"What you girls cooking over there? Damn!" came a cry from next door. An older Black man's face popped up beside a vine covered fence.

"Hey, Mr. Colbert. We're having a party. You're welcome to join us," Tenika shot back. "Just a whole lot of lesbians and a little chicken. May not be your kind of not your thing, but…"

Her neighbor gave a throaty laugh, and ducked out of sight once more. Tenika turned back to Frankie. "You were saying?"

"Just that I'm totally and completely fucked," Frankie continued morosely. "My boss found me sleeping at a stakeout. Now I'm in purgatory at the Video Library. It's a fucking desk job." She sighed and drained the bottle in her hand. "So, basically, my career is over."

Tenika glanced over at her friend. "You fell *asleep*? On the job?"

"I know, I know. Believe me, I've never fallen asleep like that before. Not once in all these years. And now, well…what can I say? I have insomnia every night. I'm so tired in the morning, I can barely drive to the station."

Tenika gave the chicken in front of her a gentle poke. "So maybe carrying a weapon and all that stuff isn't a good idea 'til you get your shit together, I mean."

"Well, that's the conventional wisdom at least. They're even making me go to therapy."

A sad silence fell between them. "You okay?" Tenika asked.

Frankie shook her head. "Not really."

"Something keeping you up at night then?"

Frankie sighed and creakily bent over to extract another beer from the cooler. She popped the top and brought the ice cold bottle to her lips. She took a long sip, then she looked at her friend. "I mean… sometimes work is hard, T. You see shit. Then you can't unsee it, right?"

"Yeah. I know."

Frankie put down her beer, and put her hands on her hips. "I had a young kid, just a girl, maybe eleven or twelve, jump off the GG when I was in the middle of talking her down. God knows how she even got out there," she said sadly. "It was…" Frankie fell mournfully silent.

Putting down her tongs, Tenika turned to face her friend. "Oh, man."

A moment later, Frankie spoke again in a low voice. "She looked just like the girl who gave me PTSD in the first place. When I found her body out at Ocean Beach. They were just kids, you know?" Frankie took another long pull from her beer. Then she shook her head. "Fucking kids, both of them."

Wordless, Tenika nodded, unable to look at Frankie now. Instead, she focused on the barbecue in front of her while she tried to manage her own demons.

A barely perceptible tear crept down Frankie's cheek, and she stabbed at it irritably. "I don't know. Maybe I need to retire early. Or find something else to do. Or…well, I don't know what."

"No, Frankie."

Frankie looked up. "No?"

Tenika shook her head. "You don't need to quit. You love this job and you're one of the good cops. They should all be like you, Frankie." Tenika paused. "We'd probably have a lot less heartbreak around here if they were."

"I don't know, T…"

"Yeah, well I do. If you hadn't stepped up and helped us last year, we would have lost the garage."

She put a heavy hand on Frankie's shoulder. "You freaking care, Frankie. So you're in the minority, first of all. And if you need to get some therapy, or take a little time off to get it together, then just do it. Trust me. That alone is no reason to quit."

"No?"

Tenika turned to her intently, waving her barbecue fork in the air. "Girl, please. We need you. That's a reason to double down and solve the problem. So you're a little humbled…who freakin' cares? Probably happens to every cop sooner or later."

Frankie folded her arms and rocked back on her heels contemplatively. "Huh."

"How's Sally with all of this?"

Frankie frowned for a moment. Honestly, she wasn't even quite sure. "Okay…I guess?"

"Yeah, well why don't you go find her and do a little dancing, huh? She showed up at this party looking hella hot. Gonna be all kinds of people checking her out. So you'd better go take care of her. You know what I'm saying?"

Frankie definitely knew. "Good point." Frankie picked up her beer bottle and moved toward the door. But then she stopped and looked back to her friend. "Thank you, T."

Tenika smiled, raising her eyes from the task at hand. "Any time, Sarge."

Smiling, possibly for the first time all week, Frankie left to find Sally. This was exactly why they called Tenika 'the Fixer.'

"'Sarge'?" asked the voice from the doorway. Tenika glanced over and standing there was her cousin Keisha. They hadn't seen each other in close to a year.

"Hey!" Tenika opened her arms wide for an embrace, but instead Keisha chose to give her a polite kiss on the cheek. Keisha wasn't a hugger. Not with her at least. But then, that was a train of thought that Tenika didn't like to pursue.

"Don't worry—she's one of the good cops. Here, have a seat," Tenika said, motioning to an empty chair nearby. "I see you already got a drink. Of sorts."

"Water's fine for me," Keisha said tightly. She sat down on the nearby folding chair and primly folded her hands, every inch the church lady. It was a glaring difference between them that Tenika was often struck by, even though they'd been raised like sisters.

"So," Tenika began, but her words disappeared into thin air. Keisha glanced around uncomfortably, a small frown on her face, as if she wasn't quite sure if she could relax. "I'm glad you made it," Tenika said, hoping to put her guest at ease. "I mean…seriously, cuz. I wasn't sure you were going to come. That's great."

"I hear you," Keisha said a little tightly. "Anyway, thanks for inviting me, T."

"Yeah, well, you're family. All that's left of it at least. Lizzy asks about you every now and then. Delilah too. Did you see them out there?"

Keisha primly crossed her ankles and eyed the open bottle of beer by her feet with distaste. "Delilah let me in. I gave Lizzy a card."

Tenika smiled over from the grill. "Good for you," she said. Keisha's strict religiosity always let issues like same-sex marriage

89

hover between them a little uncomfortably. Ultimately, she was accepting, if reserved.

Tenika glanced at her cousin. Keisha was wearing a green linen suit and matching green heels, and her white blouse looked freshly pressed. Not only did Keisha not drink, she wasn't a lesbian, and she wasn't all that into dancing either. *Good she got here before the band started playing,* Tenika thought to herself.

Keisha appeared to be barely breathing.

"So…" Tenika began. "How've you been?"

"Fine enough."

"And Benny?"

"Benny's just fine."

"Still working with you?"

"Still working with me." Keisha's grown son, Benny, had joined Keisha in her job as a security guard at the Maxwell building in Uptown Oakland. Keisha was the highly organized, firm and politely friendly presence at the front desk, while Benny was the 'walker' who made the rounds down the darkened halls upstairs at night. Mother and son had determined it was best for all concerned if they varied their shifts, so Keisha worked by day and Benny worked by night.

"Don't see him much, though, I'll say that," Keisha remarked.

"But he's still living with you?"

Keisha gave a tired grimace and nodded. "Oh, yes. He's living with me, all right."

"Huh." Tenika continued to focus on her grilling. "And that's seriously okay with you?"

Keisha's eyes flashed fury in the direction of her cousin. "What am I going to do, Tenika? Throw him out? He's my son! And if I do, where's he going to go? You've got rent starting at two grand in this city." Giving herself a shake, she composed herself once more. "Crazy nonsense," she muttered in a half voice.

Keisha took a dainty sip of water, which dripped a little on her suit. Dark wet splotches quickly spread across the perfect green linen. "Oh, Lord almighty," she muttered, brushing at the splotches with annoyance.

"Here, I've got it." Grabbing a napkin, Tenika handed it to her cousin who dabbed at her spots to no avail. "Do you need a rag? Can I get you something?"

Keisha waved her away with annoyance. "Don't go trippin' on it, T. Just…go grill something."

The two sat in silence as the grill flared up before them. Tenika moved the chicken and beat back the flames. Above all else, she couldn't piss off Keisha. Not now and not here. For once in her life, she actually needed the woman and her usually sound advice.

"So listen, Keisha …" Tenika began with uncertainty.

How in God's name am I supposed to get into this?

The subject of having a baby swam before her, vast and unknowable. And largely untouchable, too. Mainly because of Walter, who was lodged in the middle of everything, a great sprawling ghost of a problem. This strange sea of discomfort had lingered between them for nearly twenty years now. Ever since the incident.

Still the truth prevailed. Tenika needed Keisha more than ever at this moment in her life. The party was her peace offering, a single rose held out to Keisha in hopes they could get back what they'd once had so long ago, when they were just little more than girls. But how to get there, exactly, remained a mystery.

"So?" Keisha asked. "What do you want, T?"

Tenika looked up, slightly offended. "What?"

Keisha folded her arms and looked at her cousin. "You know what I'm talking about, girl. You need something. You never call me unless you do."

Tenika smiled. "I love you, Keisha."

"I love you, too, except when you're acting like some fool. So what is it this time?"

Tenika sighed and glanced toward the doorway. She shook her head wearily, then she lowered her voice. "It's Delilah," she said quietly.

Keisha's voice rose up in amazement. "What, you two are having trouble already? Didn't I just go to your wedding?"

Tenika shook her head. "No, no. There's no trouble. And the garage is fine. Everything's fine. The problem is just..." She poked absently on the chicken cooking in front of her, letting her words die in her mouth. Finally, Tenika forced herself to admit the truth. "The problem is she wants to have a baby."

A look of dismay came over Keisha's face. "Lord, have mercy."

"Exactly."

Keisha paused. "You didn't tell her about Walter, did you?"

Tenika couldn't look at her cousin. "Nope." She paused. "We don't talk about that, remember?"

Keisha leaned forward in her chair. "Oh, but, T. You've got to *tell* her. Before this gets out of hand."

Tenika looked at her cousin imploringly. "I know that! And believe me, I want to. But...you know how it is." She lowered her voice as she glanced around the yard helplessly. "We had an agreement, you and me."

Keisha nodded. "I know," she said wearily. Then she fell silent.

Tenika looked out at the urban landscape beyond her fence. "I keep telling myself it'll be a fresh start. Just put it out of my mind. Forget it every happened."

Keisha didn't answer.

"Like...it's all in the past, right? We just move on and we begin again," Tenika continued firmly.

Still Keisha said nothing. Then slowly she rose. "Well, you can tell yourself that, T, but it doesn't look to me like you've moved on. Not one bit."

Tenika nodded with a sigh. "I know. I'm trying to. But I guess I haven't." She paused, the grease-covered tongs in mid-air.

"What's the church say about it?"

"What?" Keisha eyed her.

"Well, Keisha, you're there every damn Sunday. Hasn't it come up between you and God?"

Keisha studied the sharp toes of her kelly green pumps, and kneaded her fingers, balled tightly in her hands. "No. It hasn't, as a matter of fact."

"So I should tell Delilah…but you've just moved on, is what you're telling me?"

Keisha looked at her cousin with annoyance. Then huffily, she rose. "I'm going to forget you brought this up, T."

Putting down her water glass, Keisha marched through the doorway, leaving her alone. And Tenika just stood there, turning chicken and feeling a vast, aching emptiness move through her heart once more.

Keisha hadn't solved her problem at all.

*

Monroe navigated the crowd, juggling a plate of food and a cold beer. They were looking for a place to pause and rest for a moment in the backyard. The afternoon was warm and clear, and the shouts of neighborhood kids came drifting over the fence. In the corner Tenika was working at the grill, and the entire yard was filled with the smoky, delicious smell of barbecued chicken.

Really, Monroe just needed to decompress. The entire meeting Rosalind episode had been jarring. As it turned out, this was the beautiful woman's name—Rosalind. Monroe overheard Kate talking about her.

Standing there, Monroe inhaled and dreamily closed their eyes ever so briefly. *Rosalind.* Even her name was beautiful, like something out of Shakespeare.

Then Monroe remembered the loaded paper plate of chicken and greens they still held in their hand, and glanced around for a place to sit. An empty folding chair by the fence beckoned. Monroe moved to it and sat.

Rosalind was undoubtedly gone by now, given her level of distress. Still, the sheer fact that she existed was good enough for Monroe. There would be more conversation. More contact. More everything.

There simply had to be.

Seeing Rosalind in that crowd, and feeling the direct connection between them light up the way it did was nothing less than remarkable. Monroe had never experienced anything like it before. Such moments were fated, they thought. There was no other way around it. It was like something out of the movies. Or at least the movie that played in Monroe's head. Even if Rosalind did retreat to a bedroom almost immediately and close the door as soon as they met.

A new thought now occurred to Monroe. Perhaps Rosalind was overwhelmed with emotion, as well. Maybe this was the twenty-first century equivalent of a woman having the vapors—and being overcome by love.

On the other hand…what if she did leave? Would Monroe actually ever find her again?

No, no no. This was indeed meant to be. Monroe could feel it.

At that instant, they looked up to see Rosalind, herself, standing in the doorway, scanning the crowd. Behind her Kate was saying something about the wine being on the patio.

Immediately, Monroe jumped up, upsetting the precarious plate of chicken balanced on their knee. The chicken took a dive and hit the flagstones underfoot, spattering barbecue sauce and flinging greens as it went.

Monroe looked at it for the briefest moment, as if somebody else entirely had just lost their dinner. Then in a sweep, Monroe simply moved on to stand directly in front of Rosalind.

"Hey!" Monroe said as Kate slipped away in the background.

"Hi." Rosalind barely looked at Monroe.

"Glad you emerged. Are you all right?"

"Oh…yeah, I'm fine. It was nothing." The tiniest smudge of mascara on her cheek indicated otherwise. It appeared she had been crying.

"Join me?" Monroe waved a hand toward the empty chairs in the corner. "I just have to repair a little disaster." Monroe now retreated to the heap of chicken on the ground, and began picking up pieces. "Don't mind me," they said gamely, bundling up the now inedible chicken into a bent paper plate.

Rosalind smiled as she made her way to a waiting chair in the vicinity. Monroe smiled over at her, amazed for a moment at the calm certainty that was washing through them in the midst of this very humbling, and yes—embarrassing act.

This had to be Rosalind's divine influence on them. Monroe grinned at her as they rose and prepared to find the nearest trash can. "What can I say? I'm all thumbs today. Anyway, can I get you something while I'm up?"

"A drink," Rosalind said. Suddenly, she was feeling emboldened. "I heard there was some white wine?"

"I'm on it," said Monroe, heading off to trash their dinner and handle her request.

Rosalind leaned back wearily in her chair, curious now to see what would happen next.

Chapter Ten

One moment evaporated into another as the pleasant fall evening unfolded in Delilah and Tenika's backyard. People ate, chatted, drank and mingled, while in the corner Rosalind and Monroe now sat awkwardly together in side by side folding chairs as the moments ticked by.

"I love your bow tie," Rosalind managed to say. Her heart was beating a million miles an hour at present. But it appeared that Monroe was equally on edge.

Monroe smoothed their tie with an anxious hand. "Thanks." Monroe swallowed. Here it was. Social anxiety, cranked up to max. "And I love your dress."

"Thanks." Rosalind hesitated for a moment. *Screw it*, she thought, now looking directly into Monroe's eyes. "I wanted to wear something special tonight."

Monroe gazed back at her, returning the smile. They appeared to be barely breathing. "Oh? How come?"

"Just because..." She glanced at Monroe with a look that explained her motivation perfectly. Mainly because she couldn't help herself.

Monroe took a deep breath. "You have an interesting name. Rosalind. It reminds me—"

"Of *As You Like It*. I know."

"You've you've heard this before?"

"Seems like everybody's a Shakespeare fan," Rosalind said. "But thanks."

"Sure."

There was another silence. Monroe searched frantically for topics of conversation, while Rosalind took another long sip of her wine. "Yeah, my parents named me after Shakespeare's character," she continued. "Just don't expect a monologue, okay?"

"Oh, no. Never."

Rosalind gave another shy grin as their eyes met once more. The silence ticked on between them, but now, somehow, it was no longer nerve-racking. Instead, it was becoming more peaceful.

Monroe smiled at the worn grass underfoot. "How do you know Kate and Lizzy?"

"The garage. I guess everyone here must."

Monroe took a deep breath. It appeared they were trying to relax. "Lizzy and T have worked on my car, for sure. But actually, I met Kate at the church where she was in Sanctuary." Monroe then added, "I work there."

Rosalind registered her surprise. She'd pegged Monroe as some kind of administrator, or maybe a fellow tech person. "Oh. Are you a minister?"

Monroe suddenly laughed. "God, no! I'm actually the music director, and the facilities manager. I handle the event rentals, the building maintenance, that kind of stuff. And...you know. The music."

"So you're a musician?"

Mm-hmm." Monroe scuffed a toe in the dirt self-consciously. "A pianist. And I compose. I went to...you know...a conservatory," they added in a small voice.

"Cool." This was cool. If there was anything Rosalind understood it was the outliers. The creators. The inventors. The engineers.

Monroe looked over at Rosalind and sank into her gaze for a moment.

"I'm in tech," Rosalind said quietly.

"Kate told me. She said you're a feminist crusader. That's amazing. I mean—you're not just writing code and addicting people to their screens. You're actually doing something in the world."

Rosalind nodded, slightly embarrassed. "I'm still getting used to the job. It all just happened in the past year. But here we are. Somehow I have a not-for-profit and everything."

"Do you like it?"

"Yeah. I do. I really do." Rosalind could feel the certainty of her words in her gut. She did like her work. She was proud of it. But more importantly, she was glad Monroe had asked her about it. It was a simple question, but it felt real. More real than any other conversation she'd had lately. "Tell me about your music."

Monroe now flushed red. "Oh, most of the time I just play the hymns in the hymnal."

"But you said you're a composer. What's your music like?"

"What's it *like*?" A look of concern passed over Monroe's face, and they fell silent. "I guess you'd have to listen to it." Monroe swallowed and raised their gaze once more to Rosalind. "If you wanted to, I could play it for you at the church. Some time."

Now Rosalind was silent as an unexpected surge of distaste moved through her. Here it was: a live offer, an invitation on the table. A proposed date with an interesting, intriguing, even attractive person. The first to make her motor race since Tasha.

This was, indeed, exactly what she had come to the party for.

"Oh," was all Rosalind said, confused by her own response. "Huh."

What was her problem? Why wasn't she leaping at the invitation?

Rosalind suddenly rose, and coolly picked up her now empty glass. This was all entirely too much for her. It was just…too much. This was all she knew. "Actually, I really have to go," she said, glancing at her watch.

Monroe's face registered mild shock. "Oh! Okay—wait," they said, suddenly rising. "I'll walk you out." But Rosalind was already retreating across the yard, heading for the sanctuary of the front door. Her car. Her home.

Monroe stopped, and for a moment, considered hurrying after Rosalind as she quickly disappeared. Or at least calling out after her. *Shouldn't they say something?*

Instead, Monroe simply stood there in the backyard, frozen. *What the hell had just happened?*

Was this the moment when Monroe was supposed to put up a fight and engage in some age-old game of pursuit? Or was this something else? Had Rosalind's earlier retreat to the bedroom been some kind of sign?

Perhaps the beautiful Rosalind was not, in fact, the one.

Their heart hammering hard, Monroe raised a shaky voice toward Rosalind, who had now all but disappeared. "I'll call you!"

Rosalind was gone. The yard's other occupants suddenly fell silent, and Monroe turned crimson, feeling curious eyes watching.

Heavily, Monroe sat down in their lawn chair, utterly bewildered by what had just taken place. Idly, they tapped their beer bottle against their knee and stared into space.

Now what?

*

Rosalind pulled away from the curb with a screech and sped toward the highway that would carry her home. Every fiber of her being was now screaming as a cavalcade of emotions swept through her. There was revulsion, thick and black, spreading under her skin. And utter shame. Shame at being this mutant person who somehow thought it would be okay to date women.

What the hell was I thinking?

Of course, Rosalind knew it would be like this. She would end up on a folding chair in a backyard with dying grass and cracked, half-empty terracotta pots sitting by sadly. There she'd be, talking to some so-called queer person who was…well…*what*?

Interesting, definitely. And smart and talented, apparently. And certainly a good and caring person. And attractive. Even their bow tie was hot. But…is this someone she could actually date? Could they kiss? Could they fall in love?

Could they actually climb in bed together naked and make love?

A cold wave of reality buzzed through Rosalind's brain. Was she seriously attracted to Monroe? And since she was…what was wrong with her? Why was she running away?

Couldn't she just give herself this one precious gift?

In a nutshell, Monroe was pretty much the last person Rosalind could ever bring home to her parents. The. Last. Person. That was a definite. Monroe was one of those obscure people who was, for starters, not Chinese. Not even Asian. Not in tech, law or medicine. And apparently not even male or female.

That was going to go down real well with her incredibly entrenched, conservative Chinese Evangelist family. All Monroe had going for them is that they worked in a church.

Rosalind's heart beat hard as she tried to stay focused on the weaving Oakland traffic ahead of her. A black car out of nowhere zoomed past her and hit its horn obnoxiously. "Zoomin" read the license plate.

Still, moments later, there was Monroe. They were still lodged firmly in her mind as she drove back home.

Monroe was everything Rosalind was not in this moment. Monroe had a quiet intensity, a strangely grounded calm she could not ignore. Not to mention a sweet sensitivity. "Do you like it?" Monroe had simply asked when the two of them were talking about her work.

Because, yes, that was the only thing that really mattered about work, wasn't it? It wasn't the money, or the prestige, or the damn perks. It was the joy of the work itself that really counted. At least, if you wanted to be happy it did.

They. Even Monroe's pronoun was sexy. She had to admit. And…yet.

There would come that awful moment when Monroe finally had to be presented to her family. Because Rosalind could obscure her dating life for a while at least. But finally, her parents' questions would take over, and she could no longer hide the critical back bone of her personal life. And didn't they deserve to know?

Regardless, they'd bully and cajole her brother until they got it out of him, unless Rosalind told them herself. They'd sense something was different, that she had somehow changed. And so they'd be off and running, hound dogs on the trail. That's how they were.

And how would it be for someone like Monroe, who she could already tell was a sensitive person to begin with?

In a word, it would be brutal.

Yeman ren they would call Monroe.

Savage.

Then, of course, they would tell them both to leave.

A tear slid down Rosalind's face as she drove on, trying to remain unperturbed. What was the point, anyway? She'd just remain celibate for the rest of her life. Or she'd go join the Peace Corps, or do the damn missionary work they kept trying to shove down her throat. Now that she'd carved out the unique niche in the business world they couldn't possibly understand.

Her family's expectation for her was the twenty-ton elephant that crowded every room she walked into. Though she only saw them on Sundays, they were a nagging constant in her life. A damp, worried weight that refused to settle down.

Someday you must get married. Bring honor. Have sons. Be a loyal and good daughter.

And now that Rosalind found someone she thought she

wanted, what did she do? She walked out. Because in the end, her mother and her father were still firmly in control.

It was a truth that galled her. And yet…there it was.

*

As the hour approached midnight, Tenika stretched her head back against the couch in a slouchy recline. Sleepily, she watched Lizzy and Kate slow dance in her living room, amidst the empty wine glasses, and the cake plates and the detritus of the party. Somehow no one was quite ready to end the party.

An old Frank Sinatra tune wound its way through the room, the two of them were held in a lock of love. Lizzy and Kate barely moved as Sinatra's reedy voice crooned in the background.

We may never, never meet again
On the bumpy road of love
Still I'll always, always keep the memory of
The way you wear your hat…

A clarinet spiraled up and took a solo as Lizzy now led Kate in a slow, sexy pirouette. She landed back in Lizzy's arms, and the two of them dissolved into a tender kiss. Tenika smiled. This was what they all got married for—this pure, sweet, unsullied potential. And here it was, unfolding right in front of her, in real time, in her living room.

Tenika glanced around, wondering where Delilah was. At this point, the other guests had gone. Now it was just the four of them. "Honey?" she started to call out. But then she stopped herself as a new, troubling thought descended.

She really had to tell Delilah about Walter.

Keisha was right, of course, just like she always was. As it stood, there was probably going to be hell to pay for not telling her until now. And to delay one moment further into this baby-making project was exactly the opposite of what should be happening. They were supposed to be pulling together in mutual support. Not clinging to the broken pieces of the past.

Tenika squirmed on the couch uncomfortably, and closed her eyes as if she could drive these troubling thoughts from her mind.

First of all, there was the reality of the whole thing. For the six thousandth time, phantom car tires screeched through Tenika's brain as she replayed the scene yet again. The little boy running between the parked cars. Her frantic dive to stop him. Keisha screaming "Walter! NO!" as Tenika hit the pavement heavily. Then her laying there. Frozen.

Next came the screech of more tires, the sick thud of impact, and the little boy's stifled cry. It was a small scream, barely audible above the loud, otherworldly sounds coming from the two of them as they tried to stop him.

It was a scream she would never, ever forget.

Then there was the aftermath. The bleeding, broken child, lying unconscious on the ground. The frantic calls to 911, and Miss Alma's stammered, shocked response on the phone. The questioning police officers who were sure she and Keisha were high on drugs. And finally, the sickening shame that had descended around her afterwards, when she finally had time to think.

It had all closed in on Tenika like walls of concrete, pinning her in place. It was her unspoken prison, the lead weight in the back of her consciousness. It was the wound she could never quite touch. And it was something she had never once told her wife about.

This was also the reason Tenika felt queasy every time she thought about raising children. How in God's name was she going to share any of this now?

Strains of Sinatra continued.

The way you hold your knife
The way we danced until three
The way you changed my life...

"T?" Tenika opened her eyes as Delilah appeared now on the other side of the living room. "Hey," Delilah said, making her way over to the couch. She sat down beside her wife, and leaned her head on her shoulder.

"Hi," Delilah said sleepily as she yawned.

Tenika took her small, warm hand in her own. Then she kissed it.

Delilah glanced over at her. Pausing, she studied Tenika's face. "What's wrong, baby?"

"Nothin'."

"Really?"

Tenika glanced up at the ceiling. "Mmm-hmm." She did her best to smile at her wife. "I'm just sitting here, watching them dance."

God knew where Walter was now, or if he was even still alive. His traumatic brain injury had finally caused his family to move away from the neighborhood the year after the accident. There were relatives in southern California apparently. Relatives who could help take care of Walter, perhaps. Tenika had no idea what had happened to any of them.

After that terrible night, nothing more had ever been said by her or Keisha about it—not one single word. So the incident remained buried, a Superfund site of toxic emotional sludge. There just wasn't much anyone could do about it, and that, apparently, was that.

Releasing Delilah's hand, Tenika rose and walked silently back to the kitchen.

It was time to clean up.

*

Delilah trailed Tenika into the kitchen, passing by Lizzy and Kate who were now kissing as Sinatra hit his final big notes. "Sweetie?" she called as she came around the corner.

Tenika was standing at the sink, gripping the counter with both hands, her head hung low. Her shoulders shook, and her long thin braids were a quivering mass across her back. She was crying, silently.

A stab of anxiety ratcheted up through Delilah's body as she strode over to her wife. "Honey? What is it, baby? What's wrong?"

Reaching out, Delilah put a hand on Tenika's arm, but almost violently, Tenika shook it off. Her back still turned to her, Tenika cleared her throat and shook her head.

"Nothing," she finally said as her voice broke. "There's nothing wrong. Just... Just leave me alone right now, okay?"

Delilah stood there, studying the back of Tenika's head. "T. Please. You never cry. Like ever. And you're standing there crying your eyes out."

"I'm not *fucking crying*."

"You're crying, T."

Suddenly Tenika whirled around, fury in her tear-stained eyes. "I'm not crying, *all right*? I just..." With a mute gesture, she waved away the rest of the sentence in frustration. Then she strode from the room. As usual.

Delilah sighed. She'd been here before with her wife, more times than she cared to recall. And the best solution, she had learned, was simply to wait and bide her time.

Tenika would be back, just like she always was. Clearly, there was a problem. And just as clearly, there was only one solution. Tenika would have to work it out for herself.

There would be no request for consolation, nor would there be any talking it through or processing it together. Her wife wouldn't reach out for Delilah in the night, or ever admit she needed any kind of help. Tenika was an enigma, pure and simple. A very self-contained enigma with unlimited depths.

"Okay, then," Delilah said with a sigh to no one in particular.

"Everything all right in here?" Lizzy asked from the doorway. Kate smiled at Delilah over her shoulder.

"Yeah. It's just T. Having the vapors."

"I see," said Lizzy with a chuckle. "She'll get over it. Shall we get busy cleaning up?"

"Oh, no. Don't—" she began, but Kate had already swept past her, and was heading straight for the kitchen sink. Immediately, she stoppered it, flipped on the hot water and squirted in some dish liquid.

"Here," Kate said, tossing a dish towel toward Lizzy, who caught it in one hand. Methodically, Kate began washing the stack of sticky plates on the counter.

"Now you? You sit and relax," Lizzy commanded Delilah, pointing to the kitchen table.

"Come on, Lizzy, you really don't need to do this," Delilah said. But Lizzy just ignored her as Kate handed her a wet dish. Turning her back on Delilah's protests, Lizzy began drying it.

The two women worked along in silence for a few moments as Delilah now sat quietly, considering things. Tenika was undoubtedly in bed already and heading for sleep.

Maybe it was just self-preservation. But maybe it was the ache of some old inner turmoil that kept her wife locked up like this. Delilah didn't know. She only knew that it was how things were. And if she wanted to bring a baby into their lives, she was going to have to be good with all of it.

There simply was no other way.

Chapter Eleven

B ART pulled up to the 16th Street Mission station, and Frankie got out. She ambled down the platform stairs, and out into the baking hot reality of another sunny afternoon in the hood.

The letter from the SFPD brass had arrived days before, but it still grated on her. But how could it not? Somehow she'd flunked her evaluation with BSU. But then, the Behavioral Science Unit had a reputation of being serious sticklers. Perhaps even ridiculously so. Frankie sidestepped some vomit on the sidewalk, and kept on her path.

For instance, after that lengthy, painful debrief about the teen suicide nothing much had happened. No one said a word to her about it, or even took any disciplinary action. She'd gone on licking her wounds, assuming the worst was over. But then that was a week before she fell asleep on the stake out.

Now here she was, walking into the dead zone of the SFPD's Video Reference Library day after god-forsaken day. After the stake out debacle, she'd even been asked to turn in her weapon. This, she assumed, was her punishment.

But no. There was more.

Now the top brass were even telling her, in writing no less, that she would have to go to some 'Trauma Reprogramming Retreat' up in who-the-hell-knew-where. Not only would Frankie be forced to go, she would have to be to reevaluated afterwards.

In other words, she had to prove she'd learned something, or improved…or whatever you got out of those things…before the department would give her back her weapon. Her beat. Her life.

There was no way out. The lieutenant's signature was on the letter. It was an order, plain and simple. Frankie couldn't think of anything she'd rather do less, but at this point, they were looking for willingness. The phrase used in the letter was that her 'beliefs were inconsistent with BSU team findings.'

In other words, Frankie didn't think she was as messed up as she actually was. Which, of course, was total bullshit. Of course, she knew she was fucked up. She just didn't want them to know. But they knew. Now they just didn't believe *she* knew what they knew. As if.

Frankie sighed. So much for trying to keep her job.

Frankie ID'd her way through the police station entrance, and made her way up to the women's locker room on the second floor. Peralta was hoisting her gun belt on her hips as Frankie opened the locker next to hers. Officer Mary Peralta was one of her least favorite people at that station, mainly because she was a snake in the grass. Furthermore, she was a cloying girly-girl who actually wore make up on the job, complete with lipstick. Frankie didn't get it.

"Frankie."

Frankie did not hide the disdain in her voice. "Peralta."

Officer Peralta looked at her and smiled. "It's Mary."

"Mary," Frankie said through gritted teeth.

"Heard about BSU and the Library gig," Peralta said with an even bigger smile. "Sounds rough," she said, eyebrows raised toward her locker. Peralta gave a woebegone little shake of her head.

Frankie said nothing and turned away as she tossed her lunch into her locker and relocked it.

"So I guess you won't be needing your body armor today," Peralta continued breezily. She flashed a lipstick smile at Frankie.

Frankie said nothing, and attempted to sweep past her with her dignity still in tact. But still the other officer pressed on. "Maybe you should try a little caffeine? If you're…you know… *sleepy*?" Peralta cracked up at her own joke as Frankie slammed the door to the locker room shut.

"Fuck you," Frankie muttered from the hallway.

Jesus Christ. It was just another day on her slow descent into hell.

*

The day had begun with thoughts of Rosalind. Or at least as many as Monroe was willing to ration themself. For that's how things were now. Monroe simply had to put a governor on the non-stop Rosalind stream now pouring through their head. For in the confines of Monroe's mind, at least, their relationship was already sizing up to be vast and all-encompassing.

All they had to do was get past the hurdle of a first date.

For starters, Monroe had woken up with the beginning of a song in their head. In the shower, it continued, unrelenting until finally Monroe started writing out lyrics with a finger on the steamy glass shower door. Which was a first. To Monroe, at least, this was an excellent harbinger of things to come.

The opening line of this song, which was most definitely about Rosalind, pounded through Monroe's head relentlessly to a peppy pop groove. It was called 'Reawakened,' and it was dramatically different from anything else Monroe had ever written. It even had a bridge. On the other hand, maybe it was called 'Your Smile.' Or maybe—well, honestly, Monroe didn't know.

The exact title hadn't been worked out yet. Still. A song had been born.

Humming now, Monroe took the front steps at the church two at a time as they hustled back to work after lunch. There was a wedding rehearsal in the sanctuary this afternoon, and Monroe was tasked with setting up and running the audio.

The Reverend was coming out of the church and caught Monroe's eye. "You look happy," she remarked, and Monroe blushed. Busted!

The fact was that Monroe *was* happy. Just the briefest thought of Rosalind, the merest knowledge that she existed, lit up Monroe like little had in recent years. Rosalind was like the sudden splash of cream in their coffee, the turbinado sugar in their tea. And they hadn't even had so much as a phone call together. But somehow, weirdly, that didn't matter.

For once, Monroe was feeling completely seen and understood. It really was only a matter of time until they went out with each other, Monroe was sure of it. Furthermore, Monroe just knew they both felt the inevitability of their connection. The two of them would, indeed, find each other when the moment was exactly right, and probably not a moment sooner.

For once, life was looking up.

*

Rosalind hung up the phone, feeling vindicated. *There.* She'd done it.

Booking a room in Harbin Hot Springs for two nights was somehow far more difficult than she'd originally thought it would be. Shoving aside the grant application waiting on her desk for review, Rosalind lay her head down into the cool nest of her arms. The problem was the place was now soaked through with memories. That alone was bound to be a little depressing. But there were other issues.

What if she couldn't help herself, and she slept with another woman up there who ghosted her? Or worse—what if she came around a corner and Tasha, her Harbin fling, was standing there?

Then there was the bigger problem—the looming specter of coming out to her parents.

Sally's words still hung in Rosalind's mind like shiny ornaments: *'If you don't tell them, you'll never attract the love that is patiently waiting for you. That's what is waiting for us all, but only when we truly open up to it. Some of us never do, of course..."*

Well, she wasn't going to be one of those terrified losers who sat on the sidelines waiting for life to happen to them. That was the old Rosalind, but this was Rosalind 2.0. She was now built for strength, and filled with determination. Even if it meant taking on her biggest fear and coming out to her parents.

Rosalind thought of the beautiful white statue of Kwan Yin, the goddess of compassion, that rested by the cold pool at Harbin. Somehow the goddess had weathered the wildfire that had destroyed the place.

Kwan Yin would tell her what to do, that much she knew. She could feel the truth of it. For there was a certain approach Rosalind had to take, especially with the aging Bà and Mama. It was such a delicate matter.

Anything was possible, Roslaind reasoned. Maybe Kwan Yin would guide her to avoid telling her parents. Maybe Sally was dead wrong, because these people were *old*. What if they both had strokes and dropped dead, right there in the living room? It was possible, given how hard Rosalind's news would hit them.

Anyway, did they truly need to know? What would it do for them, besides destroy the last stringy illusions of comfort they got from imagining their daughter was straight. (If she heard one more thing about the Lee's nice son, Charles, the real estate developer, she was going to scream.)

Somehow Rosalind knew she was wrong, but still...her illusion stubbornly persisted. And why not? It was helping her get through this particular day. She'd see what the next step was once she got to Harbin.

Rosalind's forehead was heavy on her arms and stuck slightly to her skin now. Briefly, tentatively, a thought of Monroe passed through her mind, blazing in and blazing out, trailing white light. She didn't need or want the thought, but in it came anyway, mainly because it had to.

Squeezing her eyes just a little more tightly shut, Rosalind did her best to banish all such thoughts. They wouldn't help. Not now. Yes, Monroe made her heart quicken just ever so slightly, but Monroe simply couldn't be the one.

That just seemed like a mathematical impossibility—an anomaly in the system. She'd never even considered being with a non-binary person. A 'they.' And Monroe was so achingly vulnerable. So real.

So…

Nope. Rosalind couldn't do it. Not now at least. Anyway, Sally didn't say who, exactly, the love was who apparently waited for her patiently. Maybe it was yet another Tasha, another lithe blonde who would just appear before her in the warm pool at Harbin and extend a hand. Or maybe it was Tasha herself.

Maybe if they did run into each other, she'd have a change of heart. Maybe there would be a total redo of their original sex-soaked, languid afternoon in bed. Maybe that might even be followed by a relationship.

The thought brought a smile to Rosalind's face, and picking up her head, she sat back in her chair and gazed at the street below. Running into Tasha might actually be all right. Suddenly an awareness settled over her.

She would be okay. It would all be okay.

Rosalind would come out, her parents would survive her news, and her brother would even forgive her. And life would quietly go on.

For wasn't that the way of the world?

Rosalind was determined to do this, one aching step at a time.

*

Sally leaned back in her chair and regarded her friend. "Delilah," she said gently, "you really have to tell her how you feel." She picked up the remains of her taco and neatly tucked it into her mouth, wiping her hands on her napkin.

A crunch of fried pork, the final bite of *carnitas*, filled her mind. This was why they came to the local taqueria, a bright, cheerful place with a line out the door and a host of motherly Mexican women in the back making tortillas in their hairnets. This was the real thing.

Delilah looked distracted. She'd barely touched her burrito. Absently she stirred the milky horchata and its melting ice cubes in front of her. "You really think?" she asked.

"I don't just think, I know." Sally put down her napkin. "It's what must be. This is the vision I had." She shrugged. "I mean, you've got to do what you've got to do, Delilah. I'm just saying, you can trust the path. You really can."

Delilah sighed and gazed at her friend. "Honestly, I have no idea if she's ever going to change her mind. What if she never does?"

There was a silence between them. Finally, Delilah continued. "Something's wrong. She's said as much, but she won't tell me what." Now her eyes filled with tears. Delilah's voice dropped. "What if T doesn't love me anymore, Sally?" she whispered.

The elderly woman at the next table glanced over at them, and Delilah closed her eyes, struggling to regain composure. Meanwhile, Sally took her hand and squeezed it. "I don't think that's it. She loves you."

Delilah's face was half crumpled. "But what if she doesn't want to be with me?"

Sally leaned forward in earnest. "Delilah—where is this coming from?"

Delilah cleared her throat and glanced around. Once more she lowered her voice. "From the fact that since I brought it up, she hasn't so much as laid a finger on me. And that is not, T. I'm telling you…something is seriously wrong, Sally."

Abruptly the elderly woman beside them got up and carried her shrimp taco bowl to another table. Still Sally pressed on.

"Okay, okay. Then all the more reason to bring it up. You've got to find out what's going on with her. You just do. You owe it to both of you, but most of all to yourself."

Delilah sat back and sighed. Distractedly, she picked up her burrito and took a small bite. Then quickly, she put it down. "And another thing. T's been on the phone twice with her cousin. I overheard her through the bedroom door. She barely ever talks to her. Keisha even came to our party, which was…like…unheard of. So those two are yakking away about something, some guy named Walter, and I haven't got a frigging clue who he is."

Once more tears filled Delilah's eyes. "These days I just feel like…like her roommate."

Sally took her friend's hand and squeezed it. "So make time to talk. You know how to do this, Delilah. You have to."

Delilah nodded and blew her nose. "Okay," she said wearily. "All right." Her tone was resigned, for there really was nothing else to be done. Uncertainty would linger until it didn't.

Raising her head, she looked at Sally. "What about you?" she asked. "Are you okay?"

Sally laughed. "Of course. I'm great." Sally sucked on the paper straw in her *horchata*, savoring the sweet, cold cinnamon sip.

Delilah blew her nose once more and regarded her friend. "Are you moving in with Frankie? Because we sure don't see you much these days."

"Frankie needed me," she explained. "She's been having a rough time with her job."

"Right. I heard about that. But…are you moving in with her?"

Sally blushed. "Maybe. I mean, Frankie hasn't actually asked. And you know how I am." Sally looked up at her friend shyly. "I don't want to blow it, Delilah." Her over eagerness had prompted Sally to move in with several bad bets in the last decade. In fact, Frankie was GF #12, a reality she was not proud of.

"This time I'm actually trying to be cautious, so *I'm* definitely not bringing it up."

"Good to be careful," Delilah noted. "Still, I think you're moving in with her. I can feel it." She chuckled. "But any time you want to come over and sleep on the couch for old time's sake…"

Sally laughed and shook her head. "I owe you guys big time. The next lifetime I swear I'm making it up to you."

Delilah swatted away her friend's concern. "You don't have to sweat it, Sally. We love you. And you're truly welcome any time."

"Love you, too," said Sally, giving her friend's arm a squeeze. Sipping her *horchata* once more, she could feel her entire nervous system relax.

Thank God for dear friends.

Chapter Twelve

Tenika picked up her wrench and cranked hard on the old corroded cap on the oil pan she was working on. After a moment, it loosened and gave, and a thick stream of motor oil poured out. This afternoon's task was replacing the leaking oil pan with a new one in the weather-beaten Nissan Maxima on the lift. It was one of those cars that had seen a little too much Bay air, and its paint was peeling and discolored.

Tenika stepped out from underneath the chassis as the used oil continued to drain. Putting her hands on her hips, she studied the floor of the garage for a long, absent moment. All afternoon, her thoughts had been a tangle in her mind. Delilah deserved an answer—a reason. A...something, in response to her entreaties about a baby. But as the days slid forward, Tenika found she had nothing to say to her wife.

Instead, she'd called Keisha twice. And twice Keisha had said the same thing. "You've got to tell that girl. What's *wrong* with you?"

As usual, Keisha had the verbal upper hand. And both times, Tenika had slunk off the phone, convinced that her cousin was right. And yet, each time she steeled herself to finally sit Delilah down and tell her about Walter she froze.

There just didn't seem to be enough time in the day, or perhaps compassion in the world to help her get past her troubles. It occurred to Tenika that she might even need therapy to exorcise these ghosts. But even that possibility, like all the others on the touchy subject of Walter, flitted in and flitted out, unfulfilled.

"You okay?" asked Lizzy as she peeled off a pair of blackened latex gloves in the work bay beside Tenika.

"Mmm-hmm."

Lizzy glanced at her business partner curiously. "You don't seem okay, T. In fact, you haven't seemed okay for…like a week now. What the heck is going on?"

"Oh, I don't know. Marriage, I guess. It's nothing."

"Seriously? I always peg you two as the perfect couple."

"No, it's all fine. Whatever," Tenika groused as she turned back to the oil pan, its oil stream now reduced to a tiny drip. Peering up overhead, she studied the trim of the oil pan for a moment. She'd need a chisel to break the factory sealed adhesive. Going over to her tool chest, she extracted her sharpest one.

"You going in there with a chisel?" Lizzy said from behind her. "Seriously?"

Tenika turned to her partner. "What?"

"It's just that steel pan has an aluminum back side. You know you could damage the hell out of it."

"I thought we had a policy of no backseat repairing around here."

"We do. I know. I'm just saying."

"Well, don't, Lizzy." Tenika's voice landed on the last word like a blade, and her partner recoiled.

"Whoa." Lizzy paused for a moment and studied her friend once more. "You sure you're okay, T?"

"Yes!" she barked. Then she stopped herself. "Well…no. But…oh, Jesus. I don't know." Her voice sunk down in a desperation Lizzy had seldom seen.

Lizzy approached her, hands on hips. "T, what's going on?"

Quickly, the wheels spun in Tenika's mind, calculating the odds. She could tell no one about Walter—not even Lizzy.

Because then Lizzy would tell Kate, and Kate might feel she had to tell Sally. Then Sally was sure to tell Delilah, unless Kate did it herself first. Because that's the way it was.

Everyone knew everything about everyone. All the time. Except no one knew anything about Walter, save for Keisha. And that was the way it would stay.

"I'm sorry," Tenika said. "I'm just worried, that's all. Delilah wants to have a baby."

"Hey—that's great!" Lizzy said enthused.

"Maybe. I mean, I suppose kids and babies and all that can be cool. But Lizzy, I'm…I'm just not cut out for motherhood. You know what I'm saying?"

"Oh, come on T. You'd be an amazing mother!"

"There are…things," Tenika said slowly, still calculating all the way. "Things people don't know about me. I—" she continued. She wavered as she looked over at Lizzy. Perhaps she'd misjudged how much she could trust her partner.

It would feel so good to finally talk about this with someone other than her church lady cousin. But then Tenika stopped. She could say no more.

Still Lizzy looked at her curiously. "Like what?"

"Like nothing. Forget I mentioned it." Tenika picked up her chisel once more and approached the aging oil pan. She gave it a few gentle taps to assess the condition of the sealant, and an edge of the pan immediately let go. A fine spray of motor oil landed on her face. "Hell," she muttered, pulling out the bandana in her pocket and wiping off her cheek.

"No, seriously, T. Don't you want to have kids?" Lizzy pressed. "That's one of the great joys of marriage, right?"

Tenika returned to working her chisel around the perimeter of the pan. "If you want them it is."

"I'm amazed you're not up for this."

Tenika glanced over her shoulder. "Don't you have some tires to rotate?"

Lizzy carried on, nonplussed. "For what it's worth, T, if there's anything I know about marriage, it's that it's one big, fat compromise. You've got to be willing to give."

Tenika stopped and shook her head at her business partner. "Now you're some big expert on marriage?"

Lizzy sighed. "Okay, okay. Point taken," she said lightly. "I just know if it was me and Kate—"

"Well, it's not you and Kate," Tenika snapped.

"T, what the fuck?"

Tenika stopped what she was doing and turned to her friend. "I'm sorry," she breathed. "I'm…all screwed up."

"You want to talk about it?"

"Nope," said Tenika. And returning to the oil pan overhead, she gave a final tap on her chisel as the dented pan came away in her hands. "Forget I said anything, okay?"

"Done," said Lizzy. But the matter was far from over in her mind. Tenika was most definitely hanging on to something, the hanging on of which was making her pretty damn insufferable.

Lizzy wondered how long it would be until she finally cracked.

*

Rosalind walked down the hill from her cottage toward Harbin's famed pools, feeling the portent of the moment. Whatever happened during the next twenty-four hours she was here, she was prepared. She had her wits about her, and her antenna highly tuned for incoming signs and signals.

The dirt path Rosalind now walked was punctuated here and there by low brush, and the brown hills that rose all around her had clearly been through something. The scars of the 2015 wildfire had left vacant nothingness more than anything else. There had once been forest here, but now it was gone, planted instead with a thousand new trees. But that was all right with Rosalind.

She, too, was in a process of reinvention herself. She knew how it felt.

Walking along, swinging her canvas tote bag gently in her hand, she imagined what might lie ahead. For instance, she would, once again, swim naked. This time she didn't even have her bathing suit in her bag. In a holy act of defiance, she'd left it back in Oakland.

The butterflies in her stomach had gravitated to her chest, and now her breathing became more rapid as she strode along. Being here was almost too much to bear. But still, she was glad she came.

Fifteen minutes later, Rosalind slipped into the meditation pool amidst a half dozen other bathers, all lounging in the shade on a perfect, sunny fall afternoon. As her naked body slid into the pool's warm bath water, she felt the tension of the previous week soften and let go almost immediately. Maybe she would get a massage. Maybe she would recline on one of the teak day beds on the deck, and sunbathe in the nude. Maybe she would swim laps. Or sit in the sauna, and then plunge wildly, deliciously into the cold pool.

Maybe Rosalind would fall in love. Today could be that day, she reminded herself. Anything could happen.

She leaned back against the edge and surveyed her surroundings. Above her head, a pale blue metal railing defined the space, as did a sign urging silence and prohibiting sexual activity. Nearly everyone was naked, just like her.

Rosalind eyed two older, silver-haired women, clearly partners. They sat together, shoulders nestled against each other and eyes closed, a matched set with their cropped hair and their beautiful, plain, unadorned faces. A younger woman with a shock of iridescent green hair and an elaborately tattooed chest floated across from her, her heels hooked over the edge. Her arms floated out beside her as she gazed up at the enormous, loaded fig tree overhead.

Just next to them was the hot springs, a steaming pool housed in a tiny open building complete with candles and a poolside altar. Rosalind had already learned she could never begin with the hot pool, which was basically scalding. She had to ease her way in, after a few cold plunges. Even then the heat of the water was so intense, it felt almost cold to her skin. Within a few seconds she was always screaming to get out. But then, if she stayed, her body would gradually soften, and loosen. She would adapt. And then the hot springs could melt every ounce of resistance she had to life. And to herself.

Maybe, she thought, this was like being a lesbian. It was a long process of adapting to what at first seemed incredibly uncomfortable. But then became easier and more and more welcoming, until finally, it was home. Rosalind would go to the hot pool before she prayed to Kwan Yin for guidance. That much was a definite. But she had to hit the cold pool first.

A few moments later, she moved toward the cold plunge in the back.

Tucked into the edge of the woods, this pool had a comfortable natural demeanor about it. It was small, but it was powerful, supplied with the flow from a white pipe of icy spring water from the stream behind it.

Rosalind picked her way down the steps, feeling its familiar sting on her skin. She stood for a moment, summoning courage. Then she dunked her body once. Then once again as ice-cold water surrounded her head with a blaze of intensity. The cold plunge was brisk, vital. Completely energizing. Rosalind let go and dropped down into a ball on the bottom of the pool, submerging herself for several seconds. Then dripping wet, she ascended the steps out and strode toward the hot pool. This was where she needed courage the most.

Clutching the wavy hammered metal railing, with its faux hippie handmade charm, she descended into the steaming water step by painful step. There was no one in the pool at that moment, and the tiny house was blissfully quiet. Rosalind pushed herself to finally descend to the bottom of the pool. Gasping at the heat, she pushed off and swam a few feet to the other side, where she splashed water on the surface of a wooden shelf at the water's edge. Pressing her face into wet, steaming wood, she hung on and felt her body finally give and let go.

This was what she had come for. It was surrender, pure and simple, and she had been waiting for it for most of her life, it seemed. Each time she came here Rosalind seemed to leave a little more of her resistance behind. She could do this. She really could.

A few moments later, Rosalind walked up the steps past the hot pool structure to the wooden bench beside the cold pool. Before it sat the statue of Kwan Yin. Despite the fire, Kwan Yin's face was still intact, and she still held her hands in a beautiful, tranquil position of prayer. A delicate necklace of marigold blossoms was tied around her neck, and an assortment of special shells, offerings and small stones were arrayed at her feet.

Rosalind sat down on the wooden bench, and gazing at the statue took a long, deep breath. Behind her, water continued to flow into the pools that not even the worst wildfire could stop.

Here goes nothing, she thought.

Rosalind was never big on praying, still she held that certain deities, Kwan Yin for instance, were worthy of her attention and her belief. And Sally apparently felt just the same way. At any rate, who knew? Maybe she actually would get some guidance.

For it was Kwan Yin who stood at the gates of heaven on the day of her own death, and rather than enter paradise she turned back, simply because she heard the cries of those still on Earth. And if anyone needed her help right now, it most certainly was Rosalind.

Please guide me, she prayed. *I need to own who I am, and I need to tell my family, even though it will hurt them deeply. How can I do this, Kwan Yin?*

How can I knowingly cause them even more pain than I already have? Goddess of Compassion, please guide me.

A lump of regret grew in Rosalind's throat as she formed these thoughts, and she could feel herself contract at the threat of tears.

Please help me know what to do.

She looked at the serene visage of the statue, and the shade of relief began to fill her heart.

Kwan Yin, please tell me what to do about Monroe. Are they the one I'm looking for? Can I really bring home a non-binary to…say… Christmas dinner, even though my mother would probably pass out and my father would become…I don't even know what?

Would it be fair to subject any of them to that?

Please help me now, goddess. I haven't got a clue what to do.

Rosalind stopped and waited now, uncertain exactly what to do next. Then finally, she rose, bowing stiffly before she stepped away from the makeshift altar, smiling at the tiny sliver of hope that now rested within.

An answer would, most likely, come.

She could feel it.

*

Monroe sat in front of the grand piano in the sanctuary of the church. It was the quietest time of the week at the church. Sunlight filtered in from the stained glass windows high above, and even the usual gloom that gathered in the ancient redwood beams overhead seemed to be gone.

The space was light and holy somehow, and utterly silent. This was where Monroe came to reconnect to themself. And to anyone else in the heavens who might happen to be listening.

Monroe leaned heavily against the piano's music rack, and rested their head in their hand. With one finger, they plunked out the melody line of the song they had written for Rosalind. Softly, they sang the lyrics.

It's pouring through me now
Light like the sun
Pure like rain
I'm reawakened
Reawakened
All because of your smile

Monroe never wrote pop music. And they *never* wrote lyrics. But here it was, delivered in a wild rush of inspiration that Monroe was still a little stunned by. That was all the confirmation they needed that they were on the right track with Rosalind.

Still, it wasn't as simple as just getting her number and calling her up. No, there were matters to attend to first. For one thing, to the state of California Monroe was still Sarah J. Monroe.

Sarah. As if.

Aside from their mother, no one had called Monroe 'Sarah' for more than a decade. Monroe had tossed out their first name all the way back in their female-conforming, lesbian days in college. At the time, having a single name was a tribute to the lesbian music phenomenon Rhiannon, whom Monroe had just discovered. It also helped that Rhiannon was originally a Welsh goddess who went everywhere on her horse. Somehow Monroe just fit.

In the past three years, Monroe slowly evolved into a non-binary soul whose essence matched their name. First the name was the thing. Then came the buzz cut, followed by the men's clothes, followed by another shift toward truly gender neutral clothing. Jeans, for instance, were good. But cut was everything. Sometimes Monroe found they wanted to go more traditionally male, with a touch of female thrown in. Baggie guy jeans with a cotton scarf thrown around their open-collared shirt became the default for a while.

Eventually, they ended up shopping online, and crafting the look and a persona that seemed to spring from their soul. All of it was a slow-burning discovery of self, and it lit Monroe up.

Now, one decade into this slow-moving revolution, Monroe was at a new turning point. For what remained was the paperwork of a formal name and gender change. It was something they had been meaning to get to since last Christmas. Yet, now the matter was more urgent than ever. This began the day after the party at Tenika's house. Something about meeting Rosalind woke Monroe up, like a sudden brisk glass of ice water to the face. Now the fact that they were still "Sarah" on their passport and driver's license seemed patently wrong. Not to mention embarrassing. They had to clean this up, and pronto.

In the past few days, Monroe had read and reread the California state requirements for changing name and gender marker, and soaked up everything they could find on the Transgender Law Center site. All of it seemed quite doable. Monroe had already decided a new birth certificate was the first order of business, for that would automatically make everything else easier. For instance, if anyone like the IRS was looking for Sarah Monroe, they would now be redirected to Monroe because of the extensive paper trail that would be in place. This way it all felt far more complete to Monroe. In fact, it felt official. And that, of course, was the point.

The process just required time spent filling out forms, filing fees, and a few trips to Oakland Superior Court. The last visit would involve filing papers with a judge, and making a case for the name and gender change in order to get a court order. If you actually had to appear before a judge, which only happened if someone challenged your request, the judges seldom gave any push back. The biggest issue was getting the forms right.

There was one small potential, though unlikely challenge. Monroe's mother, LuAnne, was bound to have a problem with all of this. Technically, of course, she could get on a plane, schlep up there from her home in Southern California and make a stink in court. If she even knew about it.

But these days LuAnne was a peripheral character in Monroe's life. They only spoke to each other once a month for a pleasant but superficial half hour. This was mainly because LuAnne was unable to accept Monroe's need to be non-binary in the first place. She tended to ask the most annoying questions about it.

"Have you met anyone nice, sweetheart?" This was followed by a weary sigh on the phone. *"I'm still allowed to call you 'sweetheart,' aren't I?"*

Given that LuAnne was safely tucked away in her suburb down south, the coast was largely clear.

A name change was important, yes, but a new gender marker designation was especially critical to Monroe. There was that bleak moment last winter, when Monroe actually braved a trip home at Christmas for the first time in a few years. The TSA agent started asking questions long enough to hear Monroe's birth gender in their voice, and confirm the F that appeared on their license. "Where are you going?" asked the agent. "And what is the purpose of your visit?"

"It's *Christmas*," Monroe had protested. "I'm going to see my mother. And my sister." Monroe glanced around, acutely aware no one else was getting these questions.

Their answer was apparently satisfactory. Or perhaps it was the lengthening cue behind Monroe that helped them slide on through. But just as Monroe was turning away, they heard the agent call over to the other agent who was busy surveying the X-ray machine. "This one's female," she said loudly.

That morning Monroe was appalled. Was nothing sacred?

So Monroe decided they would not set foot in one more airport security line until their gender marker and name had been officially changed. There was going to be an 'X' on that line of their driver's license if it was the last thing they did. Just the mere thought of a relationship with Rosalind made it imperative.

It was the honest thing to do.

Chapter Thirteen

Officer Mary Peralta strolled up to the counter of the Central Video Reference Library and smiled viciously. "Frankie."

Frankie looked up and sighed. "Peralta." There was no good reason this officer should be here.

"Oh, come on. You can do better than that. It's Mary."

Frankie just regarded her dully. "Mary," she said.

"Do you really hate me that much? Come on! I'm your fellow officer," Peralta cajoled. Her voice was dripping with insincerity. "We're even on the same team, Frankie. Being women. Being dykes."

Frankie looked down at the counter in annoyance, her hands on her hips. "Can I get you something, Officer Peralta?" she asked through gritted teeth.

"Yes. I need some footage." Peralta glanced at the piece of paper in her hand. "Golden Gate Bridge cameras from the afternoon of September 16th. About 5PM."

Frankie knew exactly what this was of course. It was her suicide intervention, as seen from the body cam of the approaching officers. The very same event that had landed her in the video library in the first place. Not to mention smack dab in the middle of a Behavioral Sciences workup, as well as some ridiculous trauma workshop she had yet to attend.

Frankie scoffed in amazement and shook her head. "Un-fucking-believable," she muttered under her breath.

"Excuse me?"

Frankie didn't answer. Peralta really was a terrorist, Frankie thought to herself as she turned silently to the computer screen in front of her and began searching. She kept her face as expressionless as possible.

Peralta's smile widened. "You must have it," she said. "I'm sure you know which one I mean."

Peralta realized, of course, that Frankie would have to review the first twenty seconds of the footage to determine if it was correct. She would have to see the sweep of the officer's flashlights over herself and the girl. Then she'd have to see the girl jump, followed by her own shocked expression. Her own inability to move. Or even speak.

And given Frankie's fragility right now, that could send her spiraling into depression or worse once again.

Frankie avoided looking at Peralta, who just stood there grinning at her, while she hunted for the footage. A moment later, she opened the file and waited for it to download. Looking up, she did her best to look right through Peralta, who was still beaming at her, her head now cocked at a calculating angle.

Glancing back at the screen, Frankie couldn't help herself. She sighed as she took in the scene that she'd already replayed a thousand times in her head. The frightened girl standing on the wrong side of the railing. Her face, contorted with fear, as she glanced back at the advancing figure of the officers who were calling out to her. Her shaking hand clinging to the strut of the bridge, while the dark bay below her churned.

That was all Frankie needed to see. Spinning the monitor around, she pushed the play button as nausea once again filled her body. Frankie hoped to God she would not lose it in this moment. She closed her eyes, talking down her own immense need to vomit. But it was no use.

Turning away quickly, she made it to the small bathroom up the hall from the Resource Library counter. Shutting the door, she heaved the contents of her lunch into the toilet. Then standing, Frankie wiped her mouth on the back of her hand.

Someday, hopefully, this hell would pass.

*

Yet again, Sally was alone.

She stared at the television screen in front of her, trying to muster up some interest in binge-watching a show about Queen Elizabeth. But the truth was she was distracted. Netflix simply wasn't working at the moment, mainly because she was worried about Frankie, who was now passed out in the bedroom. They'd barely spoken in the last few days, and they hadn't made love in so long Sally could barely remember.

And now this.

Frankie had come home from work an hour earlier, whopping drunk and unsteady on her feet. She was even slurring her words. Frankie had mumbled something about a cop named Peralta, and how she'd made her look at some tapes. Then she passed out, her clothing still on.

How Frankie had managed to actually drive herself home remained a mystery. This was the first time Sally had seen her partner go so far off the deep end.

So now here she sat, feeling utterly alone. Except that she wasn't, of course. The guides were always lurking nearby, eager to help. That much Sally had learned in her life as a psychic medium. When the going got rough, you simply called on help.

Reaching over to the drawer on the coffee table, she pulled out the familiar gold and yellow deck of goddess cards. Frankie kept them tucked away out of sight here, mostly out of embarrassment, but Sally didn't mind. That was just Frankie being Frankie.

She split the deck in half and shuffled them freely for a moment or two. Then plucking three cards from the deck, she held fast to her intention to get some clarity. *How could she actually help her partner right now?*

Sending up a prayer for help, Sally turned the cards over one by one. In the past position, Hathor was reversed. Hathor, the goddess of Receptivity, always showed up when she was too stressed out, or worried. Or more likely, feeling guilty. Sally was still plagued by an old haunted sense of shame, about what she wasn't even quite certain. But one thing she knew for sure. Even in her current sad state, loving Frankie helped her stay grounded to her strength more than any relationship she'd ever had.

There were no ghostly twinges of guilt or shame when it came to Frankie. Only the ever-present wish to love her, relentlessly.

Sally now turned over her next card, representing conditions right now, and was not surprised to see Abundantia was reversed. Abundantia, as her name implied, was all about plenty—the over-flowing cornucopia of life from which we could always draw. And that was just plain perfect. If there was ever an underline to be added to the idea of receiving, this was it. For Sally was often worried these days. *Was she honestly doing enough? Was she actually helping Frankie? Or just getting in her way?*

Of course, she was helping. She was already doing plenty, as Abundantia reminded her.

Sally leaned back against the couch pillows and smiled up at the ceiling. Abundantia represented the ultimate in the feminine art of receiving. Just seeing her on the table, reversed no less, made Sally's whole body happy. In other words, the goddesses were telling her to just relax and let Frankie love her. Open up and shake off her worry. This was all that Sally had to do.

The third card was no less than Mary Magdeline, who always represented Unconditional Love. Something stirred in Sally's chest, and rising, she went into Frankie's bedroom to lie beside her lover's gently snoring body. Everything really was going to be all right, even if things looked askew at the moment.

They would, indeed, get through this. Just like they always would.

*

Tenika's feet crunched a path along the dry brown autumn grass overlooking the Bay. Dogs cavorted here and there as their owners walked them in the gathering dusk. Making her way out toward the battered, weather-beaten picnic table at the edge of Point Isabel, Tenika pressed on. A cold wind off the Pacific pushed against her face, bringing tears to her eyes, but she didn't care. At this exact moment, a little discomfort was welcome. And even kind of appropriate.

Tenika was busy making a decision. In fact, she was making the decision she now thought she should have made weeks ago, when the idea of having a baby was new and untested. Keisha's words at the party still rang through her head. Sitting down on one of the picnic table benches, Tenika leaned back, folded her arms across her chest and watched as the mild chop on San Francisco Bay turned pale gray-blue and the sky behind it grew rosy. The Golden Gate Bridge was a small sliver in the distance, stretching out from the black amorphous shoreline of Marin County to meet the jagged, complex skyline of the city.

San Francisco had a kind of George Jetson slickness to it now, all angular and modern. Still, the Sutro Tower rose on its own lonely hill, the last stalwart in a battle between urgent expansion and the city by the Bay, as it once was. The site was sobering to Tenika. She sighed and loosened her arms that had been clamped across her chest.

Maybe she should do what Keisha was doing. Just put it all behind her, forget about Walter, and embrace having the baby for once and for all. Hell, there were a thousand reasons to get behind having a baby, beginning with the fact that Delilah wanted one so badly. Anyway, babies were cute, and warm, and chubby, and they smelled like talcum powder. And when they smiled at you, you were basically a goner.

But then she considered what Keisha had said. *You've got to tell her.* That had been her first instinct, too. She needed to tell Delilah because that was the right thing to do, wasn't it?

Deciding to have a baby demanded full and complete honesty, didn't it?

Tenika now began replaying all those visits she used to make to Walter's house, back when he was still in diapers and she would feed him in his high chair. His soft almond skin, and his black eyes, and the way he just looked at her in that simple, guileless way, opening his mouth like a baby bird for more mashed sweet potato. It slayed her every time.

That was the real reason to have a baby, she thought. It was all about their innocence. Their precious innocence. The very same innocence that was lost on that horrible July afternoon. Maybe if she and Delilah had a baby, she could finally forgive herself. Maybe she really could start again. After all, that was what Keisha was doing, right?

Maybe motherhood would be the magic key that had been missing all these years.

Tenika leaned back against the picnic table and exhaled, considering her options. There wasn't much more she could do, that was the simple truth of it. She just had to let go of trying to be so pure and perfect herself. She wasn't. Tenika knew she was flawed, deeply flawed, but Delilah didn't have to know yet, did she?

Did Tenika seriously have to reveal every last secret she had? After all, what good would come from dragging up the Walter incident now?

No, she should just agree to have the baby and move on. Just like Keisha had. The memory would still stick to her, of course, like some blurry, fat, aging tattoo. But she didn't have to pay it any mind.

Tenika could simply reinvent, like her cousin had. She could move on.

She rose from the bench now and with the bay at her back, she started walking back to her car.

She knew what she had to do.

*

An hour later, Tenika flattened herself to the floor of her bedroom, and reached into the darkness under their bed. Her fingers groped along past the old tissues and the dust kitties, until they grasped on to what she was looking for. She extracted the tattered old accordion folder and dusted it off with her hand. Then she stood up a little creakily.

Mercifully, Delilah wasn't home yet. She was working late on some evening appointments at the studio.

Tenika took the folder and sat down by the bedside table. The lamp shed a pool of light over the contents as she flipped through her uncle's aging paperwork, all arranged neatly in alphabetical order. Somewhere in here was what she'd been looking for.

His stash of penny stocks, purchased clear back in the seventies and then left to Tenika in his will, were always meant to be some kind of insurance. She could always sell them if and when they needed to, assuming they were worth anything. For this much Tenika was clear on. Having this baby was not only critical, it would be expensive. Seriously expensive. Like their entire retirement fund expensive. And that was before paying for college.

Tenika had just spent the previous hour reading about artificial insemination and sperm banks. Because God knew how this baby was going to happen otherwise. She was pretty sure they didn't have some nice young gay man in their midst who'd just love to father a child, or she would have thought of him by now. Chances are they'd be storing sperm in a cryotank before they were done, and going through month after month of hormone shots. None of which their health insurance covered.

It was entirely possible, of course, that the penny stocks her Uncle Henry had purchased were worth less than a latte these days. On the other hand, they could be worth thousands, cause that's how it was with penny stocks. Really, there was no way to know until you looked them up.

Closing in on the 'P' section, Tenika poked a finger into the accordion folder and flipped through a few papers. Peering in, she stopped. Uncle Henry's stocks and bond certificates were not only yellowed with age, they looked remarkably quaint. A classic blue decorative border surrounded each sheet, like something out of an old bank deed from the fifties, and the sheets themselves were yellow and slightly brittle. They smelled like dust.

Tenika read the inscription in the center of the page. "This certifies that the holder owns 400 shares of capital stock in Smithers Direct Industries." Various lines of legalese followed, along with her uncle's signature above that of the president of the company.

Now it was time for the moment of truth. Tenika walked the investment documents over to the aging computer set up on their shared bedroom desk. Sitting down, she planted her feet, stabilizing herself against her mounting fear. She so didn't want these to be worthless, because if they were, then she wasn't sure exactly what Plan B might be. At this moment, at least, there wasn't one.

Carefully, Tenika typed Smithers Industries into the Google search bar along with 'value of penny stocks per share.' Immediately, a list of links popped up, and Tenika clicked on the top one, assuming it was correct. She began to read.

OTC Markets Group Inc. ("OTC Markets") had discontinued the display of quotes on otcmarkets.com for this security because it has been labeled Caveat Emptor (Buyer Beware).

Shit. Seriously?

Tenika sat back and pushed her glasses up the bridge of her nose as unabashed dread passed through her. She'd had a feeling

Uncle Henry wasn't leaving her much beyond the garage. That would have simply been too much to expect.

Then suddenly, something caught her eye. Leaning forward, Tenika studied the name of the company in the top Google listing. Smithers Industries was not the name on the stock certificate. It was actually Smithers Direct Industries.

Her hand shaking, Tenika erased the errant Google entry and pushed the return button. Carefully, she typed in the correct name of the company. The screen on the aging computer remained blank for a moment as it slowly processed her request. Then up popped a link: "Share value for Smithers Direct Industries."

Tenika clicked on the top entry, barely breathing. After the customary ten second pause, during which her heart began to beat harder and harder, the offering page opened before her.

$77.45 per share, it read. Beside this, a small green arrow pointed toward the sky.

Tenika felt a sudden shudder of adrenaline rocket through her body, as she began to realize the significance of these figures. She had inherited 400 shares, which at the time had cost her uncle just a little more than $600, as he had pointed out repeatedly.

They were now worth almost $31,000.

This couldn't be right.

Tenika brought the aging stock certificate closer to her glasses and studied the fine print. Then leaning forward and peering at the screen in front of her, she tried to find the mistake. But there wasn't one.

Finally, she sat back and embraced the amazing truth. She and Delilah were now far more flush with cash than she'd realized. They could, indeed, have the baby.

Tenika brushed a tear away from her eye and laughed out loud. Then she set to cashing in her shares immediately, before anything could change.

This was almost too good to be true.

*

"Rosie, is that really you? Are you home? Like…in America?" Monroe's voice spiraled up in delight as they clutched the phone. At first, they'd thought it was their mother because her name came up on their phone. But then Rosie's voice, clear and bright, came charging through the line. *Rosie is back.*

It had been nearly three years since their sister had called. And just as long since she'd been home. Rosie was Monroe's favorite of the four siblings. She was always the baby who'd tagged along, pestering her older sisters and their brother loudly for whatever she could get, like the constant stream of Reed's Cinnamon Candies that always landed in her mouth.

Yet, Rosie was also exuberant, undaunted in her pursuit of whatever the next fun thing might be. Just thinking about her made Monroe smile.

"Yep, they let me out early for good behavior," Rosie joked.

She had just returned from the Madagascar bush where she'd spent the last three years teaching English to the Malagasy. Her lack of access to the Internet, or even electricity, most of the time meant she'd called home an average of six times per year—and always to their mother. There was a lot to catch up on.

For one thing, Rosie had missed the entire chapter about Monroe's gender shift. The previous Christmas, when she'd managed to find her way to a phone and actually call home, Monroe had spoken to her for a few moments. Standing in the kitchen, trying hard to hear her over a scratchy phone line, Monroe could just make out Rosie's voice. She sounded small and far away, but her happiness and her usual verve crackled through the line.

Meanwhile, Monroe's mother hovered by the phone the entire time, soaking up every last word her precious youngest was saying. That night Monroe said nothing about their gender shift, mainly because their mother was right there. But now they were alone on the phone together. For once, they could talk.

Monroe let out a slow breath. "I'm just glad you made it home safely, Rosie. You still have all of your limbs in tact?"

Her sister laughed. "I think you've got me confused with the zoological people. They're the ones hanging with the wildlife. I was in a classroom most the time and okay; the kids were a little crazy sometimes, but no limbs were lost."

"So…" began Rosie. "How have you been? Tell me everything. Are you happy?"

"Yeah. Really happy."

"Sounds like you're in love," Rosie surmised.

"Well, I did meet someone, but—"

"That's fantastic! Go get her, Sare!" Rosie enthused.

"Monroe."

"Right! Sorry, Monroe. *Monroe.* Damn. Sorry."

"It's okay." Yet again, the awkward dance of connecting the family with their current reality had arrived. "See here's the thing you don't know about me yet," Monroe began again.

"Listening," said Rosie.

Monroe could hear her sister rattling something clunky around. Rosie was probably doing the dishes in their mothers slightly battered kitchen. Immediately, Monroe could see its ancient flowered dishtowels, and the cracked linoleum flooring, and the grease-spattered silhouette of a cat over the stove.

Monroe took another deep breath. What was ordinarily easy now became hard, and that had everything to do with family. "So I guess you could say I've evolved with the whole Monroe thing. I met this woman a few weeks ago, and she's…" Monroe hesitated. "Well, she's really great."

"So?"

"So, I haven't asked her out yet, but that's because…" Monroe hesitated for the briefest second, unsure if they should proceed. *Screw it.* This was Rosie. Her sister. "Because I'm actually in the middle of changing my gender marker and my name in court. I'm non-binary now, so I'm making it official."

The words came out in a rush and landed in silence. Monroe could hear Rosie hesitating on the other end for the briefest second. Something caught in Monroe's throat, and now they felt a little stab of fear. "Rose?"

"I'm here. Wow…that's great." There was a marked lack of enthusiasm in Rosie's voice.

"I mean, I thought you'd want to know," Monroe added quickly, trying to fill the broadening gap now spreading between them. "It's just that's hard to travel, and TSA gets all hung up, and…oh, there are a million good reasons to do it. Anyway, I don't want to start something with someone until it's all official on paper. You know?"

Monroe's question hung there, like old laundry left on the line just a little too long.

Rosie cleared her throat. "Does Mom know?"

Monroe sighed. *Shit.* Trouble now sifted down over them, like an uncomfortable mist. "No," Monroe said in a small voice. "And don't tell her, Rosie. Please. She's…" They paused. "Just don't get into it with her, okay?"

It now dawned on Monroe that their mother could have already gotten into it at length with Rosie. In fact, she was probably standing there, listening in.

"Rose?"

"Yeah. Yeah, sure. I hear you." Her sister's tone was unconvincing.

They made small talk for the remaining moments. Rosie told her a little about her life in Madagascar, but the conversation remained flat, and scarred by what had already passed between them. Finally, Monroe hung up and put their face in their hands.

They had to get the papers in front of a judge immediately—as soon as they could. Before their mother could come up to Oakland and screw everything up.

Chapter Fourteen

Rosalind pushed the button on the microwave, and slowly her lone baked potato began to rotate. She sighed as she looked out the kitchen window. About now, her mother was probably bringing out the big steaming plate of Chinese long beans in garlic sauce, followed by the Ma Po Tofu and maybe even a plate of their favorite tea-smoked duck from the restaurant down the street.

Around the table would be all the familiar faces. Bà, Mama and her brother would be there, of course, and maybe even her Aunt Betty and her Uncle Fred. Aunt Betty would have brought her trademark five-pound bag of naval oranges from the Safeway. They would discuss Wilfred's business track endlessly, and whether he was showing enough respect at work. They would pressure him to find a girlfriend, and argue among themselves if he was eating enough. Yet, there would be no mention of her whatsoever. Perhaps her vacant chair would not even be at the table.

But then, it was just another night in the Choi household. She hadn't been invited home for Sunday dinner now in nearly a year—ever since the now infamous *Chronicle* story. Nor had she even been willing to go if she had been invited. Rosalind had been home exactly three times: for her mother's birthday, and twice after her father fell and broke his arm. Then the shock of his fall down the stairs had created a temporary truce.

But once the cast was on and his arm reset, Bà went back to his corner and she went back to hers. Once again, they stopped speaking. Her father still insisted she had brought them all dishonor. He had standards, he said, and Rosalind had violated all of them. Her mother had tried to convince him otherwise, but Bà would not change his mind. He wouldn't even listen to her brother, Wilfred, whose place as the treasured golden son usually guaranteed results.

In all honesty, Rosalind could live without her father's blessing. She had no regrets about the course she'd taken with her former employer and the media, and she wasn't particularly keen on making a big groveling apology to her family. She was an independent adult who had a right to pursue the career she had chosen, even if they didn't like it. Still, her path was hard, especially at times like this. And it was lonely.

Rosalind lifted the plastic lid on the rotisserie chicken she'd just brought back from Costco, and removing a leg, placed it on a waiting plate. A moment later, her potato beeped, and she arranged it on a plate beside the chicken. She regarded her dinner. All she needed was a vegetable.

Opening her refrigerator, Rosalind surveyed its scant contents as if something delicious might have magically appeared. But no. It was still the refrigerator of a person who worked all the time: a few yogurts, some salad dressing, a bottle of mineral water, a tired lemon and a bottle of champagne given to her when she started the foundation.

God, she was tired of this.

Truthfully, Rosalind missed her family, even with all their foibles. Her father just had to weaken someday. Or else she did.

Unable to stop herself, Rosalind pulled out her phone and texted her brother.

You guys having dinner?

A bubble of gray dots appeared.

Yeah, this is fucked. You should be here.

Rosalind sighed and put her phone away. That little exchange made her feel no better at all. Carrying her plate to the table, she picked up the knife and fork she'd set beside her place. Mechanically she began to eat.

A moment later, a thought struck her: *Go see Wilfred.*

Perhaps it was divine guidance. A little nod from Kwan Yin, who'd finally seen fit to send a bit of help her way. Or maybe it was just that Rosalind understood that somewhere, deep in her soul, she could no longer do this alone. She was on a path as sure as a guided missile, this much she knew. It was just a matter of taking each step as it presented itself, and sometimes that meant asking for help.

Pulling out her phone, Rosalind sent another text to her brother.

You want to grab a glass of wine this week?

His gray bubble appeared instantly.

Totally. Ordinaire?

A moment later, she put the phone away, a firm plan in place. She would meet her brother, and so begin the quiet healing she needed for herself. She was a renegade, an outlier who wasn't ever going to please her father or even her mother. But maybe that was okay. All she really had to do in this life was take care of herself, and find her allies where she could.

Idly, Rosalind wondered where Monroe was right now. Were they, too, sitting in front of a sad little chicken dinner in their cold, lonely kitchen? And if so, was it possible that Monroe was thinking about her?

With this thought, Rosalind picked up her fork and knife and began to eat dinner once again.

Eventually, all of this would resolve itself one way or another.

*

Delilah hurried up to the doorway of Kamdesh. Through the window of the Afghani restaurant, she could see the lone figure of Tenika sitting at a table by the wall. Her heart skipped its usual beat. Glancing at her reflection in the window glass, Delilah pushed her hair off her shoulders and straightened the strap of her dress. She wanted to look especially good tonight.

Really, she had no idea what had moved her wife to call her so spontaneously, and suggest dinner out. Delilah was just finishing up her last tattoo at the time. But somehow she could feel the urgency. It was just there in Tenika's voice.

"You busy after work?" she'd asked. "Just wanted to take you out." Tenika's voice broke slightly.

But try as she might, Delilah hadn't been able to get any more information than that. At any rate, Tenika only wanted to go to Kamdesh to have lamb when she felt like doing something special.

Far from being some high-end restaurant with linen tablecloths and tiny, rarefied dishes, Kamdesh was a huge family place with fluorescent lighting and a sea of glass topped tables and black chairs. Their house specialty, quabili pallow, was a braised lamb shank sitting on a small mountain of rice topped with sautéed raisins and carrots. One of these generous plates was easily enough food for two people.

A wide array of people filled the tables around them, from Muslim families just in after services at the mosque up the street to hipsters and techies arriving by electric scooter. Children idly played with salt and pepper shakers, while adults sat back and enjoyed the respite, sipping their glasses of tea. The entire atmosphere was serene, happy, relaxed.

"Hey!" Delilah called from the doorway as she walked toward her wife. Tenika sat up a little straighter and smiled at her. As she approached, Delilah searched her face, looking for clues. It almost certainly had something to do with the baby project. But what?

Leaning over, Delilah gave Tenika a kiss on her forehead. Then she sat opposite her and tried to quell her excitement. Something big was about to happen. She could feel it.

"So…" she began. "What's going on, honey? You're in your festive lamb-eating mood."

Tenika held up her hand and smiled mysteriously. "I'll get to that. First, see what you want to eat."

A moment later, their order was taken and they settled in for a moment to gaze happily at each other. Delilah couldn't help but notice. Tenika's eyes were sparkling with some kind of anticipation. Her heart surged again, just as it always did when they had their special spark of connection. "Now are you going to tell me?" she asked.

Tenika gave a modest grin and raised her eyebrows. "Well, I'd say you know me well enough by now, baby. What do you think I'm going to say?"

Delilah searched her face, still looking for clues. "You're not—" she began. But then she stopped herself. As far as she knew, Tenika was still down on the entire baby-making project. Delilah definitely didn't want to bring it up, lest she unleash another hornets' nest. "I honestly have no idea," she finally said.

Tenika took her hand and began tracing her finger along the fine lacy tattoo on the back of it. "Well," she began, "first of all I haven't told you nearly often enough how much I love you." Tenderly she looked at Delilah, and Delilah suddenly felt a lump growing in her throat. Tears sprang in to her eyes.

This was unexpected.

"Thank you, honey," Delilah said in a small voice. It was so unlike Tenika to be so downright gushy.

"Anyway I do. Love you, I mean," Tenika continued, looking into her lover's eyes. "And I've come around, Delilah. I've been thinking and I want that baby that you want. I'm ready to do this thing."

Delilah's heart surged even more intensely, and she leaned forward almost knocking over her water glass. "You *do*? Really and for real?"

Tenika sat back with a smile, and nodded. "There's more, baby."

Delilah shook her head in amazement. "*What?*"

"You know those penny stocks I inherited?"

"Your retirement, you mean."

Tenika's smile was big enough to light up the whole restaurant. "Well, maybe. Here's the thing, you know you only live once and all that, right?" She lowered her voice. "Guess what the damn things are worth?"

Delilah's eyes grew wider. "Tell me."

Tenika looked around and leaned in closer to her wife. "More than thirty thousand," she whispered to Delilah.

Delilah's hands flew to her face, and she gave a shriek that made the table next to them turn around. "Honey, are you *SERIOUS?*"

"Oh, I'm dead serious."

Leaping across the table, Delilah grabbed her wife by the shoulders as a wildfire of glee spread through her body. "We can do this. We can DO THIS, T!"

Tenika glanced around, chuckling. "Lower your voice, but yes. You're damn right we can do it. And we will."

The two women looked at each other, smiling in amazement. Slowly they drew together for a modest kiss, aware of their surroundings. "More on that later," Tenika noted and Delilah laughed.

Now she sat back in amazement. "I can't…I mean, *are you sure*, T? I just can't believe this."

"I'm sure all right. I couldn't believe it either. So I called a broker and double checked this morning. Put in the sell order already."

Delilah began fanning herself as a hot flash overtook her. "Look at me!" she exulted. "I'm having hot flashes and I'm not even on the drugs yet!"

At that moment, their lamb shanks arrived, perched on top of their pillows of nut-colored rice. Fat raisins and slivers of carrot accented the dishes. "Wow," Delilah breathed, overcome with the news. "I just can't believe this."

"Well, believe it," Tenika said, picking up her fork. "And you better get busy over there, if you're gonna be eating for two and all that." She chuckled at her own joke.

Delilah picked up her fork. Then she put it down again, still amazed. "T, we're gonna be mothers. We really are."

"We're gonna be mothers," Tenika noted, calmly taking a bite of her lamb. She shook her head and closed her eyes, savoring the lamb. "Damn that's good."

"Wow," Delilah breathed.

She'd be processing this for days, weeks, and who knew how long. Even if the treatments failed and they never conceived, at least they'd come together and tried their best. And that, alone, was worth the price of gold. If nothing else worked, there was always adoption.

Yet another bucket list item with her beloved was about to be checked.

*

Hot water pounded on Keisha's neck and shoulders, and for a moment she closed her eyes and blessed its pure abundance. Today she was grateful for hot water, and lots of it. Benny had been giving her such a hard time lately. Grunting a hello every morning, and staying away until late at night. Lord knew what he was up to.

Keisha closed her eyes. It was best not to think about her troubles, she reminded herself. Instead, for one more delicious moment, she enjoyed her shower and the way it loosened her hard-working muscles.

Her mind drifted over to some of the building's tenants who she saw in her work every day. The silver-haired divorce attorney who always smiled at her, unless she was going to trial, in which case, she generally looked a little grim and determined. The cosmetic dental assistant who always slipped her free toothbrushes and tiny tubes of toothpaste. The ad agency copywriter who seemed to be barely twenty years old.

Bless them all, she thought. *Bless them all, Lord Jesus.*

Slowly she soaped her shoulders. And as she did, a voice summoned Keisha from nowhere.

Go apologize to Walter, it said.

Keisha opened her eyes. The very gravity and clarity of the thought stopped her cold. *Where did this come from?* Visiting Walter was about the last thing she intended to do. For starters, she didn't even know where he was.

Closing her eyes, Keisha probed, uncertainly. *Jesus, is that you talking to me? Cause if you are, I don't even know where—*

Go apologize to Walter, the voice repeated. *And take Tenika with you.*

This time the voice was more of a command. A simple, kind command, albeit, but one she simply couldn't fight.

This time Keisha responded out loud. "I will if you want me to, Jesus, but I'm just saying that Miss Alma, Walter's mo—"

The voice repeated itself a third and final time. This time its tone was unequivocal. *Go apologize to Walter. And take Tenika with you.*

Okay, she thought. That was crystal clear. A certainty settled in Keisha's gut as she turned off the shower, and stepped out, dripping wet. She reached for a towel. There was no arguing with Jesus.

All she had to do was get her cousin on board as well. Which would be…well, interesting.

Keisha shook her head and chuckled a little. Tenika was definitely in for a surprise.

Chapter Fifteen

Frankie tucked her hands up under her armpits and braced herself. The news was not good. "Why do I have to do this?"

Her boss pushed back in his chair and stared at her dully. "You really want me to go over this again, Kennedy?" He gazed up at the ceiling as he shook his head. Then he leveled a hard look at Frankie. His tone was flat and his exasperation was real.

"Like I said, if you want to get out of the library, it's non-negotiable. BSU says you have to go. So just suck it up, drive up there, and do the freaking workshop, all right?" He leaned forward. "Read my lips, Kennedy. It's non-negotiable."

There was a pause between them, and the Lieutenant's body language now suggested the subject was now off the table. He was already leafing through the next file on his desk, effectively ignoring Frankie.

She sighed and rose. "Okay," she said to no one in particular. *Christ.* Of all the indignities.

It wasn't bad enough she'd been in video purgatory for nearly three weeks. Now she had to sit around holding hands with strangers and talk about her feelings. That would be thirty-six hours of pure Kumbaya hell for Frankie, she was sure of it.

But an order was an order. She had no choice but to comply. Not if she wanted to keep her retirement intact. No, Frankie would just deep breathe her way through the whole thing. Or possibly start her day with a few stiff shots. Or…well, who knows? Maybe she'd even just sit there and listen. And possibly even learn something. Though, obviously—to her at least—that was doubtful.

After all, the insomnia had not improved and the flashbacks were coming as fast and furious as ever. Frankie had had one that morning while she was driving into the city on the Bay Bridge, which was disconcerting to say the least.

She walked down the hallway, silently contemplating her CO's final orders. The workshop was less than one week away. She didn't even have to talk to Sally about this. She already knew what she would say.

You know you need it, Frankie. Just pull up your big girl panties and spend a little time thinking about yourself for once.

Because that was it, of course. Frankie's tailspin had a lot to do with focus. It had literally been a few years since she'd even thought about the larger, invisible aspects of life. Things like her grief over losing her late wife, her on-the-job PTSD, and the early PTSD induced by her childhood.

Visions of her father and his belt always came up at moments like this. Which is exactly what Frankie was hoping to avoid. So far, at least, avoidance had been the best strategy.

Frankie sighed. She just wanted to go home and bury her head in Sally's soft, ample breasts and be comforted. Then she wanted to have extended, seriously sweaty sex. This thought cheered her slightly. It was actually the first time she'd felt like making love in weeks.

But getting Sally in bed would have to wait for now. There were still three more hours ahead of shuffling videos around. Or more likely, listening to crickets since so few people actually came through the door.

All of this just because of one poorly timed nap on the job.
Shit.

Turning into the Video Library, Frankie did her best to shake loose her impending feeling of doom. And as she took her seat behind the counter, a thought struck her.

She needed her girlfriend now more than ever. She really, truly did.

*

Monroe clutched the state issued forms NC-200, NC-125, and NC 230, *Decree Changing Name and Order Recognizing Change of Gender* and tried not to sweat. A check for four-hundred-seventy dollars was folded in their wallet, and they had all the necessary pieces to apply for the necessary court order. Or at least they thought they did.

Unlike a lot of people, Monroe wasn't hiring a lawyer for this process. For one thing, the filing fees, petition charges and such had cleared out most of their savings. Anyway, between the Transgender Law Center and various YouTube videos they'd been devouring lately, mostly from a chipper transman named Jackson Bird, Monroe figured they had the situation in hand. And if they didn't, well they'd soon find out. Then they would regroup.

Still, Monroe was nervous. Very nervous. Taking a deep breath as the line slowly budged forward, Monroe shut their eyes and sent up a little prayer, mainly for ease. And a little bit of courage.

The gender marker change was long overdue, after all. It really would feel good—and right—to be able to go out in the world with all that paperwork finally done. Still, Monroe was struck by the small quivers of fear that now radiated through their body.

A few moments later, Monroe's number flashed on the small LED monitor overhead. Approaching the window of the Court Clerk, Monroe unstuck their forms from their sweaty fingers and handed them over.

"That should be everything. For a gender marker change? And a name change?" Monroe asked hopefully.

The non-descript, balding White man looked over the forms, grunting slightly as he leafed through the pages. Then he eyed Monroe carefully. "Driver's license? Birth certificate?"

"Oh…right. Sorry." Monroe pulled a wallet from the back pocket of their jeans, slapped down their driver's license, and extracted the aging birth certificate from their backpack. Then they gently handed the document through the opening in the bulletproof glass.

The gentleman behind the counter took the forms and disappeared. Monroe watched him plod away. He was moving at the pace of molasses, and it was unclear exactly where he was going. Monroe glanced around. The line behind them was growing.

Sticking hands in pockets, Monroe began to whistle softly in an attempt to calm down. But still their heart beat hard beneath their maroon plaid shirt and puffy down vest. Perhaps they were the one applicant—possibly ever—who would be soundly rejected.

Perhaps there was some missing piece of paperwork that was going to be hellishly difficult to find.

Perhaps they hadn't written a big enough check—and there wasn't actually enough money left in savings to cover the rest.

The list of Monroe's fears seemed endless right now. Yes, they were real, but in the end, they were only fears. Monroe knew that. If this whole gender change and name change were truly meant to be, it would simply happen. That's just how the Universe worked.

The same went for a possible relationship with the lovely Rosalind, which might or might not be waiting for them. All of it was an enormous crapshoot. At this thought, Monroe felt smaller and more alone than ever.

The unsmiling bald man returned with copies of the forms in his hand. Monroe peered over the top of them, and saw that all were now stamped with large black letters; "Filed." Immediately, a surge of joy rocked Monroe's body. Still, the dreaded money ask awaited.

The clerk handed the originals back to them and peered at Monroe. "Four hundred eighty dollars," he said.

Heaving a sigh of relief, Monroe dug out their wallet. They extracted the check they'd written earlier, and began hunting for an extra ten-dollar bill. There was one folded in the back. Relief flooded through Monroe's body as they handed over the cash.

"There's one final step. The system will issue an Order to Show Cause," the clerk explained. "You'll either get your request granted by a judge, or if someone files a complaint, you have to come in for a hearing. Then we'll send you the court date by mail."

The clerk's words barely made an impression on Monroe. A judge would almost certainly assign a gender and name change without any question.

Right now, this was all going ridiculously well.

"Okay! Terrific," said Monroe as relief continued to flood every cell in their body. They gathered up their papers and stuffed them back into their backpack.

Moments later, Monroe swung into the driver's seat of their truck as their phone rang. At that moment, they were feeling downright jaunty as they glanced at the screen. It was Rosie, Monroe's sister, calling from their mother's house.

Monroe's tone was light and jubilant as they picked up. "Hey, kiddo! How's it going?"

"Fine. You sound happy…"

"Damn right," Monroe enthused. "I just applied for a name and gender marker change. This is actually happening, Rosie. *It's. Really. Happening.*"

There was a pause. "Gender change?"

"Oh, the whole non-binary thing," Monroe explained. "Remember? We talked about it."

Rosie's voice got quiet, which Monroe knew was never a good sign.

"You have to get a gender change—like, with the state—for that?"

"Well, if I want it to be real I do," Monroe said.

Rosie sounded small and far away. "Oh. Yeah. Right."

Monroe paused. "You all right?"

"Yeah. I'm fine. It's just that Mom's standing right here. It's her birthday and she wanted to talk to you."

Shit. Monroe's good mood now immediately turned to dust. They had completely forgotten about their mother's birthday. And now they were doubly screwed. Because if there was one person who would love to kill Monroe's plans for a new identity, and could figure out how to do it, it was their mother. She was far from understanding any of this.

"Honey? Sarah?" Monroe's mother was already on the phone. "What's happening, dear? What's this business about a gender change? And what on earth are you changing your gender to? You're not…"

"Mom, don't worry. It's all fine. And not Sarah. It's Monroe, remember? We went over this? Several times?" Monroe gritted their teeth, trying to quell their ire.

Their mother knew, of course, their name was Monroe. She just chose not to use it. Just like Cher refused to call Chastity Chaz back in the day.

Shit shit shit. Panic flooded Monroe's body.

Why had they said anything to anyone in their family—even Rosie—before the paperwork actually went through? Now here was LuAnne asking questions.

"Sarah, honey? Are you going to be…a man?"

"No, Mom. Don't worry about it." Monroe paused. "And happy birthday. Can I speak to Rosie, please?"

"Sweetheart, I'm just ask—"

"Please, Mom."

Monroe's mother sighed. "You were born a girl, and you'll

always be a girl, Sarah. As if I should have to remind you."

Monroe remained silent. Finally, her mother gave a sigh that whispered across the hundreds of miles between them. It was as if she were right in the room, and it socked Monroe straight in the gut. Monroe took a breath, summoning every ounce of self control they had. "Can I please speak to Rosie?"

There was a pause. "Here, she wants to talk to you," Monroe heard her mother say, handing the phone back.

"And just for the record, my pronouns are 'them' and 'they,'" Monroe said tensely to whoever was listening. But now Rosie was back on the phone.

"I know! Jesus. You don't have to bite my head off."

"I thought you were Mom. Sorry."

"It's okay."

The two were silent for a moment. "I'd better go," Monroe said.

"Yeah."

"Bye."

"Bye." Monroe hung up and sat there in miserable silence. Then slamming their hand down on the steering wheel, they felt the complete and total moral outrage of the situation. And their own shocking powerlessness as well.

The world could apparently accept Monroe just fine, so why in the hell couldn't their own mother?

This was almost definitely going to get worse before it got better.

*

Wilfred picked up his wine glass of freshly poured nitrate-free rosé and toasted in Rosalind's direction. "Here's to you, sis. And whatever it is that you're doing, exactly?"

Rosalind rolled her eyes, proffering her own glass of Merlot in his direction. "Santé. And by the way, I'm helping women in tech stand up for their rights. Which you knew."

"Yeah, yeah. Whatever." Wilfred smiled sheepishly.

The two touched glasses and drank. Wilfred was a wine snob and before he actually took a sip from his $16 glass of carefully selected, 'natural' wine, he swirled it quickly and took a sniff.

Then he sipped and savored. "Hmm," he said. "Lemony. A little rhubarb, too."

"With a hint of chocolate?" Rosalind grinned at her brother.

"Please, Ros." Wilfred rolled his eyes, but he too smiled, for this was their perennial joke. "Everything does not have a hint of chocolate, and you know it."

"Duh. I just like to razz you."

"Consider me razzed." Leaning back in his seat, he took a bite from the plate of the sardines and sourdough bread that occupied the small table between them.

It was a pleasant evening out on Grand Avenue. There were only a few other tables occupied around them as wine sippers sat watching the world pass by and the daylight fade to night.

"So?" Wilfred began.

"So what?"

"So what's it going to take?"

"Huh?" Rosalind looked at her brother innocently, as if she didn't understand what he meant. Though she knew, of course, exactly what he was talking about. Unlike her, Wilfred hadn't turned his back on their parents. He was still showing up dutifully for Sunday night dinner. He was still considered a 'good son,' worthy of the family name.

"Ros, seriously? It's me you're talking to, dude."

"Okay, okay." She waved his words away as if trying to erase them. "It's just...it's complicated."

"What's so complicated? You changed your career. You made a splash. You got some ink. You met Rachel Maddow. You just tell them you're sorry and it's over. Ros—I mean...you should see Mom. She gets all tense at dinner, and now she has stomach trouble. And Dad's giving her the worst time, like the whole thing's her fault. Meanwhile, he's doing his angry warlord thing and refusing to say your name. And I'm sitting there like, where the fuck is my sister?" He looked at her plaintively.

Wilfred was two years younger than Rosalind, and a software engineer with one of the online payment systems in San Francisco. He'd been at this job for exactly three years, and he'd already bought a place in the city for a million five. Wilfred, being more conservative, had soundly bought into the path that had been handed to him after graduating from Yale. Living in the box their parents had assigned to them suited him just fine.

"How hard can it be to just come home and talk things over?"

Rosalind played with the glass in her hands, swirling it. She watched the traces of wine trickle down the interior of her glass. Then she studied her younger brother, sitting across from her in his expensive button-down shirt, and his tech-approved designer sneakers made from an 'interesting' fabric.

Rosalind couldn't come up with anything to say in that moment. Finally, she raised her face to him. "Look, I'm sorry."

"I know you're sorry, but so what? Some damage is being caused here. And like I said, what's so freaking complicated? I don't get it."

Rosalind took a long sip, then put her wine glass on the table. "So, brother, here's the thing. I need to tell you about something."

"What?" Wilfred lowered his voice. "Just tell me you didn't get arrested or something. And if you did, who the hell paid your bail?"

She almost laughed out loud as she looked at him. "Calm down, bro. No, arrests." Rosalind hesitated. Was she finally going to do this, and tell her brother the truth about herself?

"I'm …" The words were stuck in Rosalind's throat, refusing to come out. *What if he got up and walked away? If Wilfred couldn't even accept her, then she'd be alone. Utterly, entirely, and completely.*

"What? Are you sick or something?" Wilfred's face suddenly creased with fear. He looked at her like a scared little boy.

"No, no! Nothing like that." Rosalind picked up her glass and took another drink. Then she put the drink down and looked at him directly. "I'm gay," she said. "I'm a lesbian."

Wilfred's eyes widened. "Whoa...Is *that* why you haven't come home?"

"Pretty much. I mean, you know how they're going to react. And I have to tell them, brother. This is who I am." She held up her hand to silence the words about to come out of her brother's mouth. "You don't have to tell me—I know. They're going to go completely crazy."

"Oh, *Ros.*" Wilfred's voice was filled with despair. Now suddenly alive with a surge of defiance, Rosalind shrugged off his sympathy.

"It's my truth," she said. "They'll just have to deal."

"Yeah, like seriously," her brother muttered. He sat back and looked at her, now a little perplexed. "Are you...dating someone?"

"No. I did meet someone. I knew there was something there the minute I met them. But it's too soon. But who knows? Maybe we're not even going to date." Rosalind closed her eyes, feeling a wave of pathos at her situation. If she told her parents, she would surely hurt them. But if she didn't, she would destroy herself.

All of it seemed impossible.

"Yeah," she continued quietly. "That's not happening. Not yet, at least."

Wilfred cleared his throat a bit formally. "*Them?* Wait a minute...how many people are you talking about here? Is this like some polyamory thing?"

"God, no!" Rosalind laughed out loud. "Monroe is gender queer. Non-binary, as they like to say. Their pronouns are they and them."

"*Jesus.*"

"I know, I know. Bá and Mama are going to go berserk."

"I'd say," nodded Wilfred. Then he gave a sigh, and he shrugged. "But presumably you know what you're doing."

Rosalind smiled weakly. "Glad you think so."

"What—you don't?"

Rosalind stared at her wine glass as shame overtook her. "I don't know. Sometimes I think I've lost it," she said in a small voice.

"No way," Wilfred said, helping himself now to a large sardine balanced on a thin piece of dark bread. "You haven't lost it. You're just going a different way. It's all cool."

She looked up at him, relieved. "Really?"

"Yeah," he smiled. "I mean—you're freaking Rosalind Choi. You're a rock star. And you're my fucking sister."

Tears sprang into Rosalind's eyes and she smiled so hard her cheeks began to hurt. "Thanks," she said, as one tear trickled down her cheek, followed by another. She wiped at them with the back of her hand. "Thank you, bro. I needed that."

"Okay, whatever." Wilfred waved away her sign of emotion. "Anyway, will you just come home next Sunday? Mom would be so fricking relieved."

"God, I don't know if I'm ready to tell them. What if they totally freak?"

"Well, they will totally freak. Like, count on it. But it doesn't mean you shouldn't do it. Just get it over with. Pull off the Band Aid, you know?"

"You'll be there, right?"

He folded his arms. "You seriously think I'm going to miss the confrontation of the century? Dad's going to go insane."

She gave him a small smile. "Was that supposed to make me feel better?"

"I'll be there! I'll be there. Don't worry about it."

"Okay," she said hesitantly. "Because Bá will probably throw me out."

"Yeah," he said half-eagerly. Reaching across the table, Rosalind swatted at her brother's arm. He pulled it away and laughed. "Just freaking defend me, all right?"

"Of course I will. I've got your back, Ros. What do you think I am?"

"Okay," she said. "Just checking."

"I've got you, sis," he said. "Even if you are a dyke."

She just shook her head at Wilfred and he smiled.

"I know," he said. "Shut up."

Chapter Sixteen

Monroe shyly pushed open the door to the Driven garage and looked around. They'd ridden their bike over, so as not to confuse business with pleasure. For the fact was that right now, Monroe seriously needed a friend. It was time to find Kate and have a talk. Even if she was at work.

"Hello? Anybody here?" Monroe called, stepping into the half-empty garage.

Tenika emerged a moment later with a fan belt in her hands. "Hey, Monroe."

"Hey." Monroe just stood there for a moment, grinning awkwardly. For the last six days, Monroe hadn't slept. Nor had they thought of much other than their newest obsession—LuAnne driving up from her southern California suburbia, and raising hell at their gender confirmation hearing.

It was unlikely, of course. So far nothing indicated their mother would actually try to stop the process. Nor that she even realized that she could. Monroe repeated this thought hourly. Yet the fact that it was even possible had them completely unnerved.

Tenika glanced through the open bay doors. "Where's your car?"

Monroe cleared their throat. "I'm uh...actually wondering if Kate's around?"

"Yeah. Hey, Kate!" Tenika called to the back of the garage.

She gave Monroe an appraising look, and her expression now was one of concern. "You okay?"

"Oh…well. You know," Monroe paused, then shrugged noncommittally.

Tenika nodded. "I hear ya," she said, giving Monroe's arm a pat. "We're all just trying to keep on keepin' on, right?"

"Basically."

"Hang in there, sis. I mean—*oh shit.*" Tenika closed her eyes, impatient with herself. "Sorry. I meant—"

Monroe cut her off with a weary smile. "Don't worry about it, T. It happens all the time."

The number of people who mistakenly called Monroe 'her' or 'ma'am' or 'she' never ceased to astound. But now it was just a regular part of their life. Monroe had decided a while ago to relax about it. Especially if people noticed their mistake and acknowledged it.

"I totally apologize," Tenika pressed.

"T, it's okay. Truly."

"Monroe!" Kate suddenly appeared from the back, a clipboard in her hand. She was as lovely as ever, wearing a pair of old jeans and pink button-down shirt, as she made her way across the garage to Monroe. "I'm so glad you came by. I'm a bit of a mess."

Kate gave Monroe a small hug, then she laughed and pushed her slightly tousled strawberry blonde hair from her face. Monroe noticed she had a small streak of dirt on her cheek. Immediately Monroe wanted to brush it away. They stifled the impulse.

"Doing the inventory," Kate explained. "And it's just so many tires. Must be hundreds back there. Anyway, I'm glad you're here. Can I get you a coffee?"

Monroe shoved their hands in the pockets of their jeans and blushed. "Well, I'd take a coffee, that's for sure. But you're obviously in the middle of something right now. But…I mean I was just wondering…if you had a minute?"

"Coffee," Kate said firmly, already heading to the conversation corner. "Over here, my friend. I could use the break." In a moment, Kate had filled the coffee maker as she reached for a few coffee pods. "Decaf or the real thing?"

"Real." Monroe dropped gratefully down on the couch as Tenika's power wrench squealed in the background. It felt good to be here, yet it also felt a little vulnerable. "Is Lizzy here?"

Kate smiled. "At the dentist, poor thing. Root canal." She turned to Monroe brightly, offering a steaming mug. "Black, right?"

"Yep." Monroe took the coffee and sipped. Then closing their eyes, Monroe leaned back against the couch and took the first full, deep breath they'd taken all day.

Kate sat down in a nearby armchair. A wave of concern crossed her face. "You look exhausted, Monroe. Is everything okay?"

Monroe studied the ceiling, almost unable to get the words out. "I'm doing this...thing. And I made a mistake."

Kate studied her friend. "Say more."

Monroe put the mug down. "So I'm getting a gender marker change to non-binary. It's no big deal, really. Just paperwork, you know? But now...well, suddenly there's a judge and a hearing. And apparently, sometimes the judge hears objections, you know, like from family members?"

Kate nodded, listening. "Go on."

"So right after I filed, I was telling my sister about it. Next thing I knew, my mother's going apeshit on the phone, trying to talk me out of it."

"Where's your mum?"

"Chino. It's outside of LA."

"That's eight hours away," Kate pointed out.

"There are airplanes, Kate, and if I know my mom, she'll find out she can object. Then she'll get her ass up here. She wouldn't miss that hearing if her life depended on it."

"Oh dear."

"Yep. Oh, dear is right."

Kate studied her friend. "But has she told you she's going to do this?"

"Well, no, but—"

"So we don't know she'll actually show up at the hearing, right?" Kate said, leaning forward.

Monroe exhaled, and their voice was thoughtful. "True. I guess I don't…really."

Kate put a hand on Monroe's arm. "Listen, Monroe. Officially changing your gender *is* a big deal. But I know you're going to be okay—even if your mum does show up. And chances are, she won't. At any rate, no self-respecting judge is going to let your mum control your life, no matter how much she complains. Not about something this important."

Monroe leaned forward urgently, reveling in this moment of just speaking the truth. "My mother and I do not get along, Kate. We really, really don't. We're just opposites on everything. There's always been tension and this just pushes her over the edge. She freaking calls me by my old name! The whole situation sucks!"

Monroe pushed back into the couch and shut their eyes. A small tear pushed out, followed by another, and they brushed at their face, giving an embarrassed laugh.

"Oh, Monroe," Kate said tenderly, patting their arm. "You'll get through this, love. I'm telling you, no sensible judge will ever let your mother have her way. You're an adult! And you've been one for years now."

Kate's level-headed logic settled over Monroe like a fine mist. They could feel their entire central nervous system relax. This much was true. Still, as ever, doubts lingered.

"But what if my judge is incredibly stupid?"

"Well, there's that I suppose…" Kate murmured to herself. She looked intently at her friend. "Do you have a lawyer, Monroe?"

Monroe looked chagrined. "I can't afford one."

"Well," said Kate, taking a sip of her coffee. "Sounds like you need to call our friend, Rebecca. She's the go-to queer lawyer, and she's a Buddhist teacher as well. Lovely woman. We send her people all the time." Kate paused. "I think she even works on a sliding scale."

Monroe sat up a little more alertly. "What? Really? Like… *really* sliding scale?"

"Just talk to her," Kate said. Already, she was flipping through her phone. A moment later Monroe's phone pinged. It was a contact card for someone who's name ended with Esq.

"Give her a call.," Kate continued. "She got me my immigration attorney. She'll know just what to do."

Monroe glanced up at her gratefully. "I knew you'd have the answer."

"Oh, love. We're all in this together, right? Anyway, worse comes to worse, she'll certainly have a little spiritual advice for you." Kate chuckled. Then she rose. "Now if you'll excuse me, a mountain of tires is calling."

Monroe beamed their appreciation at their friend. "Thank you, Kate. You're truly a life saver. I've been so worried—I haven't slept in days."

"Ah, Monroe. Call me sooner the next time, eh? We're always here."

The two friends hugged then, as Tenika's power wrench squealed once again, Monroe walked away ten times lighter.

*

A few hours later, just as Monroe was hanging up from chatting with their new lawyer, the phone rang. It was their mother.

"Hi, LuAnne."

"Sarah?"

Monroe sighed. "Hi, Mom. My name's still Monroe."

"That's your last name, dear."

"What is it, Mom?"

"What do you think it is? You've obviously lost your mind. What makes you think this gender business is a good idea? Honey—this isn't like a tattoo. You can't just get rid of it if you change your mind. Once you've gone male, or whatever it is you're doing, you're over. Sarah no longer exists."

"Exactly," Monroe said calmly.

Unexpectedly, her mother let out a little sob on the phone. "But why?" she asked in anguish. "You were always such a good little girl. What did I do wrong?"

Monroe shut their eyes. Why in God's name had they even answered their phone? They knew this was coming.

Still Monroe's mother carried on, oblivious to Monroe's silence. "I tried to raise you right. I did everything I could think of. I know your father left, but I did the best I could for you and your sister." LuAnne sighed dramatically. "But who knows? Maybe I worked too much. I just had to because—"

"LuAnne, please stop."

Monroe's mother paused.

"Just stop. There's no need for this." Monroe exhaled, trying to calm the knot of tension that had built in their gut. "Look. I'll explain it one more time, then that's it, LuAnne. My gender has always been wrong. It just has. I'm not a girl. I'm not a guy. I'm just... me. And I don't actually have a gender. This is my choice." Monroe paused and tried to keep their voice calm, their tone even-handed. "This is who I am. And unfortunately, it's not up to you."

LuAnne's voice ratcheted up, shrill with fury. "Don't you tell me what's up to me."

"Mom, I'm a freaking adult!"

"But you don't know what you're doing, young lady. You could be—"

Monroe looked at their phone and for one brief moment, they hesitated. Then their finger came down on the red button and the call was over.

Finished.
Done.

Kate was right, of course, and Rebecca backed her up absolutely. If LuAnne made her way up to Oakland, and actually managed to get into the courtroom, she would never prevail. Chances are she wouldn't hire a lawyer. Just like Monroe, she could never afford one.

This was all about Monroe rising up, seizing the day, and taking what they wanted and needed once and for all. It was simply meant to be, this name change. This gender marker change. It was an undeniable part of their life path.

Meanwhile, Monroe would run their public notice of a name and gender change in the most obscure publication possible. That had been Rebecca's first excellent idea.

Suddenly, Monroe felt newly empowered. Rebecca and Kate were both right.

Everything really would be fine.

*

"You're quiet tonight," Sally remarked.

She and Frankie were sitting on the bench in front of Frankie's house, a bottle of Chardonnay and a few half-empty glasses between them. Sally had her shoes off and her feet up on the edge of a nearby planter filled with still blooming petunias. Frankie was sitting beside her in her most worn jeans and a simple gray t-shirt, the clothing of total comfort.

Before them, a sliver of sunset was visible behind the houses across the street. It was darkening into shades of deep rose and purple, prompting them to bring their wine outside after dinner.

"Oh, it's nothing," Frankie said.

Sally smiled, clearly amused. "Really, honey? Are you still trying to get away with that?"

Frankie waved away her girlfriend's words. "Let's just enjoy the evening, shall we?"

"What did your boss say?"

Frankie looked at her. Sally was so perceptive, she scared her sometimes. "How do you know I talked to my boss?"

Sally just shrugged. "I just think something happened at work, and you're not telling me," she said evenly. "But it's not like you have to tell me everything."

"Yeah, I don't," Frankie asserted, her voice taking a small tone of defiance.

Both women sat quietly for a moment, sipping their Chardonnay.

Finally, Frankie cleared her throat as a wave of uncertainty overtook her. She really was trying to do better with Sally. She honestly was. "Look, here's the thing. It doesn't matter what my boss said. He gives me a command, and I have to do it." Her voice softened. "I know that's hard to understand."

"Sounds like he wants you to do a workshop," Sally remarked.

Frankie whirled toward her. "Would you just quit it?"

"What?" Sally asked, wide-eyed. But then she smiled. "That wasn't a hit I got. By now I actually know you, Frankie. Better than you'd wish."

Sally's work as a professional medium and psychic had disturbed Frankie from the beginning of their relationship. Frankie always insisted the invisible world did not exist. Or at least she did until Sally began systematically blowing her mind every now and then.

"All right, all right!" Frankie threw her hands in the air. "I surrender. *Jesus.*"

Sally sat quietly, expectantly, a little like a cat about to be served a big dish of cream. "Please continue, dear."

"Yes, it's a damn workshop. Some touchy-feely 'we're all traumatized and we're going to get over it by holding hands' freaking love fest. Sounds ridiculous, if you ask me."

"But you're going."

Frankie sighed. "Next Friday."

"Good," said Sally. "You need it." At this, Frankie shot her a dirty look.

"I'm sorry if this is inconvenient," Sally continued, "but the fact is you need more help. You know you do, Frankie. This sounds like just the thing."

Frankie crossed her arms and stared out at the sunset, refusing to answer. How did she know Sally would say this?

"Oh, Frankie, come on. Do you want me to sit here and lie, and withhold my feelings?" Sally continued.

Frankie gave a long, painful sigh. "No," she said in a small voice.

"It's only a workshop. I mean, it's not a life sentence. Just try and keep an open mind, honey." Sally looked at her lover. "You might be surprised," she added more gently.

Frankie gave Sally a dark glance. "Well, I'm not getting a psychic reading, if that's what you're thinking."

"Who mentioned a reading? I wouldn't *think* of offering you a reading!" Sally laughed at Frankie now. "I just know that something is going to happen that will lead you in an entirely new direction."

"I am not leaving the Force," Frankie said tightly.

"Fine. Whatever," Sally said. "Your new direction will be just right, Frankie. It's going to take you into places you seriously want to go."

Frankie resisted Sally's words, and yet at the same time, she craved them. "Like out of the video library?" she asked.

"Totally out of the video library. That's what I'm saying, honey. Just trust your process, because you're in a huge one right now. And it's really, really important." The two women looked at each other. Frankie was suddenly filled with yearning. Desperately, she wanted to believe the words that Sally was telling her.

And yet, there was that damned reason. The very same boulder blockade that always came up for Frankie at such moments. Regardless, Frankie let go a little as Sally put her arm around her girlfriend. Nuzzling her, Sally kissed her ear.

"It's all going to be okay," she soothed. With this, Frankie lowered her head to Sally's shoulder and closed her eyes as she fought the tears that welled inside.

It was all going to be okay. Sally said so.

"You'll be fine. Better than fine," Sally whispered into Frankie's ear. "Trust me, honey."

The two of them sat there, heads nestled together as the sunset turned crimson. There would come a point at which Frankie would finally, completely, totally melt. And even Frankie knew it.

It just wasn't clear exactly when.

*

Tenika and Delilah studied the web page of sperm donors that was open before them. "I don't know..." Tenika shook her head. "Are you sure this is how it's done? You just pick a guy with some appealing characteristics, and order a shot of sperm?"

Her wife glanced over at her. "Well, how else would this happen, honey?" Delilah's gaze returned to the screen. "Hey, look. Here's a biology researcher who went to Howard."

Tenika rolled her eyes. "First of all, how do you even know it's true?"

"You doubt?"

Tenika's forehead wrinkled with concern, and the crease between her eyes deepened. She pushed her glasses up her nose. "Well, anyone could say they went to Howard," she pointed out. "This all just feels so mechanical. So...cold. I mean, do we really care where the dude went? What about his values? What about his politics? Is he even a nice person? Maybe those are the questions we should be asking."

Delilah cocked her head at her wife. "There is no line for that on the form, babe. No 'Rate your personal integrity on a scale from 1 to 10.'"

"Anyway, I wouldn't worry about it," Delilah continued, studying the listings once again. "Our child is going to have two excellent mothers."

Tenika sat back uncomfortably and folded her arms. "Are you *sure* we don't know any nice gay guys who can get the job done? There's got to be someone. This is the Bay Area!"

Delilah gave her a weary expression. "Baby, we've talked about this. At length. We really don't know anyone. Come on, T." Delilah turned to her wife. Pausing, she looked at her critically. "What's the matter, honey? You getting cold feet?"

"No," Tenika was quick to say. But in truth, she was.

The fate of Walter was never far from her mind these days. By now, who knew how old he even was? The accident happened more than twenty years ago, so Walter was most definitely an adult by now. Tenika kept imagining him in an adult day care facility, wearing a giant diaper and unable to do the simplest things.

Hell, he probably can't even tie his shoes, she told herself.

Still, there was much that Tenika didn't know. At the time of the accident, the level of damage he had sustained was unclear. How he would grow and develop would remain a mystery until he became an adult. But, of course, Walter was long gone. Not long after the accident, the family left, as if wanting to distance themselves from Keisha, Tenika and the entire painful experience.

So by now, anything could have happened. It was even possible that Walter was a totally functional adult. Maybe he was a kid who'd once been hit by a car, suffered a concussion and that was it. Maybe he was even successful.

Tenika truly had no idea.

Still, the old shroud of shame once again slipped over her shoulders at times like this. It was a remarkably comfortable shroud. One that had been in place for many, many years.

Turning back to the computer, Tenika shook off her thoughts and did her best to refocus. "How about an athlete? Can we order a guy who likes to play basketball or soccer or something?"

Delilah gave her an appraising look. "Sounds like you're back on track."

"I am," Tenika nodded and swallowed, fighting back her fear. "I guess I get...you know...a little scared."

Delilah put her hand on her wife's thigh, and refocused on the screen. "Me too, baby. That's why we're doing this together."

"Right."

Together they continued to study the applicants, looking for just the right one.

Chapter Seventeen

Rosalind sat back in her desk chair, and regarded the spew of work across her desk. Despite the two new staffers sitting outside the glass wall of her startup office, she felt very much alone right now.

For one thing, they were unpaid interns. Eager, fresh-faced girls just out of college who could somehow manage to not make a living. What they didn't know far outweighed what they did know. They seemed to be able to answer phones, use apps and research things online. But so far, that was about it.

Rosalind pinched the space between her eyebrows, in an attempt to ward off an impending headache. Starting the non-profit had been such a rush in the beginning, fueled by the storm of national publicity she'd gotten in the days after *The Chronicle* story broke. Really, bringing down the tech boys at her old job had been the easy part. Anyone could have seen what they were doing, once they looked clearly enough.

This—right here, right now—was the hard part. The non-stop process of getting and keeping funding, combined with feeling her way along in the dark as she tried to determine where to focus next was exhausting. But at the same time, it was also incredibly rewarding. If she didn't feel like the entire project could collapse at any moment, it would be a total joy ride.

But no. That lurking anxiety was a constant stone in

Rosalind's gut. Why, for instance, should the female whistle blowers she depended on trust her enough to come forward with their stories and risk their jobs? Not to mention their careers and their reputations? Especially when she was still making up this entire process, one day at a time.

Still, there was a hunger out there for this level of transparency, for this kind of accountability. So Rosalind's mission kept crawling steadily forward, one unlikely day at a time.

#techwomentalk had been a remarkable success so far. More than eight women had already gotten local and national publicity in the US, with another three in Canada and a few overseas. As a result, more than five startups had been busted for criminal activity. It didn't even bother Rosalind when all those entitled men she was working to educate threatened her with lawsuits.

That's what all the fundraising was for, of course. It was for the lawyers she now needed just to keep the lights on. Rosalind gazed at the disarray on her desk. The empty take-out containers. The scratch pad where she'd been calculating her expenses. The bottle of caffeine tablets. The worked over spreadsheet on the open screen in front of her. It was a still life of stress in the modern era.

All of it was a reminder of how much she'd gotten done so far. And how much further there was to go.

No, Rosalind was doing the right thing at this moment in her life, that much she was sure of. The key was just to keep her foot on the gas. Eventually, hopefully, all the smart, capable women in tech like her—women with degrees from MIT, Harvard and Yale—would finally stop putting up with being shut down at work. Especially when they stuck their necks out and told the truth.

That was her dream. And so far, even in a small way, it was working.

The phone rang now, and Rosalind reached for it. She'd been trying to stay off her phone lately, after reading an article about how constant phone exposure weakened her ability to think creatively. Her phone was in the bottom of her bag, and she had to dig around to find it.

Finally extracting the ringing phone, she glanced at the screen as she swiped to answer. It was her mother. The knot of anxiety in Rosalind's gut twisted just a bit more.

"Mama," she said. "How are you?"

Her mother answered in Chinese, as she always did, hoping they might keep the conversation there. But, just as she always did, Rosalind switched them back to English. Yet again, she told herself that her mother could use the practice.

"Why you not call me, Lijuan?"

Rosalind resisted the urge to correct her mother with her American name as an unexpected wave of grief made her eyes tear up. "I'm glad you called," she repeated, ignoring her mother's question.

It struck her then that it had been a very long time since her mother had called her. Too long. Even now Mama's voice, quieted with age, seemed so familiar. And so very, very dear. Rosalind instantly felt ashamed.

Wiping a tear away from her eye, she realized she was on the verge of seriously weeping. She missed her mother, plain and simple.

"Mama, I want to come to dinner on Sunday," she heard herself say.

Whoa...really? Already?

Yes. Really. She would go to dinner and honor her family. And she would come out to them. And she would take the punishment they almost certainly would mete out. It was time. She would do this out of respect for herself, but also for them.

As if suddenly passing into a brilliant beam of sunlight, Rosalind could see and feel the truth. By not talking to her parents, by staying away, by not sharing her life, she was running away. For all of their faults, and their old country ways, and their stubbornness and even their small-minded Evangelical prejudices, Bá and Mama were still her parents. They, too, deserved her respect.

This was the undeniable reality she could no longer run from. She loved her family. And she missed them.

"I will make *Mapo Doufu*," her mother exulted. "You come home. You make your father happy." The relief in her mother's voice was palpable, and it struck Rosalind now just how much abuse her mother had taken in her marriage. In the last year, it had mostly been on her account.

With a trembling hand, Rosalind wiped away another tear. Then she sniffed hard, pulling herself together.

"Are you sure he will be happy to see me, Mama? I heard Dad was still pretty angry."

"Men always mad about something," her mother replied.

Rosalind chuckled. "Yeah, I guess so." Maybe her mother was beginning to get it. "I don't know, Mama. You're sounding like a feminist."

"What this *femnizz*?"

"Feminist. Don't worry about it, Mama. We'll talk."

"You come Sunday?"

"I will come Sunday."

Rosalind paused, taking in this moment for all it was worth. A bridge, however temporary, was now in place. She could let her mother's love come streaming back in, warming her and comforting her just as it always had. It was love she had been yearning for, and she wrapped herself in it like a warm, soft blanket. Rosalind hadn't realized how much she'd missed it.

"I love you, Mama," she said.

"You come Sunday, " her mother repeated. Then she hung up.

Rosalind sat back in appreciation of this singular, perfect moment, when everything felt aligned just as it should be. For she did, indeed, love her mother. And most importantly, she knew without a doubt that her mother still loved her. Even if she didn't say so.

*

Frankie crossed her arms tightly against her chest and waited with dread for her turn to share. It was day three of the PTSI Recovery Initiative Workshop. She hadn't had alcohol since she'd arrived, nor had she used a cell phone, laptop, wifi, or a telephone in the last seventy-two hours. At this point, she was feeling weirdly empty and beyond raw.

So far, Frankie had spent hour after hour with her fellow first responders, sitting in lectures about trauma, the brain and addiction recovery. She'd even begun processing a few harsh memories. Of course, she knew this was useful; she could feel the value of all of it. Still, Frankie didn't want to be here.

Even 'Taco Tuesday,' a beer-free event in the drab cafeteria, complete with sandpaper tortillas and bland salsa, was painful.

Mainly Frankie was going with the program simply to get herself out of her video library gig. At least that's what the Lieutenant had promised. Still, in the small, quiet hours of the night, as Frankie thought about it, she knew she belonged here. And that sooner or later, something had to work. Honestly, Frankie was tired of being held captive by her ghosts.

There were only a handful of active cases like herself at the workshop. The other dozen people here were dispatchers, fire fighters, and law enforcement folk who'd already completed the workshop. Now they were simply there to support Frankie and the other participants.

It was a reality that made her intensely uncomfortable. After all, who *were* these gung-ho people who wanted to help her so much? And why the hell should she trust them?

One of them was her roommate Bonnie, a soon-to-retire Crew Chief on Central California EMT squad. Bonnie had been among the first to arrive at a mass shooting in a high school down by Manteca. That day, as Bonnie hauled out body after body, she said something inside her had died. So she got sent to the PTSI workshop as well. And now here she was, nearly two years later, gamely helping all these other injured people.

A soft butch with a spiritual bent, Bonnie read Thich Nhat Hanh late into the night with her itty-bitty book light clamped to her paperback. This was the fifth time she'd used her vacation time to support the workshop. Bonnie was warm and humorous, and Frankie had to admit that aside from being so eager to help her, she was actually all right.

Frankie leaned back in her folding metal chair, her hands still tucked up tight in her armpits. In the chair beside hers, a fire fighter tried to recite one thing he'd learned about himself the day before. Finally, he mumbled something about realizing he was "actually pretty shy in groups." Then sighing with relief that his turn was over, he turned expectantly to Frankie.

Shit. Frankie's mind blanked.

She closed her eyes and waited for her carefully prepared answer to come swimming back. But it had completely disappeared. "I…uh…damn." Frankie faltered, looking around the room for help. Then she fell silent as the room regarded her curiously.

"Go on, Frankie," urged one of the facilitators.

She licked her lips. "Yeah, sorry. I…uh…" Frankie studied her boots as blazing white blankness filled her brain. She looked at the others, feeling lost. "I just suddenly forgot what I was going to say."

The facilitator, a large bosomed mom-type named Mary smiled at her gently. "Take your time, dear."

She just had to say one lousy thing—it could be anything. She could even say what the firefighter said. She could lie, even.

Frankie closed her eyes, and inhaled. *Why was this so fucking hard? After all, did it really matter? Did it even remotely matter in the larger scheme of—*

Frankie's thoughts were now interrupted. First she thought of Sally, who'd put up with her drinking herself into oblivion, her frequent retreats to the living room couch, and her refusal to leave the house except for work. And yeah, they did go to one party, but that hardly counted.

Sally had been a damn saint through the last three months, and Frankie knew it. In fact, she loved her even more for this. What followed this was a sudden flash of insight.

Shaking her head, Frankie found that weirdly she could now begin to address the group. "I realize my trauma…the reason I'm here…it's just really old. I mean, yeah, there was a dead kid on the beach. But, you know, there was also my sister, Diana. Did I mention Diana?" A few people sitting in the circle shook their heads, so she continued.

"Diana died when I was seven. She had leukemia. And… fact is, she really looked like that dead kid. And she looked like the girl who jumped off the Golden Gate bridge in front of me, too. They all looked alike, you know?"

Frankie's voice wavered and her breath came hard as tears threatened to overtake her. "All those girls. They all looked so… young. Innocent, like…" she whispered. "Like Diana."

Tears suddenly were pouring down Frankie's face. "I'm—sorry." she fumbled, wiping her face on the sleeve of her fleece. "Didn't mean to get so…granular." She gave a nervous laugh.

Wordlessly, the therapist sitting next to the facilitator handed over a box of Kleenex. After a moment, she spoke. "Do you have more, Frankie?"

"No, no…it's okay," she answered. And it was. For suddenly, something had shifted.

The truth was startling. As if it had hit her from behind.

It wasn't her fault. None of this had ever been her fault.

Even falling asleep in the patrol car—even that hadn't been her fault. Just like Diana's death, and the depression that had locked up her mother in the years that followed.

None of it was because of her.

Frankie had just been a witness, and nothing more. There was truly nothing she could have done. This is what she knew now, and the insight was worth gold. Suddenly, there was the tiniest bit of light breaking at the end of the tunnel.

The day before Frankie had actually gone into the chapel and sat there for a while in the quiet, just thinking. It was the last place she'd ever thought she'd wind up. Yet here she was, pulled in by the promise, the relief of surrendering for once to something bigger than herself.

For a good half hour, Frankie just sat there quietly, taking in the utter stillness of the place and for once relishing it. She wasn't distracted. She wasn't even anxious or restless. Instead, she felt curiously alive. She also felt soothed and profoundly safe, as if all the bad memories and dark thoughts in her head might suddenly back down and leave her in peace.

Sitting in that chapel had been some kind of panacea for her badly broken spirit. It was here Frankie began to see how exhausting it was to hold the whole world on her shoulders. And how unnecessary.

Later, when Frankie finally left the chapel, she'd smiled, noticing the other first responders who'd wandered in as well. At least half of them were sitting here and there among the pews, soaking up the silence. That, alone, had been a revelation.

Now Frankie wiped her face on her sleeve and looked around. "I'm good," she said, nodding to the person to her left. And for once, she actually was.

Frankie smiled and shook her head. You never knew where so-called serenity was going to come from.

*

"Has it always so complicated, this lesbian baby-making thing?" Tenika shook her head uncertainly, as they sat there in yet another cool, off-white medical office. "I mean first the dye test, then the pills, then the trigger shot, then the ultrasound. This is beginning to feel like a marathon."

Delilah reached over and took her hand. "I have no idea, babe. We're just doing what we're told."

"Back in the day didn't women just use turkey basters at home?"

"Yeah, and how many of them actually got pregnant?"

Tenika sighed. "Good point." She looked over at her wife and squeezed her hand. Nervously she released her hand. "But I get it. You're excited. Hell, I'm excited, too."

Restlessly, Tenika uncrossed her legs and now crossed them the other way. Her foot tapped a nervous outline on the linoleum of the floor.

At the moment, Delilah was grinning in anticipation. Now that her hormones were jacked up, she was all feelings all the time, she said. First she was scared, then worried, then jubilant, then pissy. Then apologetic, weepy and contrite. Delilah was stuck on a runaway train of emotions, and it blew both of their minds.

But then, this was to be expected, the doctor said. For starters, Delilah had been required to take ten Letrozole, literally an entire handful of the estrogen inhibitor. And that was before the prep injection that made her hormones rev like a race car engine. The trigger shot needed its own special cooler as well as a portable sharps disposal system.

Tenika had administered the shot to Delilah's belly two nights before, shoving her glasses up her nose repeatedly as she took aim, then hesitated and rechecked the notes. After a whole lot more dithering, she finally delivered the shot.

It had been a thirty-six-hour emotional roller coaster for both of them.

Getting the sperm delivered came with a rigmarole all its own. First they had to listen to a voice message from the donor they'd chosen as he described himself: "*I'm a healthy Black man, about six foot tall. People say I'm handsome. I mean, I'm not like some model or something, but I'm okay. Good enough probably…"*

The donor sounded like a normal, average guy. Maybe even a nice guy. Not a braggart, but not an apologetic sort, either. His recorded message reminded Tenika of someone her brother might have hung out with. All the characteristics were there in his voice.

"He's our man," Tenika had finally said, and Delilah agreed.

Then the sperm had to be overnighted by Federal Express from southern California. They had only a few hours to get to the clinic for the IUI procedure, when the sperm would be injected directly into Delilah's uterus. Which now, they could say with certainty, was swimming with eggs.

Fed Ex had been heroic, delivering the all-important (and very expensive) tube of sperm in smoky wildfire weather. Fires burning to the north had made visibility for cargo planes landing at OAK tricky, causing delays. Both Tenika and Delilah had toggled back and forth, refreshing and checking the tracking until they could see the delivery was finally on the ground in Oakland. In no time, it was being driven to their fertility doctor's office.

Then they both tore out of their jobs and headed for the doctor's office. In the end, their potential son or daughter was delivered in a small, ordinary looking plastic tube about two inches long.

'12042' it said in big black letters.

Tenika had looked at it in disbelief. Here was their child. Or, if they believed the literature, potentially two of them, for the chance of twins with fertility drugs was higher than usual.

Now the two women peered at the test tube lying on the stainless steel tray beside them.

"You excited?" It was only the seventh time Delilah had asked this question in the last hour.

Tenika folded her arms. "Yes, babe. I'm excited. Like I said. Repeatedly." Still, as she said this, the usual misgivings clouded her mind.

How could she not help but have misgivings, knowing what she knew about herself and about the inestimable fragility of children? They could slip through your fingers and be gone in an instant. Tenika swept her thoughts away with a shake of her head, and gave a half-hearted smile at her partner. "Of course I'm excited. Why wouldn't I be?"

Delilah was still studying Tenika's face when their physician walked in. "Let's get this party started," the doctor said jauntily as she pulled on her latex gloves and pulled up the stirrups on the examining table. "Just scoot down toward me, Delilah, and put your heels in those stirrups if you would."

She picked up the tube as Delilah got into position. Then she looked up at the two of them brightly. "I think we've got a winner here," she said. "Of course, you never know…"

"Guess we'll see, won't we?" Tenika remarked.

Then Delilah grasped Tenika's hand and closed her eyes as the procedure began.

*

The summit of the small mountain was just ahead in the gritty pre-dawn light. Frankie's boots crunched along in a silent march with her fellow first responders. It was the last day of the workshop, and they were all headed up the trail to do the closing ritual.

This would be followed by a celebration breakfast. It was off site at a local restaurant known for its pancakes. Frankie was looking forward to the breakfast, and not just because the food at the workshop had been miserable at best. Instead, she found she was actually, legitimately in the mood to celebrate.

Something had definitely happened in her four-day exodus to the woods. Finally, Frankie had seen the cost of the enormous burden she'd lugged around for all of these years, first with Tiffani's death, then with the girl on the beach and her lifeless eyes. And finally, with the jumper, whose terror cut into her each time Frankie thought of her, hanging out over the Gate.

But now, all of it seemed less relevant. Less immediate. And certainly, less personal. Perhaps it was the intense two-hour EMDR session she'd done the day before, or the reciting of all the PTSI stories around her, one after another. All of it helped her realize how common her problem was. And how curable it was. For the first time Frankie could remember, hope lit her up like a light.

Frankie had already decided she was done with the negativity, the depression and the resentment. Even the grief. She'd done her time with all of it, and she was ready to move on. They reached the clearing just ahead and put down their day packs.

She stepped up to the edge of the clearing and took in the view. Beyond them, a Sierra sunrise was just breaking over a distant lake. It was flanked by tall imposing mountains much higher than the one they were on. They were monumental in the way only the Sierras could be. It filled Frankie's heart just to stand there, taking it all in.

Suddenly the entire experience—even getting to know Bonnie and the other first responders—seemed magical, inspired, and wise.

A surprising thought now struck Frankie. Perhaps she, too, would come back to the workshop as a peer counselor. After all, why not? Clearly there was something to be gained here. Something she'd actually like to share with other first responders who had PTSI.

Two of the peer counselors who'd gotten there ahead of them tended a roaring fire in a carefully prepared stone fireplace. Walking back to it, Frankie stepped up to the leaping flames and warmed her hands as the fire took hold. The smell of smoke and the heat that radiated toward her, reminding her of camping expeditions she'd taken as a kid.

It was here, in just a few moments, that they would have the opportunity to burn anything they didn't want to take with them when they left. Reaching into her pack, she extracted the envelope stuffed with small file cards she'd prepared. On each one Frankie had written a memory, a belief, or a viewpoint she no longer needed. The stack was chunky in her hand. There had to be at least a dozen cards.

She smiled at the stack in her hand, and to herself. Frankie was one tough nut to crack, just like Sally had said. Sally knew far more about her than she'd ever realized until now. Suddenly, Frankie couldn't wait to get back to her girlfriend, to see her smile, to feel her body beside her in bed. And to make love with her and see the sunlight come flooding across her face as she did.

Frankie was truly in love. Perhaps now more than ever as her heart once again returned to peace.

Her reverie was interrupted by Bonnie. "Want to kick things off and put your cards in the fire?"

"Definitely." Frankie removed the stack from her pocket, and glanced through them as she stepped up to the edge of the fire. Its heat licked her face and her throat as she pulled out the first card, and then the next, and the next after that. One by one, the cards dropped into the fire, rotating slowly as they shifted from white to tan to brown to black in seconds.

She watched the words '*Guilt over Diana*' curl up and dissipate into ash before her eyes. Each one of these cards, written in excruciating blurts of pain, told the story of her life until now. Yet, of course, the story wasn't over. Far from it. She could now say that it was all just beginning.

Frankie smiled as she dropped the last of the cards into the fire. "Done!" she declared jubilantly, high-fiving Bonnie who stood beside her, watching.

Bonnie smiled at her enthusiasm. "You did it, Frankie."

"Yeah," she chuckled. "In spite of myself."

Bonnie shrugged. "Ah, we're all like that in the beginning. Bottom line is you did enough."

"Guess I did." Frankie smiled and turned to her roommate. "Thank you, Bonnie," she said. "For everything."

The two women hugged, then stood side by side on their shared mountaintop as the others put their cards into the fire, one by one.

So it was on an early winter morning in the Sierras, as the sun rose beyond the mountains, that Frankie discovered she really, truly could start again.

And so, she did.

Chapter Eighteen

Rosalind turned onto the block of the house she grew up in. It was in Fremont, a middle-class suburb forty-five minutes south of Oakland, home to a large Asian population. It was here that Rosalind's mother happily served on the vestry of the Baptist Church of the Blood Crucifix. It was here her father tinkered with his zero-gage model trains, and did tai chi in the park with the other aging Chinese men and women.

It was also here that she was about to wipe away her past, and most likely be forced to leave her family forever.

Pulling up to park, Rosalind looked at her watch. It was ten minutes to six. She was early. Her brother had already texted to make sure she was coming, but she didn't see his car yet. Rosalind glanced in the rear view mirror and checked her make up. She looked at herself uncertainly as her heart pounded in her chest.

She'd wait until Wilfred showed up. That seemed safest. Then they could walk into her parents' house together. That was probably the only way she was going to be able to do any of this.

Her gut wrenched as she sat quietly and waited. She was too nervous even to flip through her emails on her phone. Rosalind closed her eyes, imagining the coming scene. Her father would, of course, completely lose it. And her mother would fall apart, most likely by sobbing and praying for mercy for her daughter.

The whole scene would basically be apocalyptic. And...if

what Sally said was true, perhaps all of this angst, anxiety and conflict truly was critical to her making it to the next level in her life. Whether or not she managed to go there with Monroe.

It was all quite clear. Rosalind was on a mission now, just as she was when she brought down True Wire. She could feel the rightness of seizing this moment, right here and now, and she needed to marshal all of her resources to make it happen. Thank God her brother was coming.

Wilfred's black Tesla pulled into view, and silently he slid into the parking spot behind hers. Taking a deep breath, Rosalind opened the car door and stepped out. She smoothed her skirt and waited for her brother to emerge.

"Okay," he said as he joined her in the street. "It's go time."

"Shut up."

He grinned. "Don't worry sis. You're going to be fine." Then he turned toward their parents' front pathway.

She touched his arm, pulling him back. "Wait a minute."

He turned back to her. "What? It's *not* go time?"

A new wave of panic rose up in her, and for the briefest moment, she wondered if she was going to vomit. Or possibly hyperventilate. She hung on to his sleeve for dear life, trying to collect herself. "What's wrong?" her brother asked.

"Just tell me something," Rosalind said, looking at him intently. "Are you still going to be my brother? I mean…are you going to kick me out, too?"

"Jesus, Ros! Of course not. What do you think?" He turned her around toward the house. "Come on. Let's just get this over with."

A moment later they approached the tidy, nondescript front door. Wilfred pushed it open. "Mama?" he called.

Then there was their mother, holding out her arms, making sounds of exuberant delight. "Rosalind!" she cried, beholding her daughter with a broad smile. Then her smile fell, and she said in Chinese, *"You are too skinny. You're not eating enough rice!"*

"No, Mama…really, it's okay." Rosalind gave her mother a warm deep hug. Her mother's arms came around her and held her then, and she dissolved into the warmth and the strength of this small woman for just one moment.

She needed this hug. God, she needed this.

Perhaps this was the last maternal hug she would ever know, she thought to herself. How she loved this small, fierce woman, in spite of everything. The bittersweet sense of this destiny, their shared bond, was stronger than ever. Rosalind pulled away and smiled at her, and her mother patted her hair, smoothing it proprietarily.

"You father in front of the TV," her mother said, nodding toward the living room.

"Bábá," Rosalind said, walking into the living room. He looked at her slowly, looked her up and down. Then he turned off the golf he'd been watching with a snap of the remote.

Stiffly, the old man rose. Walking over to his daughter, he gave her a small hug. A hug of forgiveness. As if to say, 'We will move on now.'

Rosalind hugged him back, surprised at the gesture. Hope rose in her heart for just the briefest moment. Maybe this would all go a lot better than she'd hoped.

Her mother called them all to dinner then, and together they walked into the living room. Her father chatted animatedly in Chinese with Wilfred, while she moved toward the kitchen to help her mother. After the plates were brought to the table the steaming Ma Po Tofu, the bowl of rice, the sautéed long beans in garlic sauce, just as she predicted—Rosalind found her usual seat. The old brown wooden chair with the blue cushion had been left vacant for her.

She glanced around the table for a moment. Here she was, among her people. However briefly, she could relax and enjoy them. Wilfred uncorked a bottle of wine he'd brought, and quickly he gathered four slightly dusty glasses from the cabinet nearby. It was a sweet gesture. And an unusual one, for most of the time her parents didn't actually drink.

"Ma?" he asked, putting a glass before her mother. A small, shy smile crept across her face, and she gave a little giggle. "Just little," she said, holding up her fingers to indicate a tiny amount. Predictably, her father refused.

Good, thought Rosalind. Some alcohol would help her mother cope. Meanwhile, she let her brother pour her a full glass of Cabernet. Then the four of them bowed their heads for the customary prayer. Rosalind's father began in his gruff voice in English.

"Send down upon us Thy heavenly food, Father, and confer upon us Thy blessing. Thou art the Bestower, the Merciful, the Compassionate. In Jesus Christ's name, to Thee we pray."

After a moment of silence, he looked up, blinked, and took up his spoon. That was the universal symbol that the family could begin. Quietly, the four of them ate their dinner.

"Rosalind," her father said after a moment. "You disrespected us."

Rosalind glanced at her mother, whose eyes were now securely locked on the plate before her.

"Yes, Bá. We have talked about this, do you remember?"

He held up his hand. "Of course I remember. But the priest tells me I must forgive you. I don't want to…" He paused. "But the priest said I have to."

She nodded, taking in his pronouncement that she was forgiven.

"Thank you," she said. "I appreciate that."

Wilfred now tried to change the subject. "What do you think of the wine, Ma?"

"Very nice," she said. It appeared she had not yet taken a sip.

"You should try it, Mama. Just a little sip. Why not?" Rosalind said. But in an instant, her father turned to her.

"If your mother does not want to drink alcohol, do not force her," he said in Chinese.

Her mother still studied the food on her plate, and Rosalind was struck dumb.

They continued on, chewing in silence.

"I got a promotion this week," Wilfred said. Immediately his father's eyes lit up. Finally—something to be happy about.

"Yes?" his father asked eagerly.

"I'm in charge of West Coast Sales. Substantial hike in income, too."

"Very, very good!" their mother exalted, while their father beamed and stuck out his hand to his son. They shook.

"Good, son," his father said. Shaking his head, he smiled. "God is good."

"I mean…I was in line for it."

"God is still good," their mother added. "He brought our Lijuan home."

Rosalind smiled over at her mother politely. "Please call me Rosalind, Mama." Her mother smiled at her benignly, as if she hadn't a clue what she'd just said. Clearly she was back to one of her old tricks, selectively understanding English. Meanwhile, her father returned to his dinner, entirely ignoring the remark altogether.

They ate on in silence. But it was always like this, Rosalind thought to herself. Idly, she wondered exactly what it was that she'd missed about the family dinners so much.

It wasn't until the dinner plates had been cleared and they sat drinking tea that Rosalind finally cleared her throat. "Mama, Bá. I have something I want to talk to you about."

Uneasily, she eyed her brother and he gave her a barely perceptible nod of support. "Yes, go on," her father said, turning to her. She could see his body tense. It was the first time all night, he'd fully looked at her.

Suddenly, for just a moment, she froze. The words, which had been forming on her lips for years now, would not come out. It was as if panic had climbed up her throat and grabbed her tongue.

"I…" Rosalind stopped, unable to continue.

"What? You sick?" her mother said, and immediately Rosalind shook her head. She saw her father give her mother a long look. It was a look of warning. A look of *I-told-you-no-good-would-come-of-her*.

Rosalind felt a flash of defiance, fueled by his expression. This look of his was so familiar, and as ever, it clearly betrayed her. Resolved to speak, she took in a deep breath. Then slowly she exhaled. *This was it.*

"I'm gay," she said simply.

Both of her parents simply looked at her. Meanwhile, Wilfred was glancing from one to another, as if he were measuring the reaction that was sure to come.

"What you mean?" her mother asked, apparently confused.

"I'm a lesbian, Mama. I am a homosexual." This was the word her parents always used, as if to call someone a lesbian or gay was too friendly. Too affirming.

Now her mother looked at her, aghast. "You…*homosexual?* No, Lijuan. No, no, no. You just need nice man."

"No, Mama," Rosalind affirmed. "I've always known it. I was just afraid to tell you."

"No," her mother said fiercely, but Rosalind just gazed at her passively.

"I'm sorry. I am a homosexual."

Suddenly, Rosalind's mother could not answer. Instead her words disappeared. Tears began to run down her face. She just stared at Rosalind's father, bewildered.

Across the table, Rosalind's father rose. "Get out," he said in Chinese, pointing to the door. "Get out and don't come back. Ever."

"Dad, come on!" Wilfred now said, jumping to his feet. "You can't do this—"

Their father turned on him in a heartbeat. "You do not tell me what I cannot do in my own house!" he thundered in Chinese. Then turning back to Rosalind, he continued in English.

"Get out!"

Her mother was sobbing audibly now, weeping as if she had just witnessed the murder of her own child. In a sense, she had.

Slowly, Rosalind pushed back her chair and stood up. "Okay," she said. She'd known this was coming, and here it was. Now she repeated the words she had practiced again and again before she had come here.

"I love you both, and I always will. I hope some day you can accept me for who I am."

Turning, Rosalind grabbed her purse and made a beeline toward the front door as blind fury met fear in a tangle in her throat. Her face was white hot, and every sense in her body was alive.

Tears began to pour down her face as she pounded down the front steps, the door swinging wide open behind her. Her brother's footsteps sounded just behind her. "Wait, Ros, don't go. He doesn't mean it. He doesn't," he insisted.

"I mean it!" her father called out, still ensconced in his seat at the table. Behind him, Rosalind could still hear her mother weeping and whimpering. She felt such a pull in that moment to go back to her mother, to put her arms around her, to comfort her.

Still, she knew she could not. What was done was done.

Wilfred was standing before her now, trying to push her back toward the house. His voice was intense. "Don't go. At least come back and talk about it. If you leave, it's all over."

She shook her head. "There's nothing to talk about. I've delivered my news." Tenderly she looked at her brother. His face was so worried, and pain was written across it. "I love you," she said. "Thanks for trying."

"I swear it, Ros. Come on, just stay and we'll get through this. I know we will," he pleaded.

"Bá just…he just needs to sit with it, bro. You know he does."

"But mama…" he said brokenly. "Please don't go," he whispered. "This is going to kill her."

Rosalind sighed and looked at her brother. She knew his words were true. How she wanted to stay, how she wanted to comfort her mother. She paused for just one moment, as if considering the idea. But then her father's dark figure suddenly loomed in the doorway—a squat, angry, heavyset man silhouetted by the lamplight in the front hall.

Behind him, she could see her mother's forlorn figure. She looked utterly lost.

"Go!" her father thundered.

Wordlessly, Rosalind pushed past her brother, and as she left, she turned to him. "Call me."

Wilfred nodded. Then, standing there with his hands in his pockets, he shook his head as if he couldn't believe what he was seeing.

Rosalind made her way toward her car, every one of her senses still on fire.

At that moment, she suddenly felt crystal clear. Getting what you want in life was by no means easy, or even a sure thing.

And yet, you always have to try.

*

Tenika hurried into the coffee shop on Telegraph, having just stepped out of her grease-stained coveralls a moment earlier at the garage.

Tenika chided herself as she made her way over to the table and her waiting cousin. For some reason, Keisha said it was urgent that she come. But she still had two brake jobs and a realignment issue to deal with before the end of the day. The last thing she should be doing was eating lunch out.

"Okay, I'm here," Tenika grumped as she sat down.

"Like, this better be good?" her cousin asked. "Sit down, T. You look like you're all bent out of shape."

Tenika rubbed her eyes. "It's been hella busy…"

"You tell me one person who isn't busy around here," her cousin noted, her eyes firmly on the menu.

A moment later, they'd made their order. Then leaning back in her seat, Tenika regarded her cousin curiously. "So what's so urgent, anyway? You okay?"

Keisha waved away her concern. "I'm fine. Benny's fine. Everyone's fine. That's not it, T."

"So…?"

"So why'd I call you…" Keisha put her hands together and took a breath. "Well, I know you don't put much stock in the church and the power of prayer," she began.

"Wait a minute, Keisha. You want me to join the damn church? We've been over this. Like, repeatedly."

Keisha's eyes flashed at Tenika. "Girl, please. That is not what I'm saying. Would you just hold on and let me explain myself?"

Haughtily, Keisha drew herself up in her chair and took a sip of water, while Tenika rolled her eyes impatiently and drummed her fingers on the table.

Slowly, Keisha collected herself. Then she began again. "Everyone's fine, as I said," she continued. "Here's the thing. I heard from Jesus while I was in the shower, and we've got to go apologize to Walter."

Tenika sat back in her chair and sighed. Then she gave her cousin a long, dubious look. Still, Keisha carried on, unabated.

"Now I know what you're thinking, T. It's always Jesus this and Jesus that with Keisha—always pushing the church at me." Keisha stopped and glared across the table at Tenika. "This is not that. I swear it. Just hear me out."

The two women contemplated each other silently. They'd been bonded in a delicate web of tension that had lasted for decades. And now, in an instant, Keisha was suggesting they tear it all down, and actually go see the subject of all that anxiety, shame, pity, and remorse.

In response, Tenika stared at her cousin. After a moment, she shook her head and scoffed. "You seriously want us to go apologize to Walter? What if he wants to sue us?"

Keisha folded her arms and studied her cousin. "He's not going to sue us."

"How the hell do you know?"

"I know."

"I'm sorry, but you do *not* know that, Keisha," Tenika retorted. "Anyway, Miss Alma and the rest of them lost track of us years ago. They probably don't even remember our names. So as far as I'm concerned, silence is golden."

She paused while Keisha sat there, eyeing her tensely and listening.

"Anyway, Keisha, this is America," Tenika continued. "The minute we do this, some asshole is going out and finding a lawyer. I could lose the damn garage. Have you and Jesus discussed that?"

Keisha's gaze was laser focused on her cousin now, and her words were like a guided missile. "Now you listen to me, T. Jesus didn't say, 'Keisha invite Tenika to go with you.' Or, 'Go ask her nicely and see if she'll come.' What Jesus said was, 'You get Tenika's sorry self in there with you, and you both apologize.'"

Tenika folded her arms across her chest and gave her cousin a dour look. "Oh, Jesus put it like that, did he?"

Keisha shifted uncomfortably in her seat. "More or less." She paused. "I just think it would be a good thing. You know it would. We've got to get closure, T. We need it." She looked at Tenika with a gaze that was almost tender. "You need it."

The two women fell silent. Nervously, Tenika jiggled her leg, staring at the table top before them. "Maybe *you* need it," she replied.

"Well, I'm going down there," Keisha announced. "With or without you."

Tenika glanced up at her. "Down where? You know where these people are?"

Keisha gave a little sniff. "I hired a detective, T. Walter still lives with his mother in Antioch."

"Oh, I don't know about this, Keisha. *Really*. This is…this is a very, very bad idea. It's risky as hell. Once you go down there, they're going to be on me in a second—even if I don't show."

Keisha gave her cousin a look of disdain. "T, you know perfectly well why Jesus suggested this."

Tenika rolled her eyes. "Come on, Keisha!"

"Tell me," her cousin said. "I know you know."

Tenika sighed. "No, I don't actually know. Why did Jesus suggest this? So I could be 'saved?'" She made little air quotes with her fingers.

Keisha leaned forward across the table and lowered her voice. "Forget all that, T. We're talking about Walter here. We're talking about that bad dream that still haunts both of us twenty years later. We're talking about moving on with our lives and apologizing. That's the whole point. And if you could get your head out of your butt about the church, you might actually see that."

Tenika fell silent. Keisha did have a point, Jesus notwithstanding. "Yeah, well…" she faltered as the waitress arrived with their sandwiches. Reason was failing her in this conversation. "Okay. I'll think about it, Keisha. But don't rush me."

"Nobody's rushing you," her cousin affirmed. "But I am going down there, whether you come with me or not."

Tenika picked up her sandwich. She didn't doubt that at all.

*

Forty-five minutes later, Keisha sat at her seat in the window of the coffee shop and she smiled. By now, her cousin was furiously fast-walking up the street toward her garage, hunched against a wave of late autumn fog that had drifted in. She hadn't agreed to go with Keisha. Anything but. Still Keisha had hope.

Shaking her head, she stirred her coffee. *I will be back,* she told herself. *And she will come with me to Antioch.*

That's all there was to it. Jesus knew, even if Tenika didn't. Those two women weren't ever going to have a baby unless she and Tenika put this thing right. That's why Jesus had shown up in the first place.

Now it was Keisha's job to make sure that it happened.

Chapter Nineteen

Monroe pulled their bike up to the rack outside the Alameda County courthouse and snapped the lock in place. Glancing at their watch, they saw they'd cut it pretty close. It was only a few moments until their hearing would begin.

Monroe hurried through the massive oak doors and the security detail, briefly flashing the inside of their messenger bag for the guy with the wand. Up ahead in the fluorescent-lit corridor, their lawyer, Rebecca was on the phone.

She gave a little wave. Then she held up a finger and turned away as Monroe approached.

Pausing, Monroe waited while Rebecca wrapped up her conversation. Apparently another one of her clients was going through a contentious divorce. "I told you not to talk to him. What's it going to take, Carol?" she asked. "I mean, let's get real here."

Covering the phone, she motioned Monroe inside. "Take your seat, and I'll be right in."

Monroe pulled open the heavy paneled door to Room 403 and stepped inside. Almost immediately, they saw her.

LuAnne, Monroe's mother, was seated in one of the benches in the back of the gallery. Instantly, their eyes met, and LuAnne stood uncertainly. Monroe stopped and sighed. Then turning around, Monroe walked right out the door to the hallway once again. "Rebecca…" Monroe said, approaching the attorney.

"What? Is it time already?" Rebecca glanced at her watch, but Monroe shook her head.

"It's my mother," Monroe explained. "She's come to make trouble. Just like I thought she would."

Rebecca set her jaw, and quickly ended her call. "Don't worry," she said as she strode into the courtroom. "We've got this."

Glancing around, Rebecca locked eyes on the only spectator seated in the gallery. "That's her?" she asked in a low voice and Monroe nodded.

Taking LuAnne in in a glance, Rebecca leaned in to Monroe. "Do what I do. Exactly," she said. Then ignoring LuAnne, who was now waving frantically at Monroe, the pair of them walked up to the front of the courtroom and waited patiently to approach the bench.

"How did she even get in here?" Monroe whispered to Rebecca.

"Where does she live?" Rebecca asked.

"San Bernardino County."

"She must know someone who's a lawyer," Rebecca said. Monroe immediately thought of her best friend Della's husband, Rob. He was a lawyer and he'd never liked Monroe. "All of this is online," she said, gesturing around the courtroom. "If you're in state and you know where to look."

Behind them, Monroe could hear LuAnne's plaintive voice. It sounded oddly out of place in the large silent room, like a strange echo from the past. "Sarah? Honey, can't we at least talk about this?"

Monroe tried to ignore the knot of fury that was now burning in their gut. LuAnne was not going to derail this process. Not if it took every ounce of strength Monroe had.

An Asian-American judge with a weary air motioned them forward a few moments later. "Hearing the case for a petition for gender and ID change for Sarah Patricia Monroe?" He peered at Monroe. "You're here for the gender X driver's license?"

"And a name change," Monroe added as Rebecca stepped forward and handed up a file of papers. The judge reviewed the papers, then he motioned the court clerk over. "This case was contested? What's the problem?" His tone was one of mild disbelief. No one ever contested these cases anymore.

"I can't believe she did this," Monroe whispered to Rebecca.

"Just ignore it," the attorney whispered back. "Truly. This is no biggie." Rebecca folded her arms and waited patiently. A dour looking court clerk in a tweed skirt and plain blouse returned to her desk, and shuffled through a few papers. Then she plodded back to the bench and handed them up to the judge.

He reviewed the packet of papers. "LuAnne Monroe?" he said, looking up.

Monroe now heard their mother's high heels tapping up the aisle behind them, and once again Monroe resisted the urge to even look at her. LuAnne took her place beside them. Rebecca glanced over and gave Monroe a barely perceptible nod, as if to say 'hold steady.'

Unable to control herself, LuAnne leaned over and tried to engage Monroe. "Honey…please, if we could just talk about—"

"You're out of order," the judge intoned from his spot a few feet above them. Immediately, LuAnne was silenced, and Monroe gave a small smile.

The judge peered down at the woman. "You are contesting this case?"

LuAnne drew herself up, and did her best to muster up her most pained expression. "This is my daughter, Judge, and this is all a huge mistake. She's not a they or a male or whatever. She just doesn't know what she is doing."

The judge peered down at the papers, then he looked at Monroe. "It says here you are an adult, and apparently have been for some time."

"There are no grounds here, Judge," Rebecca added.

The judge nodded. Then pulling out his stamp, he stamped the document and swiftly gave it his signature. "Agreed," was all he said. "This person is a legal adult, so it is entirely their decision." He banged his gavel, and that was that.

Silently, LuAnne stood there, unable to move. Unable to even respond.

"Ma'am?" the court clerk said, now handing LuAnne back her papers. Wordlessly, she took them. Then sadly, she turned to go.

As furious and as fired up as Monroe had been only a moment earlier, they couldn't help having a little empathy for their mother now. For suddenly, the truth was blatantly clear. The poor woman didn't have a clue.

She just didn't.

The three of them filed out silently. Rebecca then stepped away as her phone began to ring once more. Meanwhile, LuAnne just kept walking toward the door.

Suddenly, Monroe was spurred into action. "Mom—wait!" Monroe rushed forward, catching up with LuAnne. They reached for her arm, but LuAnne yanked it away angrily.

Doggedly, Monroe followed her hurrying mother up the hall. "Look, I'm sorry you're not happy about this, Mom. It's just something I have to do."

LuAnne gave a heavy, martyred sigh as she finally stopped and spun around. "I don't understand it. I really don't. Neither does your sister."

Monroe stuck their hands in their pockets, and fell silent for an awkward moment. "It's okay," they finally said. "I mean, it's okay if we don't understand everything about each other."

The two of them looked at each other, and slowly a soft truth settled over Monroe. Their mother cared about them intensely. Meanwhile, LuAnne stood there, looking utterly defeated.

Once more, Monroe reached out and patted her arm and this time LuAnne allowed it. As Monroe's fingers gently closed around her forearm, she shut her eyes. A single tear ran down her cheek, followed by another.

"It's all going to be okay, Mom. We're going to be okay," Monroe said, giving her arm a squeeze. Then they took her hand, and LuAnne's fingers entwined with their own. "You'll get used to this. We have to just give it time."

A moment of silence ticked by. "Anyway, we need each other," Monroe concluded. And now LuAnne nodded in agreement. "I need you," Monroe said.

LuAnne stifled a sob. "Oh, honey..." She shook her head miserably. "Thank you for telling me," she said in a half voice. Monroe nodded, giving her hand a squeeze.

"And Mom?"

LuAnne opened her eyes. "What?"

"My name really is Monroe now. If you could call me that, it would be great."

LuAnne nodded grimly. "Okay." Then she paused. "I'm sorry," she finally said, giving a small sob.

"It's okay. I understand."

LuAnne took her former daughter in her arms, and standing there in the bureaucratic gloom of the courthouse hallway, they gave each other a long hug.

Then Monroe pulled back and looked at their mother. "You going home now?"

LuAnne shrugged. "I guess so."

"Have lunch with me first?"

"All right," Monroe's mother said softly. "I mean, all right, Monroe," she added with a chuckle and Monroe smiled.

"Thank you."

Mother and child gazed at each other. "You're welcome, honey." The next phase of Monroe's life had just officially began.

*

Frankie and Sally lay in bed together reading and drinking coffee, as Saturday morning unfolded around them. They'd already made love, and now sections of the Sunday paper were scattered around the bed. Frankie's bedroom was their gentle cocoon, and as ever, Sally was grateful to be there.

She looked over at her lover, reading the sports section beside her. "I don't know," Frankie sighed, putting down the paper. "The Warriors are toast. I mean—look at this. Steph's got a broken hand, Klay's out, Dray is hanging on by his fingernails. I've never even heard of any of the guys in the starting lineup. They're all rookies!"

Sally smiled. "As I've been saying, life is change."

Frankie folded up the paper distastefully, and tossed it aside. "You got that right. Sheesh!" She reached for Sally now, and the two of them nestled under the covers together. Sally threw a long leg over Frankie's hip, and Frankie's hand came to rest on her impossibly soft thigh. They kissed.

Then Sally pulled back and studied Frankie for a moment. "How are you doing, honey? You seem a lot better since the workshop."

Frankie rolled on her back, contemplatively and gazed at the ceiling. "How am I? Well…" She gave a long exhale. "I *am* better. I feel stronger, more in control. Not drinking seems to be weirdly helpful."

Turning back to Sally, she smiled and pulled her close once more. "And I'm here with you. That, alone, is pretty great."

The two lovers kissed for a long moment, their tongues finding each other. Sally loved dissolving into Frankie's kisses. It was the very best kind of foreplay.

Frankie pulled back now. "Can I tell you something?"

"Sure. Anything." Reaching up, Sally brushed a few curls from Frankie's face.

"You know something? I really loved that workshop. I never would have guessed it, but somehow it was exactly what I needed." Gently, her hand found Sally's hip. "I liked it so much, I could even see doing more with them," Frankie added lightly.

"Seriously?" Sally pushed herself up on her elbow, and studied her lover. So far Frankie hadn't shared much at all about her time on the retreat. Yet, now there was an uncommon vulnerability in her face.

"Yeah," Frankie nodded. "It really was excellent. And they had these peer counselors, all first responders who've done this work. They come back just to support the active cases. I mean, it's incredibly well designed." Frankie paused.

"It's crazy, Sally," she continued. "I went in there prepared to hate the whole thing. But now I want to go back and do more. I think I could even be a peer counselor."

Sally beamed her response as it struck her. This was exactly what she had seen in the goddess cards. Frankie would eventually move on in an entirely new direction. Perhaps even a healing direction.

"So it all worked out, then. In spite of you?"

Frankie chuckled. "Yeah, I guess I deserve that." She pulled Sally down to kiss her once more. Then Frankie pulled back. "All I know is that I'm better for it." She gazed happily at her lover. "Baby, I'm so sorry I've put you through all of this. I love you," Frankie added.

Sally flushed with happiness. "Honey, it's okay. You were having a really hard time. Anyway, I understand. You do very, very difficult work. You really don't have to apologize."

"No. No, I do," Frankie said more intently. She gazed at Sally as she ran her fingers through the ash blonde cascade of her curls. Her fingertips traced her ear and came to caress the softness of Sally's cheek, and it struck Frankie now.

This is what love feels like. Real love.

"You've been amazing this entire time," Frankie continued. "You've stood by me, helping me deal with all of it. Practically living here just to keep an eye on me," she said. "You really took care of me, and I want you to know how grateful I am."

Sally felt her heart quicken at her lover's words. It was a little hard to take them all in at once, for suddenly here was Frankie unplugged. Let loose from her usually very tight mooring. Frankie was opening up to her in real time.

Sally swallowed. "Well, sure," she said a little shyly. "Of course I'm here for you." She took Frankie's hand. "I love you, too, honey."

The look that passed between them then was all Sally had been hoping for. Theirs was a union now. A perfect union. It was the sort she'd imagined all those years ago when she began dating women.

This is it, she thought.

This is really it.

*

Tenika rolled over and sat up, careful not to wake her sleeping partner. Getting up silently, she padded barefoot into the living room. Then snapping on the light, she lowered herself on the couch.

The house was quiet in the early morning darkness, but her thoughts were on fire.

Sitting there in her t-shirt and her pajama bottoms, she felt completely lost. It was as if all the hope had just drained right out of her life. Keisha's invitation to go see Walter still burned through her mind. And here she sat, still trying to figure out what to do.

There was no doubt that meeting with Walter would help Keisha. Hell, if Keisha wanted to go, she should go. It had clearly become a spiritual matter for her. The problem was…where would this leave Tenika?

If she didn't go to see Walter, she would always wonder if it might have helped. For it was possible that the visit could bring her massive sense of shame to some kind of uneasy peace.

Yet if Tenika did go, and she saw exactly what had become of Walter, she might return with even greater guilt—the kind that could gnaw away at her for the rest of her life. Not that it wasn't already. Shame, she knew, was debilitating, no matter how you looked at it.

Then there was Delilah, who had no clue about any of this. Lately, she'd been acting worried, and staring at Tenika like she was trying to x-ray her thoughts. Clearly, Delilah knew something was up, so it was only a matter of time until Tenika would finally have to tell her the truth.

And then what?

Perhaps Delilah would feel lied to, or at least so excluded for all of these years, that she might think about leaving. This could be the end of the whole relationship.

There was the matter of Tenika being unfit to be a parent, at least in her own mind. Didn't Delilah deserve to know this critical piece of information about her own wife?

The answer, of course, was a resounding yes. Tenika sighed. The shit truly had hit the fan.

If she lost Delilah, then she would lose the precious baby that could at this very moment be taking form in her wife's body. Some other mother would come along and raise him or her. And that thought was now unthinkable.

There was a potential baby in Delilah's womb. A real, live, living person who might not have her DNA, but he or she would most certainly have Tenika's heart. And that's all that mattered anyway, right?

Tenika put her head in her hands as her thoughts swirled round and round in a toxic stew in her brain. What was she thinking, assuming she could parent a child? She'd already proven to be a complete failure at child care. But the last thing she wanted to do was to lose her wife. Or this baby, who might or might not exist.

What in God's name am I supposed to do?

Tenika glanced at the clock through the kitchen doorway. It was close to 5 a.m. Yet again, she'd barely slept. Leaning back against the couch, she closed her eyes. Her words to Lizzy a few months ago popped into her mind.

'Happy wife, happy life.'

It seemed like ages ago she'd said this.

Back at that exact moment in time, everything had been calm, wonderful even. She hadn't yet gotten into the baby-making project with Delilah. And she'd pretty much lost touch with her cousin. That night over beers at the White Horse, she'd gone on and on about how you had to 'keep it real…but do it with respect.'

Tenika grimaced at the memory. Now that just seemed like so much bullshit.

She wondered what it would take to get back there again. Of course, there was only one answer and she already knew exactly what it was. She had to tell Delilah the truth. And that meant she had to get clear on exactly what that truth was in the first place.

Then she'd simply have to face the consequences, come what may. There were no ifs about this.

By now, Tenika had gotten wonderfully used to the idea of a baby in their life. Especially a little guy she could shoot some hoops with. Or maybe they'd have a girl who ran around in pink party dresses, and wobbled her tricycle down the sidewalk. All of it sounded perfect to Tenika. Amazing even.

She swallowed hard as she imagined the scenes. That precious little-kid hand in hers as they walked to the ice cream store together. The daughter or son she'd eventually teach to drive, and to repair their own car. The soccer games, the Halloweens, the birthday parties. Helping with homework. Teaching how to brush teeth.

Tenika wanted it. She wanted *all* of it. That was perhaps the most surprising thing of all. This parenting thing just came out of the blue, and it was so very right. And that was mainly because being with Delilah was so very right.

She stood up now and put her hands on her hips. She actually knew what she had to do.

Tenika needed to go with Keisha to see Walter. Then she needed to share the whole miserable story with her wife.

That's all there was to it.

Chapter Twenty

Kate looked up from her bookkeeping as the door into the garage creaked open. She smiled and waved as she stood up. Rosalind was in the house.

"Hey there!" Kate called, walking toward her customer-turned-friend.

For once, Rosalind wasn't wearing her usual tidy professional skirt and flats. Instead, she was in casual mode in a pair of tailored jeans, some Birkenstocks and an oversized button-down shirt with a monogram on the pocket. She looked exhausted.

"Kate," she said, with a note of relief in her voice. Rosalind swung her shiny, long black hair off her shoulders as she came in for a hug.

Kate gave her an appraising look. "I know just what you need," she said with a nod. Then taking her by the hand, Kate led Rosalind over to the conversation corner. "French roast or Espresso?"

"Espresso. A double please," said Rosalind. She gave a wry laugh. "That probably says it all right there, huh?"

Kate nodded, as she pressed the button on the coffee maker. "I'm guessing you are dealing with a lot?"

Rosalind dropped gratefully onto the couch and gave a long exhale. "Well, some things have happened," she began. Then she glanced around at the empty garage. "Where are Tenika and Lizzy?"

"It's their lunch break, so I sent them off to order new signage. Anyway, tell me, love," Kate said. "What's going on?"

"Well, I still have a job, that's good," Rosalind began. "But… you know…"

Suddenly her voice disappeared, and she swallowed hard, seeking a bulwark against her grief.

Kate sat down beside Rosalind as she put the steaming cup of espresso on the low table before them. Then she looked at her friend with an expression of concern. "What is it, dear?"

Rosalind studied the buttons on her blouse, saying nothing for a long moment. Finally, she looked up at Kate. "The worst possible thing has happened," she finally admitted in a small, tight voice.

Kate's hand landed on her arm. "Are you all right?"

"Yes, I'm fine. I mean, physically fine. But I came out to my parents and…they threw me out." Two fat tears that had been gathering in her eyes dribbled down her smooth cheeks. "They *threw me out*, Kate. They won't even speak to me now. Neither of them!" Rosalind now began to cry in earnest.

Kate gave a sigh. "Oh dear, I'm so sorry," she said, gathering Rosalind up in a hug. The two women held each other for a long moment as Rosalind cried into Kate's shoulder.

Rosalind sniffed and blew her nose in a ready tissue that had been in her pocket. "I can't imagine why I'm so shocked. I knew it was going to happen… It's just who they are."

Kate looked at her friend sympathetically. "But, Rosalind, you've got to be you, love. You know that. You can't go through the rest of your life in hiding." Kate paused. "They were going to have to learn the truth someday."

"I know," Rosalind said in a voice still shuddering with tears. "I know. It's just really, really *sad*."

"Of course," soothed Kate, giving her arm a consoling pat. "And they may come around. Nothing is forever, even if people say it is."

"Oh, you don't know my father," Rosalind countered. "It could be forever with him."

"Then he doesn't appreciate you for who you are. And that's the most important thing."

A dispirited silence hung in the air between them. Finally Rosalind blew her nose. "I guess so," she said.

Once more Kate gave her a hug. "You'll get through this. It's terrible, I know that. But you are a survivor, Rosalind. You're a very, very strong woman and you will get through this," she said into her shoulder.

"Sally told me I wouldn't fall in love until I told them…so I did." Rosalind pulled back. "Kate," she said more urgently. "I want to find my person. I really do." She collected herself, blowing her nose once more. "Otherwise, I left my family for nothing, you know?"

"Of course!" agreed Kate. "And what about Monroe?"

"What about them?"

"Have you called?"

Rosalind hesitated. "Not yet."

"Because?"

"Because…well, because of this. Somehow I just had to get clear with my family." Rosalind blew her nose once more and looked at Kate shyly. "But now, yeah…I guess I'm ready."

"Just what I'd hoped you'd say," said Kate as she rose. "I'll text you Monroe's number. It's only a matter of time for you two. Or…wait!" Kate stopped herself mid-stride, then she doubled back to the conversation corner. "Do you need a place to celebrate Christmas?"

The idea took Rosalind by surprise. "Oh—I hadn't really thought about it."

Kate was in the zone now, carrying on as if she'd barely heard Rosalind's reply. "I suspect Monroe could use a place to go, and it sounds like you could, too. Come to our house for Christmas dinner. I'll make a Christmas pudding, and Lizzy can do a Secret Santa as well. We'll have Tenika and Delilah, and Sally and Frankie, too." She paused, eyes sparkling. "It'll be mad fun, Rosalind. You'll love it. Perhaps you might even bring Monroe to the party?"

Rosalind blushed and laughed. "Now, Kate, let's not get ahead of ourselves, here."

"Oh, let's do exactly that!" Kate smiled. "Why not? At any rate, do tell me you're going to come. It would be such fun to have you."

"Sure," said Rosalind easily. "I'd love to." Picking up her coffee, she took a long sip. Then she breathed in the relief of having a friend to talk to. This was all it took sometimes to get hold of herself.

Thank God for Driven, she thought. *And thank God for Kate.* "Kate, thank you. I really needed this."

"My pleasure. We love having you here. And now you have Monroe's number…and well, you know what to do, Rosalind."

"Okay, okay!" Rosalind put up her hand. "I'm on it." Then she smiled broadly at her friend, and rising, gave her a grateful hug.

Driven had come through, yet again.

*

Tenika's truck bounced along the back streets of Antioch, her GPS guiding them as they went.

"Make a left here," Keisha said, pointing to the intersection ahead.

"We've got the GPS on, Keisha. You don't have to keep telling me," Tenika snapped.

"Well, excuse me for living. I'm just saying—"

"Just don't, okay?"

Keisha gave Tenika a look and stared through the windshield in front of her.

Tenika was in a foul mood, a dark combination of dread mixed with fear. At any moment, the two of them would pull up to Walter's family's home. Here they would finally learn what had happened to him all those years ago. Keisha had taken the final step of contacting his mother, Miss Alma, whom she'd found on Facebook.

Apparently Miss Alma remembered them, and they were welcome to come by. So Tenika had taken the afternoon off, telling Lizzy that she had a doctor's appointment. Then together the two of them had set off to Antioch.

As they drove through the sea of split level homes, with their gated windows and the graffiti tags and empty storefronts on every block, the reality of this life interrupted dawned on them.

"Maybe they would never have come here," Tenika said. "If… you know…"

"What? They would have had to move out sooner or later. And it's not like West Oakland is a whole lot better. You know that, T."

"Yeah, but it was our place, you know?"

"They would've gotten their rent jacked up like everyone else."

"I suppose," Tenika sighed.

"Let's just focus and get through this, please?" Keisha shook her head. "Lord almighty," she muttered darkly.

"All right, all right," Tenika grumbled just as the GPS noted the house was just ahead on the left. She pulled up and parked outside a squat house that appeared to be built in the sixties. It had an overgrown yard, and a mixed breed terrier of some kind was chained up outside, sleeping in the shade.

The dog raised its head warily and looked at them. Then it started barking furiously as it leapt to its feet. It held them off for a tense moment as they got out of Tenika's truck. The two women glanced nervously at each other.

Just then the front door opened, and an elderly Black woman peered around the edge of the wooden door. Seeing them, she opened it wider. "Keisha?" she said, coming out on the steps.

"Miss Alma?" they both said.

Her hair was now gray and pulled back in a bun, and her body thicker, but Tenika still recognized her. It was Miss Alma, all right. She was always a slightly mysterious figure to both of them, claiming to be part Chocktaw. Standing there with her hands on her hips, Miss Alma looked remarkably the same.

Keisha moved toward her and reached out for a hug. The elderly woman gave her a hug, and smiled at them both.

"Oh, chee-*chee!* Look at you girls...you're all grown up," she exclaimed. "Tenika! Look at those braids," she noted, shaking her head. "Just yesterday you two were little girls."

Tenika touched her braids a little vulnerably and swallowed. This was Miss Alma all right. She sounded exactly the same.

Miss Alma paused, still struck by the sight of them. "Isn't this something? We've got Walter to thank for this, you know. He got me going on Facebook."

Tenika and Keisha looked at each other. "He did?"

"Oh yes, come on in. I'll get some iced tea." Miss Alma led the way into their house. "Have a seat," she said. Then she disappeared into the kitchen just beyond.

Silently, they sat down on the sofa in her darkened living room and waited.

Miss Alma returned a moment later with a tray of iced tea. She put it down on the dining room table. "Help yourself," she said, and each woman took a glass. "I brought you something," Tenika said, holding out a small brown paper bag to her hostess.

Miss Alma took the bag. "What you got here?" When she opened it, she let out a cackle of delight. Inside the bag was a pound of her beloved candied ginger.

"You still like it?" Tenika asked.

"Sure do," Miss Alma said as she placed a piece in her mouth, and offered the bag to each of them. Then she settled on the love seat beside the couch. The three of them sat there silently, sucking on their candied ginger.

Settling her hands on her lap, Miss Alma looked at them expectantly. "So what brought you two girls all the way out here to Antioch? Keisha said you have something to talk about."

Tenika cleared her throat nervously, but it was Keisha who began. "It was my idea, Miss Alma. I—we, well..." she paused, grasping for words for a moment. Tenika looked at her cousin uncertainly, wondering if she should jump in. But Keisha silenced her by putting up her hand.

Keisha cleared her throat and crossed her ankles. "If you want to know the truth, Miss Alma, Jesus told us to come here today. To apologize and make amends to you for what happened. For what happened to Walter all those years ago, I mean."

Now Miss Alma's smiling countenance suddenly grew grave, and she looked at them somberly. "I'm listening," she said.

"It was just—" Keisha faltered, her usual professional demeanor now gone. "Well, you see...we...uh ..." Finally, she looked at Tenika, unable to continue.

Tenika sat up a little straighter and pushed her glasses up her nose. "What Keisha's trying to say is that we're very, very sorry for what happened. You have no idea how sorry we are, Miss Alma. I've been...I've been hanging on to this for years. Been so ashamed I didn't know what to do with myself. But like I said, we both apologize. Truly."

"We do," Keisha added. "That's why we came out here. And to find out how Walter and you both are."

Tenika rambled on. "When you all left after the accident, we never had a chance to apologize. I'm sorry it's taken so long. I mean...we—or I...didn't know what to say. And then Keisha got this idea to come down here."

"Jesus told me to come down here," Keisha added firmly.

"Yeah, Jesus told her..." Tenika echoed.

A moment of silence followed, and it seemed the old woman

might finally say nothing. But she just sat there, apparently absorbed in her own thoughts.

Finally, Miss Alma's face softened. "I've often thought about you girls." She shook her head. "You changed my life, that's for damn sure. And Walter's life, and all of it. But, I know the truth. It took me some time, but I found it. You were only girls. Just little girls. You didn't know any better, and your own mamas weren't around…and I trusted you with my boy. So this is what happened."

An uncomfortable moment ticked by as the three women sat with their current reality.

"What I mean to say is that it's not your fault," Miss Alma continued.

"Is Walter getting along okay?" Keisha asked.

Miss Alma nodded. "Yeah, he's okay. He lives here with me, but he's independent. He has a job in a greenhouse over near Black Diamond Mines. It's, you know, mowing, weeding and such. That's about all he's good for. Doesn't really know any other life."

Tenika and Keisha looked at each other. The reality of what had happened to Walter was bad, but it wasn't the worst thing possible.

"Is he happy?" Tenika asked.

"I think he is," the old woman said, nodding slowly. "He likes the plants."

Keisha cleared her throat again. "I wish it had all happened differently, Miss Alma."

"Me, too," added Tenika. "There hasn't been a day gone by that I haven't wondered about Walter."

"You been thinking about Walter all this time? Lord, girl, that was twenty years ago," the woman exclaimed. Then, improbably, she gave a laugh. "Hell, that's more than I thought about him."

Then Miss Alma looked at the two of them and she shrugged. "I know you girls did the best you could," she said, shaking her head. "Never can figure out God's plan, can we?"

"Yeah, I guess not," Tenika said.

"Thank you for understanding, Miss Alma," Keisha added.

"Yes, thank you," Tenika echoed. "And for forgiving us."

Miss Alma shook her head. "You've got to forgive people," she said. "You just do."

Tenika and Keisha looked at each other. And in that moment, Tenika was suddenly profoundly grateful—for her life, her friends, her wife. For Keisha. And even for Walter and Miss Alma.

Because right here, in this dark little living room in Antioch, she was learning firsthand about love.

*

Frankie's boss got up, walked across the office and closed the door behind her. She shifted nervously in her seat. He almost never shut his office door, so this couldn't bode well. During his impossibly long walk back to the other side of his desk, Frankie's mind raced.

I am about to get fired.

Somehow—God knows how—I was deemed 'disruptive' at the workshop.

Or maybe Peralta set up a smear campaign against me...

Whatever the case may be, a new wave of anxiety spiraled through Frankie's body. In the past week since she'd been home, she'd realized just how much she loved this job, these people. This institution she'd been so connected to for all these years. Now it was potentially disappearing, and along with it, the critical pension she'd been building up all these years.

To lose all of this would be a deep and lasting tragedy in Frankie's life. As bad as losing Sally.

Frankie took a long breath, then slowly she released it as she watched her boss fiddle with his watch for a moment, as if she wasn't even there. He had to be playing with her, she thought.

He had to be.

Didn't he?

Finally, the Lieutenant took his seat and leaning back, he gazed at her evenly. "How's the trauma?" he asked. As usual, he pronounced this very important word in her life with his broad Boston accent, so it came out as 'tramma.' Usually, he said it with disdain.

But today he seemed strangely compassionate. "I read all about your time up there, Kennedy. At the PTSI workshop. BSU sent a report."

Frankie's gut twisted another inch. "And?" she asked.

"Well," he said, "how do you think it went?" His expression remained strangely serious. She'd assumed her boss would be impressed, even proud of her. But not one thing in his behavior was signaling this.

Frankie swallowed and her mind spun in reverse now. She'd been counting on a good report from BSU. An excellent one, even. "Oh…uh, actually I thought it went…well?"

Her boss remained expressionless. He raised his eyebrows slightly and slowly shook this head, as if to indicate how clueless he was.

Now Frankie was confused. *What the hell was going on here?*

But then suddenly, a large smile burst across her boss's face. "Ah, Kennedy," he said, slapping his desk, "I'm just messing with you! You got an excellent report. Highest rating they give. They want you to come back as a peer counselor as soon as you can. Good work."

Relief flooded her body and she managed a weak laugh. "Really? *Really?* Thank God!"

"What?" he chuckled, "You thought I was going to fire you?" The Lieutenant shook his head and laughed again. "Not a chance, Kennedy. BSU was on it, and you did good."

"You got me, Lieutenant. You got me good," Frankie smiled. "And I just want to say thanks, because that workshop? It was excellent. For real."

"Okay," he said, smiling into his paperwork. "You're cleared to return to undercover work effective immediately. You get your weapon back and everything. So…" He spread his arms wide, as if to say the case was closed. "Now get out of here."

Frankie rose to go as simple happiness pushed through her.

"Hey, Kennedy," he said, and she turned back to him once more.

"Go home and do something nice for your girl. You know, take her out to dinner or something. Thank her."

"I'm way ahead of you," Frankie said. And she was.

She was seriously on it.

Chapter Twenty-One

M onroe nervously drained their double espresso, and checked the door to the café once more. Servers bustled by, delivering organic breakfasts while entrepreneurs bent over their laptops, vacantly stirring their lavender lattes.

The café known as Julie's was at max. And at any moment, Rosalind would walk in, sit down and their first date would finally begin. Taking a long inhale, Monroe closed their eyes, hoping the butterflies that buzzed through their gut would just settle. One more, they looked up as the bells on the front door chimed.

There she is.

Walking over, Rosalind smiled shyly at Monroe, and pulled her trim leather jacket a little more tightly around her. *God, she is hot*, Monroe couldn't help thinking. Jumping up awkwardly, Monroe gave her a half hug that was stiffly returned.

The two of them looked at each other and smiled nervously. It was all right there in front of them. The curiosity, the desire, the longing to finally find their person, who might, actually, be right here. Not one iota of it had changed since the first moment they laid eyes on each other. Their shared frisson was still as electric as ever.

"Can I get you something to drink?" Monroe asked, swallowing hard.

"I can do it," Rosalind said. Then she walked over to the counter and inspected the tea menu.

Breakfast had been Monroe's idea. It was a noncommittal safe zone, just in case the two of them looked at each other and the thrill was gone. But so far, it appeared, the thrill was still firmly in place.

Monroe studied Rosalind in her Sunday casual look of perfectly fitting jeans. A fine gold chain adorned her neck. The light glinted off of the smooth cascade of her black hair, and her body looked so sleek, so refined. And strong, Monroe noted. She exuded pure strength, this woman. Rosalind was elegant and polished in all the ways that spoke of power, confidence, and simple beauty. Really, she was breathtaking.

Monroe watched her walk back to their table, as if memorizing her every move. She seemed truly at ease now, and a hundred times more relaxed than the last time they'd met. Rosalind smiled warmly at Monroe as she sat down. She, too, seemed to be relaxing.

"So," Monroe began with an exhale, "how have you been?"

"Well, first, I actually need to say something to you," Rosalind replied.

"Okay."

Monroe studied her face. There was a thought there that they couldn't quite read. Bracing themself, Monroe prepared to hear Rosalind deliver the dreaded line, "I only want to be friends, okay?" But she didn't. Instead, she said this:

"I owe you an enormous apology. And I'm so glad you called."

Whoa. This was not the feared closing. Instead, it was an opening. Monroe leaned in. "Say more?"

"I'm sorry I was so rude to you at Tenika's party; there was no reason for me to walk out like that. You were being perfectly nice. I just…choked, I guess."

"Rosalind, please. It's totally all right…"

Rosalind continued, her dark eyes gazing steadily into Monroe's own. "I was attracted to you," she continued. "Anyway, let's just say a lot has happened since then."

"Wow," Monroe said a little breathlessly. They couldn't believe what they were hearing. This gorgeous woman was attracted to them? She used that very word. She said, 'attracted.' It was official now.

Rosalind paused, not wanting to be too intense, and Monroe leapt right in. "I mean, I figured you weren't feeling well or something. It's really okay. You don't have to apologize."

Rosalind now reached across the table toward Monroe, and as if by magnetic pull, their fingers naturally found each other. Then both of them studied their hands, now entwined, as if they were observing something strange and phenomenal.

"Listen," Rosalind said, raising her gaze to Monroe. "I just wasn't ready a few months ago. I hadn't fully come out. But I have now. That's the fact of the matter." She paused, and took a breath. Then shyly she blushed. "To tell you the truth, I was scared. And I just wanted to tell you this. I guess…to get it over with?"

Monroe nodded, wordlessly. They were suddenly filled with a sense so huge, so overwhelming, they almost forgot to breathe for a moment. "I… I…wow," Monroe faltered.

"I mean, you don't have to date me," Rosalind continued. "I'd understand if you didn't want to. I was so out to lunch the last time we met and everything, but I was hoping—"

"I want to date you," Monroe interrupted. "Believe me, I do! That's all I've wanted since the moment I laid eyes on you. You're…well, look at you…"

Now Rosalind fell silent, as a small, shy smile crept across her lips.

"You're *beautiful*," Monroe breathed. They locked eyes on each other now, an electric wave of energy ricocheting back and forth between them.

"I didn't call you because I had my own issues to deal with," Monroe said. "I just got my name and my gender marker legally changed. After I met you, I just knew I had to do this. It didn't feel right otherwise."

Now it was Rosalind's turn to register amazement. "You did? Really?"

"Anyway, it's all official now. I'm Monroe, just one name. And look—" Monroe whipped their wallet out of their back pocket. Then they fished out their driver's license and handed it to Rosalind. Under gender, it now said 'X.'

Slowly, Rosalind read it and handed it back. Then she rested her chin in her hand and gazed evenly at Monroe, which made Monroe's heart practically stop. "That's so cool," she said dreamily.

Monroe smiled, tucking their wallet back into their jeans. A surge of strength and pride passed through them. It had been so worth it to make that change, just this exact moment. "So," Monroe continued, "how was coming out to your family?"

Immediately Rosalind's demeanor changed, and her gaze fell to the tabletop. "That's not such a happy story."

Monroe's hand squeezed Rosalind's. "Tell me."

"They threw me out," Rosalind said simply. She glanced up at Monroe, as if measuring their response.

"*What?*"

"Yeah," she nodded. "They're fundamentalist Christians. This is like their worst nightmare." Rosalind paused. "But, you know, you've got to do what you've got to do. Right?"

Monroe nodded. "Yeah...but Rosalind, that's terrible. I'm so sorry."

Rosalind sighed. "I guess it's all part of the process. At any rate, it's not stopping me." She looked directly at Monroe, who now put their other hand on top of Rosalind's, as if trying to ward off any more stress in her life.

"You're doing the right thing," Monroe said. "You know you are."

"I do." The two of them just looked at each other, melting into each other's gazes as Rosalind's small white pot of tea was delivered.

"None of it is easy," Monroe continued. "For either of us. My mother came all the way from Orange County to fight my name and gender change in court, but...you know, I actually learned something about her that day."

"What was that?"

"She can be incredibly small minded, my mother. But actually, she does love me in her own way. Just like your parents love you, I suspect. Maybe they just have to sit with this for a while."

Rosalind shook her head as she poured herself a cup of tea. "I'm not waiting for that to happen. They're just..." Her words trailed off and disappeared.

"At any rate, here *we* are." said Monroe, giving her hand another squeeze.

They smiled at each other, and Rosalind nodded, her face once again lighting up. "Yeah. Here we are."

And gazing at each other, they both let go into the vast expanse of possibility now spread out before them.

It was a place of nothing less than wonder.

*

Tenika was brushing her teeth in the bathroom, thinking about whether to hire a bookkeeper for the garage, when Delilah came into the bathroom. Leaning forward, Tenika spat and rinsed. Then suddenly, her wife's arms came around her from behind as she stood there.

"Hey," Tenika said, leaning back against her with a smile.

Lightly, Delilah nuzzled her neck and kissed it softly. "Hey."

"To what do I owe this pleasure?"

"To love," Delilah said, and resting her chin on Tenika's shoulder she gazed at her in the mirror. Tenika regarded her wife tenderly.

"Thanks, baby," Tenika said. It had been three days since she and Keisha had driven to Antioch and met with Miss Alma. She still hadn't told Delilah about Walter, and she knew she needed to. At this point, she was just looking for an opening.

"You know what?" Delilah said gently.

Tenika studied her in the mirror. Delilah had a certain smile on her face, the one that usually meant something important was about to happen. Tenika turned to her. This could only mean one thing. Tenika's heartbeat suddenly sped up.

"What?"

"I just bought this." Delilah pulled a small white and blue box from her pocket, and put it on the counter in front of them. It was a pregnancy test kit. "My period is two weeks late, honey."

A shock of recognition passed through Tenika's body. It was as if the future had just come barreling in, almost unannounced. "*What*? Why didn't you tell me?"

"I'm telling you now. So don't go anywhere, okay? We're going to find out what's happening like…right now."

Tenika put her hands up. "Oh, believe me, I won't move an inch."

Pulling the test from the box, Delilah unwrapped it. Then unzipping her jeans, she sat down on the toilet and held the test stick between her legs as she let go with a stream of urine. "Now we just have to wait three minutes," Delilah explained. "Which will probably be the longest three minutes of my life."

"I get that," Tenika concurred as Delilah handed over the test stick. Delicately Tenika rested it on the counter. She turned back to her wife, who was now zipping her pants. "Honey?" she said.

Do it now. Don't wait another minute.

Tenika swallowed hard. "Baby, I need to tell you about something."

Suddenly, Delilah's whole demeanor changed as she recognized the shift in the conversation. "Uh oh," she said, her voice falling. "What is it, T? What's happened now?"

Tenika glanced at the developing test strip on the bathroom

counter. So far it was still negative. Then she forced herself to look back into the eyes of her waiting wife. "Look, I—"

"Whatever it is, do we really have to get into this right now? Can't it wait?"

"No. No, it really can't wait, honey. Just let me explain."

Impatiently, Delilah folded her arms and sighed. "Go on," she said, her voice full of resignation.

"Now I know I should have told you about this sooner, but—"

"What the hell is it? Would you *just freakin' tell me*?" Delilah was bobbing around before her, twisting a long auburn lock in her finger.

"Okay! Okay. All right." Tenika paused and took a breath. Then she closed her eyes, as if keeping them open might confirm her worst fears. "So twenty years ago...me and Keisha were kids, right?"

"Well, teenagers. But go on."

Tenika eyes remained clamped shut as the dreaded words came tumbling out, one after another. "So..." she began. "Back one night that summer, we were babysitting and Walter—this little boy we were babysitting? He got away from us." Tenika's voice dropped to a whisper. Tears filled her eyes as she continued. "He ran out in front of a car, and before we could stop it it hit him ..."

There was nothing but silence following her words. Tenika half opened her eyes, making sure Delilah was still there. She was. Her wife was simply looking at her, transfixed.

"He has a traumatic brain injury. Baby, he's never been right since." Tenika's voice broke and she struggled to keep control.

Delilah just continued to look at her, appraising the situation. Tenika barreled on in the silence, unable to stop her torrent of words. And mostly unable to tolerate her wife's stillness.

"That's why I've been so damn cagey about all of this, baby. I mean, me and Keisha apologized just the other day to his mother. Went to her house out in Antioch. She forgave us and everything, but I…I just don't know if I can be a good parent to our baby." Tenika stopped as tears welled up again. "I'm afraid," she croaked.

Delilah shook her head in wonder. "That's what you've been so weird about, T? That's it?"

Tenika looked up at her wife. "Well, yeah."

Delilah looked at her tenderly. "T, listen to me. How old were you then?"

"Fourteen."

"You were only a child, honey. But you're an adult now. You're a totally different person. Anyway, you can do this. You're going to be fine. You don't have to be scared, you really don't. Now come here." Delilah opened her arms, and Tenika found her way inside them, and the two of them hugged tightly for a moment. Then Delilah took a tissue from her pocket, and wiped the last of the tears from her wife's face. "It's okay, baby."

"Really?"

"For real."

Now glancing over Tenika's shoulder, Delilah gave a shout. "Oh! Oh my God! Honey, look!"

There before them on the counter, a second pink line had filled in next to the original line on the pregnancy test stick. The result was positive.

Tenika turned to her wife wide-eyed "That's it? This is really happening…like, now?"

Delilah was jumping up and down now. "It's happening! It's happening now, T!"

Tenika stood there, still a little dumbfounded. "We're actually gonna do this?"

"We are! It's totally happening now! I'm pregnant." Delilah let loose a yell of pure unbridled happiness. It was a primal whoop that came from somewhere deep inside of her.

"Honey, quit jumping around like that!" Tenika yelled, grabbing her arm. Then both women burst out laughing.

They kissed, a kiss of power, tenderness and pure unadulter-
ated Grace. The future was moving along, and bringing them with
it. And for once everything felt absolutely, utterly right.

"You sure it's okay? About Walter?" Tenika asked a moment
later as they were nestled together in bed.

"Oh course, I'm sure," Delilah said. "That was then and now
is now, T. And we are going to be mothers."

"We sure as hell are."

"And you know what else?"

"What?"

Delilah snuggled just a little closer, putting her head on
Tenika's shoulder. "We're gonna be good mothers, honey."

"Maybe we'll even be great mothers," Tenika offered.

"Yeah! We're going to be great mothers."

Tenika kissed Delilah on the top of her head. "Anyway, I get
it. We're going to be just fine."

Pulling her wife in for a kiss, Tenika could feel the truth of this.
They would, indeed, be fine.

*

The maître d set off to a small, quiet table for two in the corner, and Frankie and Sally followed. Scott's was a special occasion restaurant—the sort where you might come when you were
ready to drink champagne, or at least acknowledge something big.
Coming here had been Frankie's idea.

Sally could feel Frankie's hand on the small of her back, gently steering her as the hostess led them forward, menus in hand.
She was wearing her special dress, the blue one. It hugged her
curves nicely, opening to a beautiful neckline that showcased her
pale, ample bosom.

Sally had taken special care to dress up that night, though she
still didn't have any idea what they were celebrating.

As they seated themselves, Sally noticed Frankie smiling at

her. Her look was almost mischievous, and Sally was now on high alert. It felt like something big was about to happen for sure.

Sally gazed at her girlfriend. In the lamplight on the table, with its soft silk shade, Frankie looked especially sharp. She was wearing a dark shirt and a beautiful suit jacket that enhanced the angles on her face. They played up her beautiful androgyny, a quality of Frankie's that Sally truly loved.

She glanced around the restaurant in satisfaction after they'd placed their drink orders. The sunset was visible through the windows in front of them. The surface of the still harbor before them had a dreamy peach gloss. "This is great," she sighed happily.

"The last few months you've been incredible." Frankie said. "So I wanted to thank you properly."

Ah, Sally thought. *This was a thank you dinner then.*

Sally took her hand. "I was happy to do it. You don't have to take me out for an expensive dinner."

"What if I want to?" Frankie smiled. "What if I feel like showing you off a little?"

Now Sally smiled, bemused by her lover but also grateful. She'd been thinking tonight Frankie might finally ask her to live with her. Because that was, of course, the next logical step in the careful expedition that was their relationship. Even though Sally now spent most of her nights at Frankie's.

She wondered about Frankie's reticence, but had never mentioned it. More than ever, Sally was aware where she'd blown it in her past relationships. Mostly she'd assumed that things were further along than they actually were. Or she'd picked the wrong partners in the first place, and then tried to force a strained dynamic to work.

Sally had done it all at this point, she figured. She'd dated the serial monogamists who couldn't commit, and the erratic borderlines who had no boundaries. She'd even dated some verbal abusers whose words had been lacerating.

And yet, here she was, truly in love. But this time with an entirely different sort of person. A person who made it all seem easy, in spite of the challenges.

Frankie was honest and reliable, a truly good woman who had strength and courage for days. She appreciated so much about Sally, even if she'd originally balked about her profession. Now even that was no big deal. Instead, Frankie had returned from the PTSI workshop a renewed person. Suddenly, she seemed far more accessible to Sally.

Again and again, Frankie kept telling her how much she loved her. It was as if some kind of quantum shift had happened in her life, and she wanted to share all of it with Sally. Which, of course, Sally eagerly received. This was just where she'd imagined they might be heading.

A waiter came by now with two glasses of champagne, which he put before them on the table.

"So I'd like to make a toast," Frankie said, picking up her champagne flute and tipping it toward Sally.

Sally raised her own glass as well. "What are we toasting?"

"You, Sally. You brought me here, to this point in my life, and I am really grateful." Frankie paused and looked into her eyes. "You are the best thing that's ever happened to me."

Sally softened the minute she heard this. Meanwhile, Frankie's just kept looking at her, deeply, intently. In her eyes Sally saw a new, softer strength, one forged out of all that had happened to her. "I love you," Sally said.

They touched glasses. "I love you, too," Frankie echoed. Then she extracted a small red silken bag from her pocket, and placed it on the table in front of Sally.

"There's this, too."

Sally looked up at her, mildly confused. This did not appear to be a gift-giving occasion. "This is for me?"

Frankie grinned. "Oh, it's for you all right. Open it."

Sally picked up the tiny bag curiously. The fabric was expensive, and there was something small and hard in it. She really couldn't fathom what it was. Whatever it was seemed precious.

Sally drew back the small silken cord on the bag and peered inside the bag, and what she saw inside made her gasp. In fact, Sally couldn't quite believe what she was seeing. A solitaire diamond on a rose gold band was nestled in among the folds of rosy silk.

Extracting the ring, she held it up with a look of wonder, unable to quite comprehend what it was.

Frankie leaned across the table, and took her hand. "Marry me," she said.

Sally's voice caught in her throat as a sob threatened to escape. "Oh…Oh *Frankie*," she murmured. Suddenly she began laughing and crying at the same time. "I thought…I thought…"

"Marry me," Frankie repeated firmly.

Sally started nodding before she could even form the words. Finally, they came out in a tumble. "Of course! I will! Yes. Yes. *Yes!*"

Leaning across the table, the two women came together in a long, passionate kiss. Then Frankie took the ring and slid it onto Sally's finger as the couples seated at the tables around them began to applaud.

Sally gazed at the ring on her finger, still unable to believe this was happening. "You're sure?" she asked, looking up at Frankie.

"Oh, I'm sure all right. I know you've been waiting for me to ask you to move in," Frankie explained. "But honestly, when I thought about it, I wanted more than that. I was just waiting to be well enough to ask you, Sally. But I am now…"

"Wow…" Sally breathed, her voice shot with wonder. "You even got my ring size right!"

"That was a freaking lucky guess," Frankie admitted. "But sometimes I really do luck out. Like right here, and right now."

"I'm right there with you," Sally said. And she certainly was.

The goddesses had been right, indeed.

Chapter Twenty-Two

Tenika peered into the oven and gave a low whistle. She shut the oven door, and turned to her hostess in satisfaction. "That is some turkey! Must be a twenty-five pounder."

Lizzy nodded and caught Kate's eye. "Oh it is, all right. Kate wanted to skimp on the size, but then we found the Safeway deal on turkeys. And, basically, I insisted."

"It was only seven ninety-nine for the whole bloody thing," Kate added. "Turned out Lizzy was absolutely right."

Tenika nodded. "At any rate, everyone's happy and we're not going to starve."

"Not with T's mac and cheese, we're not," Delilah added. The two of them grinned at each other.

"It's West Coast-style—the kind that's so loaded with cheese, you have to slice it," Tenika said.

At that moment, the doorbell rang. "I'll get it," Kate said, spinning off in the direction of the door. Meanwhile, Lizzy was busy pulling up music on the stereo. Nina Simone came crooning out through the speaker, setting the mood.

A moment later, Frankie walked into the kitchen, red cheeked from the unexpectedly brisk afternoon, as Sally trailed behind her. Frankie had a wool scarf tossed around her neck, and she held out a bottle of French champagne to Lizzy.

"Whoa—the good stuff!" Lizzy said. "Thank you very much!"

"There are things to celebrate," Frankie noted with a grin.

"It's Thanksgiving, for one thing! Hello chosen family!" Sally called out, giving Kate a kiss on the cheek. Then she turned and gave Tenika a hug.

"Hey, sis, glad you two made it."

Sally smiled at her friend and former host. "Are you kidding? We wouldn't miss it."

Delilah gave her old friend a hug. "Speaking of missing things, we are seriously miss you, Sally. Our house isn't the same without you."

"I don't know what's going on up at your place," Tenika said to Frankie, "but it definitely feels like Sally doesn't live here anymore."

Frankie and Sally looked at each other. Radiant smiles lit them both up as they studied each other. "I think we'd better tell them, honey," Sally quietly urged, and Frankie nodded.

Wordlessly, Sally held out her left hand with its glittering engagement ring. Immediately, Lizzy gave a cheer as the murmuring crowd in the kitchen gathered around. Lizzy looked up at them with eyes shining. "Hey, is this for real?"

"As real as it gets," Frankie said, and Sally nodded.

"Can you believe it? I can barely believe it…" Sally gushed.

"Ah, Sally," Kate said, bringing her friend in for a hug. "That is just so great."

Delilah leaned in as well. "Ring, please," she said. She studied her friend's hand and turned to Frankie. "Nice," she said, approvingly. "Very nice. Look, honey."

But Tenika was busy hugging Frankie. "You both deserve a lot of happiness," she said. "Congrats. Seriously, you two. Way to go."

"Yeah," Frankie said, hands in pockets as she rocked back on her heels. Her expression was a mixture of shyness and simple joy. "I asked her, and she said yes," Frankie remarked, as if she were still amazed. "Can you believe it?"

"Oh, I can believe it, Frankie. It's love, pure and simple," Tenika replied.

Frankie and Sally pulled in for a kiss, and around them their friends all cheered.

*

Monroe strode up the pathway to Lizzy and Kate's house, a bottle of Cabernet in their hand. Beside them walked Rosalind, carrying a bowl of Chinese long beans simmered in garlic "I hope this is okay," she said. "I mean, it's not traditional."

"It's awesome. Everyone's going to love it," Monroe reassured her. Then pausing midway on the path, Monroe turned to her. This was their third date, and the two still had yet to kiss. There had been one brief, end-of-date kiss…but not a real kiss.

Despite the fact that every night for the past week, Monroe had thought about kissing Rosalind endlessly. *Why rush*, they'd chided themself, letting their natural shyness take over.

But suddenly, it was clear. Now was the time.

Monroe looked at their date in the gathering twilight. "You look so pretty tonight." Really, they couldn't believe this stunning woman, with her gentle, soft strength of steel was their date. *How did this happen?*

"Thanks," Rosalind said, meeting Monroe's gaze. "I'm glad we're here together."

Whoa. It was like every word she said pushed another part of Monroe's circuitry into high alert. *This woman was just incredible.*

"Yeah, me too." Monroe swallowed, aware of the sudden portent of the moment. "And it's great that you brought the Chinese Beans. They're very…you, Rosalind."

She looked at Monroe, her eyes not moving from their face. Finally there was nothing more to do. Leaning over, Monroe took her arm lightly and kissed her. Then Monroe kissed her willing lips once more, their two tongues touching as they opened to a deeper, more passionate kiss.

Rosalind pulled back now. Putting her bowl of long beans down on the metal bench by the door, Rosalind took the bottle of wine from Monroe's hand, and placed it beside the beans.

Then she twined her arms around Monroe, and drew them in for an even longer, deeper kiss. The two of them were still at it a few moments later when the front door swung open.

Finally, Kate cleared her throat, and immediately the two of them stopped, embarrassed. She had been standing there watching them with a large grin spread across her face.

Monroe looked up in mild alarm. "Oh!"

Rosalind gasped, then she laughed. "Kate—hello!"

Kate gave a little chuckle. "Care to come in, you two? Or would you like to stay out for a bit more snogging?"

Monroe and Rosalind looked at each other and laughed. Then chastely, the two of them gathered up their items and followed her inside.

*

By the time the group was seated, everyone had fully inspected Sally's engagement ring. And it had already been established that no wedding date was set yet, but that Frankie and Sally would definitely marry in the coming year.

Monroe's arm was now casually draped across the back of Rosalind's chair, and Rosalind's leg was nestled comfortably beside their own. The pheromones were pinging back and forth between them as a large steaming platter of sliced turkey made its way around the table, followed by a gravy boat, the long beans and a large bowl of stuffing. Rosalind was discussing Chinese bean recipes with Sally, who sat beside her.

"It's a tradition in my family, really for Sunday dinner mostly. But, I've decided traditions are good, no matter when and where they happen, right?" Rosalind said.

Suzanne Falter

"They always bring back the best memories," Sally noted. Now Lizzy rose, wine glass in hand.

"Ahem!" Lizzy began, and everyone around the table gradually fell silent as they looked at her. These friends, these dear friends who'd been through so much together, were as connected as they'd ever been in that moment. The love in the room was palpable.

"Here's to my family," Lizzy said. "I mean, I've got a mom and some siblings, and I think of them on this day...Christmas Day, as we like to call it in the East Bay." Lizzy paused. "And yet, every one of you came into Driven at one point or another, and you sat on our couch and you told us your story. So really, I'm here to toast you all. Because, honestly, one by one, you guys have become my family." She looked around nodding. "This is our family."

"Here, here," Kate agreed. "It is indeed."

Raising her glass, Lizzy added, "Here's to us! Merry Christmas!"

The women lifted their glasses and drank, calling out "Merry Christmas!" and "To Driven!"

"I'm with Lizzy on that," Tenika said, standing with her glass raised. "Here's to our family. To the best one I ever had. And," Tenika paused, clearing her throat as she looked around the table. "I got a heads up for y'all because this family is about to get bigger."

"I'm about to get significantly bigger, too," Delilah added.

Lizzy started. "Wait a minute—*what*?"

Kate grabbed Delilah's hand. "You're...*pregnant*? Honestly?"

Delilah took Tenika's hand and stood up beside her. "We are pregnant!" she confirmed, raising their hands in the air as everyone cheered and applauded. Then she raised her glass of sparkling water to the group. "Here's to our family," she said. "Long may we love and be loved."

In an instant, the turkey was forgotten and everyone was crowded around Tenika and Delilah, congratulating them. Sally's eyes welled up with tears as she hugged her old friend. "I just can't believe it," she said. "Me getting married and now you having the baby…this is all so perfect!"

"It's the baby you saw when you read my cards, Sally," Delilah told her. "I want you to know that's why we're here right now. Because of you and that reading, Sally. For a while there, I was sure it wasn't going to happen. But I kept remembering what you said, so I kept the faith."

The two looked at each other, eyes brimming. "The goddesses are never wrong.," Sally said. "And here we are."

Delilah sniffed back a little sob. "Yeah," she said, her voice swollen with emotion. "Here we are." The two embraced for a long, long time.

Meanwhile, Lizzy patted Tenika on the back. Then pulled her in for a hug. "You're going to be a great mother. I can feel it," she announced.

Tenika looked at her a little shyly. "Oh, I've had my doubts, Lizzy. Believe me. But it seems like it's all in flow this time."

"You've got this parenting thing," Lizzy told her. "You just have to trust yourself, T."

Tenika glanced up at her business partner. "Isn't that the Universal lesson?" she quipped. Then she smiled. "Anyway, I guess it's meant to be."

"So it is."

And as the group settled in once more to enjoy their Christmas dinner, Monroe turned to Rosalind. "See?" they said. "This is what it's all about. Why it's all ultimately worth it. The coming out, the paperwork. All that anxiety, the lawyers, the hassle…"

"The fear," Rosalind added.

"Yep, all of it. Because this is what we get, Rosalind." Monroe gestured at their friends, new and old. "We get *all of this*. And you've got to admit, this is pretty damn cool."

"Yes, it is," Rosalind nodded. She did get it. And it was cool, indeed.

Someday in a perfect world, her parents would be happy to meet Monroe. And she and Monroe would find a welcome home. Or at least, they'd manage to have a nice lunch in a restaurant sometimes with Monroe's mother.

Someday everyone would understand, and so the world would chug along, as they returned to the business at hand. For now, at least, her family conflict no longer mattered so much.

All of them had found their home. They'd found their soft place to land. And so they could all go on, doing just what they were meant to do. Living in the world as who they each were.

And loving each other, for all they were worth.

Also by Suzanne Falter

Fiction
Oaktown Girls series
Driven
Committed
Destined
Revealed

Transformed series
Transformed: San Francisco
Transformed: Paris
Transformed: POTUS

(All titles by Suzanne Falter & Jack Harvey)

Non-Fiction
The Extremely Busy Woman's Guide to Self-Care
The Joy of Letting Go
Surrendering to Joy
How Much Joy Can You Stand?
Living Your Joy

Many thanks to those who directed me to find my way through lives and scenarios that were unfamiliar to me. Thank you Andrea J. Lee for being my 'cultural consultant' on Asian immigrant and Asian-American families. Chris Paganelli aptly guided me on the process of cashing in old penny stocks. Ollie Mills guided me on the non-binary life. I also wish to thank PSM and Jack Harvey for their ongoing support...as well as my ace production team. Danielle Hartman Acee gave her all, as usual, on copyediting, proofreading, formatting and marketing the book, and Caroline Manchoulas crafted a gorgeous cover.

Finally, my thanks to all the many diverse women of the East Bay queer community, and the deep support of my wife. You provide a loving, supportive inspiration for us all.

About Suzanne Falter

Suzanne Falter is an author, speaker, blogger and podcaster who has published both fiction and non-fiction, as well as essays. Her queer fiction titles include the funny romantic suspense series Transformed. She also writes and speaks about self-care and the transformational healing of crisis, especially in her own life after the death of her daughter Teal. Her non-fiction books include *The Extremely Busy Woman's Guide to Self-Care, How Much Joy Can You Stand?* and *Surrendering to Joy.* Suzanne's essays have appeared in *O Magazine, The New York Times, Elephant Journal,* and *Thrive Global* among others. Her free flash fiction can be found at www.suzannefalterfiction.com, as well as on Facebook, Twitter, YouTube, and Pinterest. She lives with her wife in the San Francisco Bay Area.

www.ingramcontent.com/pod-product-compliance
Lightning Source LLC
Chambersburg PA
CBHW020605180626
46810CB00007B/2654